GATHERING LIGHTS

A NOVEL OF
SAN FRANCISCO

LARAINE HERRING

ALSO BY LARAINE HERRING

Into the Garden of Gethsemane, Georgia

Ghost Swamp Blues: A Novel

The Writing Warrior: Discovering the Courage to Free Your True Voice

Writing Begins with the Breath: Embodying Your Authentic Voice

Lost Fathers: How Women Can Heal from Adolescent Father Loss

Monsoons: A Collection of Writing

GATHERING LIGHTS

First published September 2013

Library of Congress Control Number: 2013945138
ISBN: 978-0-9852607-7-4

Author photo by MH Ramona Swift, ©2013

Cover by Mike Iverson

Presented by The Concentrium
Phoenix, Arizona USA
www.theconcentrium.com

for Keith

*It is an odd thing, but everyone who disappears
is said to be seen in San Francisco.*

*It must be a delightful city, and possess all
the attractions of the next world.*

– *Oscar Wilde*

...arket, 2238 N. 31st Str.

WANTED: Fiddle playing sky diving hippie chick. Pls come home. No questions asked. 537-4464 anytime.

CARTOONISTS---Anim

REMMY X

No one has been by to steal the Street's sign in many years. It used to get stolen every few days, but back then nobody needed a sign to tell them they had arrived in the middle of it all. We knew where we were and the ones who came to gawk at us by the carload did too. Once I ran alongside a tourist bus holding up a mirror. Nobody on the bus got the joke, but I had a belly-jiggling long laugh about that for some time, even though I'd forgotten to wear gloves and the sides of the mirror cut into my hands.

I am running out of food for my Street. I didn't realize how much it required to keep living. I stay here to tend it. I keep my stoop clean, brush the cobwebs from the shadows. I make offerings every day of my poems and my newspaper, the *Hashbury Daily Times*. When dusk comes and I'm on my way home with my dog Shep and my typewriter, I toss change to the ones who now line the streets where I used to huddle, a shroud of gray blankets and reaching fingers. I guard my post at the corner of Haight and Ashbury so I can always be watching, always be holding the strings together for all of us who walked on her streets, from the wingtipped to the sandaled to those whose bare feet are bruised and bloodied.

The Haight is a hungry ghost, she is. Her belly never fills up. It's always growling, rumbling, taking more than you have. It's indiscriminate.

A wild animal. No matter how long you've been putting food out for her, no matter how long you give her shelter in your heart and hearth, one day she's going to consume you. When you let a wild thing into your home, only the biggest fool of all gets upset when she takes what she wants.

- X out.

2007

"Turn there. That's the hotel." Frank Connor meticulously folded his San Francisco street map and placed it on his lap. He gazed out the passenger side window at the cacophony of Union Square. "I told you we shouldn't have taken the car. This is the most car unfriendly city in the world."

Helen Connor clicked her fingernails against the steering wheel, the glare from the band of diamonds on her wedding ring finger slicing her vision. "How else could we have gotten here, Frank? You're afraid to fly. Did you want us to walk?"

She'd missed the light. Honks from angry drivers startled her. The wash of pedestrians had entered the intersection even before the light changed. If she hit one, at least they'd have something to talk about on the trip. He could tell her how she never paid attention. She could tell him how he never wanted to go anywhere. She could speak, in that low, monotone voice he deplored, and tell him how she used to have fire. Used to have desire. And how all of its current breathtaking absence was due to him. He could tell her that she never knew the right things to say to him after his nightmares, the right way to touch him, the right way to brew his tea. He could speak, in that low, monotone voice she deplored, and tell her that he had made a mistake seventeen years ago. That he had been afraid no one else would come along. She would nod and say yes, she had thought the same thing, and hadn't it been a pity. They would part then, melancholy smiles on their lips, and dance into the dark.

But of course, they will not say any of these things to each other, because that is not what they do, Frank and Helen, not the way they have structured their relationship, not the way they have determined that things are supposed to work, not at all the way they have managed to stay together for seventeen years, four months and three days. Frank would know how many hours and minutes. Helen would not be sure whether it had been twenty or ten years. Or maybe fifteen. Years run so smoothly together.

The light changed again. She inched the nose of their paid-for Prius into the street, then slammed on the brakes, almost causing an accident. The red BMW behind her honked.

"Did you see that?" asked Helen.

Frank readjusted his seatbelt. "What?"

"That girl."

The BMW honked louder.

"You have to move, Helen," said Frank.

"She just came out of nowhere."

"There are hundreds of people."

Helen craned her neck to look out the back window. Where did she go? Tourists in summer coats and scarves milled around the corners. The Don't Walk sign flashed an angry orange. The girl with the dirty blonde hair and wild eyes was nowhere.

"You didn't see anyone?" she asked. "She leapt right in front of us."

"I see lots of people. This is a big city."

The BMW crowded against her tail, then began to inch around her into oncoming traffic.

"You've got to move," said Frank.

She released the brake, almost scraping against the BMW. The driver, wearing aviator glasses and a blue blazer, flipped her off and sped away.

She gripped the wheel and turned right into the valet parking lot for the Hotel Gladmore, a Travelocity deal at only $135 a night, conveniently located on the edge of Union Square. Perfect for a weekend getaway, claimed four out of five travelers.

"There's no complimentary parking?" asked Frank. Or maybe Helen only imagined Frank said that. It would be something he would say. She's going to complain about having to give her keys to a stranger, thought Frank.

"What?" he said.

"I didn't say anything," she said.

"Oh."

They piled their luggage on the brass luggage cart and handed a ten to the bellhop. She had over packed. He had under packed. One would think that between the two of them, they would have had enough.

The suite was indeed grand; the hotel positioned at the edge of Union Square and the Stockton Street Tunnel entrance to Chinatown. They were high enough in the hotel so they could see the top of the flagship Macy's and imagine the ferries leaving for Sausalito in the fog of early evening. They had both thought it wise to curb expenses on this trip, their last in whatever stage of their marriage they currently occupied. They had thought, well, if we can work it out, we'll be in a lovely place, and well, if we don't, we'll be in a lovely place and have some money left over for the legal fees. It had made sense in Phoenix when they planned the trip, but now that they were here, neither one felt it was money well spent. The Travelocity travel gnome had assured them they would never roam alone and had provided additional trip ideas with a City Pass and a Red Line Cruise voucher.

Helen sat on the bed and ran her fingers over the sage green bedspread. She couldn't shake the girl's eyes from her skin. There had been someone. "It's a king," she said. "Plenty of room to stretch out."

He was lining his toiletries up on the marble countertop. Razor,

Gillette. Shaving cream, Mennen. Deodorant, Arrid. Extra dry. He hated being wet. Travel toothbrush. Toothpaste, Crest Tartar control. Floss, mint waxed. He needed to claim his section of the countertop before Helen spread out her vast assortment of gels, sprays, mousses, brushes and lipsticks. She never left enough room for even his meager needs. Helen watched him lining up the toiletries like he was playing with action figures. He'll put them on the right side of the sink next to the outlet so she won't be able to use her flat iron without moving them.

"There's an honor bar," she said. "Want something?"

"Nah." He moved his razor a sixteenth of an inch to the left. "If you want something to drink, we can go down to the bar." He thought the relative darkness of the bar, even at only 4:00 in the afternoon, would make it easier to sit with her, make it easier not to memorize all the lines on her face, the way her smile turned up first on the right side of her mouth before she erupted into the laughter that still, even now, made him think of hand bells. He should think of the things he would miss about her when they went their separate ways. That will help him be less angry. That will help him wish her well. She'd been leaving him, he realized, since the first day they met.

"You want to go to a bar? In the afternoon?" They would be those two people who sit in the dark next to each other not talking. Better, Helen felt, to sit in their suite not talking than to display their distance to the entire city. He was afraid she'd make a scene. Afraid she'd cry, even though she'd assured him that she was done with that. Afraid she'd surprise herself and cling to him. He'd already told her how much he hated when she touched him in public. He'd told her that on more than one occasion, lying every time. He never wanted her, she realized, not even on the day they met.

"OK," she said. "Let's go to the bar."

Frank had not expected this. She knew that and watched him inhale quickly. "OK then."

She had not expected that, but smiled, she hoped, without revealing her surprise.

The bartender was setting up for happy hour. The décor was 1920s chic, with the modern conveniences of wi-fi and 2 for 1s in seemingly bottomless ebony tinted glasses. The burgundy velvet wallpaper reminded Helen of a sofa her aunt had kept covered with plastic in the never-used parlor of her ancient house. Frank thought of thrift stores and people trying too hard. Even at 2 for 1, San Francisco drink prices shocked Frank. He bought in bulk. Boxed wine. 108 rolls of two-ply toilet paper. He had to. Helen would spend the necessities budget on non-essentials, items such as organic turmeric powder and mineral make up. Helen and Frank never did agree on a definition of essentials. Maybe they could talk about that in the dark—Frank with a glass of dry chardonnay, Helen with a glass of deep berry Merlot. Maybe that was where they went wrong first.

Frank tipped his glass toward Helen's. The lips dinged as they met. "To San Francisco," he said.

"To San Francisco," she said, and when they drank it was together in the manufactured dark, both watching the gloved intertwined fingers of the happier couples coming in from the late summer cold, shoulders touching, hips touching, even through multi-colored layers of clothes.

They both refused the offer of a second drink. Helen knew the bar was getting too crowded for Frank. The kids were all attached to multiple electronic devices, texting with a thumb faster than she could dial her phone. She wasn't old. Not yet. Old was other people. Old was people's mothers and grandmothers. She was turning forty tomorrow. Not old. Beginning.

She'd been pretending she hadn't noticed how many of her friends' mothers and grandmothers were dying. She'd been pretending she hadn't noticed no one carded her anymore in the grocery store. She made a joke once to the checkout clerk—a safety-pinned girl with purple hair. "I used to get carded all the time," she'd said. The safety-pinned girl looked at her as if nothing could be more impossible to believe. She remembered reading Joseph Campbell's thoughts on midlife crises when she was in college. Something about middle age occurring when you get to the top of the ladder only to realize it was up against the wrong wall. She remembered vehemently declaring she would never climb the wrong ladder. She would be aware. She would not let her life slip away.

The fingers of Frank's right hand still curled loosely around the empty glass. He was gazing at something a few inches past her face. He had crow's feet too, she thought, and his hair was creeping down from his head onto his back. Rather than cause her to turn away, her jaw softened. She saw him as she might see an animal, vulnerable and alone. Now was as good a time as any. If they had the conversation now, perhaps they could both enjoy the weekend. It had always been the unspoken things that separated them most.

She spun her wedding band on her finger. "Frank."

His gaze settled on her sparkling finger. "Let's go for a walk," he said.

"A walk?" Helen resisted the urge to shout.

"It'll be nice. See some of the city."

The softness she had felt for him dissipated. He was resisting even what he wants. He wants her to be the one who starts the conversation, but he can't even let her finish a sentence.

"I'd like to ride the trolley," he said.

"Really?" Helen wondered about getting another drink. She could drink two more so Frank wouldn't feel like he was wasting money. She tingled thinking of the effects of three deep berry Merlots in the afternoon.

"Yeah." His fingers were still curled around the empty glass. "Didn't

I ever tell you I have kind of a thing for trolleys?"

"No. You never did."

"Meant to."

Helen caught the bartender's eye, but Frank had already stood, wrapped his brown scarf around his neck, and held out his hand to her. "We'll have to wait in line, you know," she said. "It's still summer. Everyone wants to ride the trolley."

"That's OK."

"But you hate being perceived as a tourist," she said.

Frank thought it would be nice for them to be perceived as one of the happy tourist couples for one more night. He had known Helen was watching him in the bar. He felt her pity, and he knew she was about to speak about a divorce. He really was fond of her, and the idea of her not being with him in the hotel room frightened him. He knew he clung too tightly. He knew he didn't love her, at least not in the storybook way couples are supposed to love each other, but he was practical. If nothing else he knew that love is more about staying than going, and even if she no longer (did she ever?) caused his heart to dance, a man could be much worse off. Maybe they just needed to adjust their expectations. Maybe they carried too much weight on their shoulders about what marriage should be. Neither of them had good role models. Neither of them knew how to be with anyone else. Maybe they could hold hands, like the kids in the Gap commercials, and dance off together in red and blue matching T-shirts.

"I just thought it would be nice," he said. He took her hand, which had gone chilly. "Let's just go get in line."

"Fine." She pulled her purse over her shoulder, grabbed her pashmina wrap, and unhooked her fingers from his.

"Do you want to go get your camera?" he asked.

Helen stopped walking. When would he have seen her put it in her weekend bag? It had been an afterthought to pack. She'd so long been out of the habit of carrying one around with her, and now that everything had gone digital, she felt even farther away from the photographer-hobbyist she had thought she was going to be. The last time she'd snapped any shots she was reminded of the one and only time she tried to ice skate. She'd just turned twelve and wanted to slip onto the ice like the skaters she'd seen on Saturday afternoon television. She'd thought she could just slide one blade and then the other out into the rink and become light. Instead, her ankles twisted inward and she fell before she made it away from the wall. Photography had once felt like she'd thought ice skating should. But not the last time. The last time she wobbled. Unfocused. Images cropped in crazy ways. The camera, which had at one time felt like a part of her body, had become as unnatural as that thin blade on her skates.

"I just thought you might see something interesting," Frank continued. "It *is* San Francisco."

"I saw that wild girl in the intersection."

"Right."

"I didn't bring it," she said. "My camera."

"Oh. My mistake."

It wasn't even six in the evening. The line for the Powell Street Cable Car was stretched around the block. Helen pretended to look at the trays of silver earrings for sale at the street vendors near the MUNI entrance. She held up a pair of dripped silver ones with tiger's eye beads at the end. "What do you think?"

"Ten dollars," said the Asian man, wrapped in a blue parka. "Two for eighteen."

Helen nodded at him. "Frank?"

"I don't think they're you."

Helen took the offered hand mirror from the man in the blue parka. The earrings were longer than what she usually wore. Shinier.

"Very nice," said the man. "I have others too. Turquoise? You like jade? I have lots of jade."

"I think just these. Thank you." She pulled a ten from her wallet.

"No bag, thanks. I'll wear them."

Frank touched the tiger's eye beads at the end of the silver stream. His lips turned slightly lower. "The beads are pretty."

"I don't mean that I didn't actually bring the camera on the trip."

"Oh."

"I meant that I didn't actually bring it out of the hotel with us."

"OK."

"OK," she said.

"So do you want to go get it?"

"Right now?"

"Sure. I'll go stand in line."

Before Helen could reply, Frank had turned away and begun maneuvering around the city map hawkers, doomsday preachers, and Union Square shoppers. She turned her head quickly, enjoying the slight slap of the silver against her cheek. When had she last worn anything showy? If you could even call these showy. In her teenage years, she'd fully embraced all things eighties. She wore pointed shoulder pads, four colors of eye shadow, huge plastic bangle earrings with matching plastic bracelets, pegged pants and granny boots with kitten heels. She'd lived long enough that the eighties were back in style—what did they call it—retro chic—something like that. Maybe she should pick up some neon pink bangles from a thrift shop while they were in town.

Why does he want her to have a camera all of a sudden? It was just a little camera, one of the cheapies from the drugstore. She still wasn't very good at downloading the pictures to her computer, and she missed not touching the film, not watching the images begin to dance alive underneath the liquids of the darkroom. Digital was too quick—you could see right away if you got the shot you wanted. It seemed like that prevented a person from really looking.

Frank had taken his place at the back of the line, which peaked in front of the Walgreens. His sunglasses were on, though there was no need. Frank didn't actually care about the camera. He adjusted his scarf, still amazed that one could need a scarf in August, and let his gaze scan the crowd. Behind his Ray-Bans, he imagined he looked confident, like someone who was unconcerned about waiting in a tourist line by himself. He imagined the younger ladies in line found him attractive in that older-guy way. What would it be like to try and date again? Would he even try? Everyone looked really young, except for everyone else who looked really old. He was neither.

He'd lost sight of Helen. The line inched forward. He didn't relish cramming his body onto a cable car with sixty other people with cameras and children. Just do this, he told himself. Just do one normal thing. One thing like everyone else does when they come to San Francisco. Helen could snap a picture of him hanging on to a safety strap and he could look at it long after they were no longer together. He didn't care about the camera, but he cared, surprisingly, intensely, about documenting this trip. He cared about Helen being occupied enough so that she wouldn't pierce him with the announcement she was leaving him when he was unprepared. She'd been dangerously close at the bar, but that wasn't the right time. It was too soon into the trip. Why was he trying to prolong the inevitable? He didn't want to be married to her anymore, but the idea of being without her made him feel like a boy again, like he felt after his brother Benjamin died. Not an I-can-do-anything boy way. More of an I-don't-know-who-I-am-anymore way.

He'd been unprepared for the thoughts of Benjamin that had wormed their way into his head once he and Helen booked the hotel for the trip. What did Benjamin and divorce have in common? Maybe his brother wanted him to give the marriage another chance. Maybe he wanted him to do something unexpected, unplanned for once in his life—take the risks that Benjamin had never been able to. Were love and familiarity compatible with each other? Perhaps they were essential. He was getting colder in the deepening twilight. What strange summer weather in this city of possibilities.

Helen thought she'd take a few shots of the hotel room—Frank's meticulously arranged toiletries, the ocean that was the king-sized bed, the broken strap on her polka-dotted weekend bag. She didn't want to ride the cable car. Up one side of the street and down the other. That felt too familiar. A route she'd been taking her whole life. Even the two-inch thick mauve carpet felt unreal. Or un-hers. Rather than connote luxury, the carpet seemed ostentatious. It put forth too much effort to be classy. If she'd had a digital camera she could have deleted all the shots except the one of Frank's toiletries—his chess pieces lined up on the white, but not too white, sink. That would be the snapshot of their marriage.

She waited for the elevator, an ancient one with a metal gate that rattled in its shaft, on the same two-inch plush mauve carpet. Her marriage was going to end in mauve, she thought, a tinted sepia retrospective flashing in her mind. She could take multiple shots of Frank's toiletries, removing one with each shot until none were left and send it to an on-line photo competition. Too cheesy a concept for even a fourth grader, but just because it was cheesy doesn't mean it wasn't true.

HER

The wild one did not know if she had the strength yet to materialize. She'd been trying for years, succeeding only in revealing an ankle or a dirty braid or a finger. Sometimes she released a scent, the patchouli and sandalwood she'd worn ever since leaving Georgia in 1967. She had a very distinct memory of the smell of iron and a touch on the bridge of her nose from someone who still held breath. She heard music, oh, did she hear music, and she could still dance to it, still feel it inside her, the wail of longing from Janis Joplin, the shrieking of Hendrix's guitar, the Mamas and the Papas' belly soul. She had boundaries, edges, borders she was not supposed to crash, though she flung her smoky form at them over and over again, hoping for a rift. She could not catch sight of herself in a mirror so in her mind she constructed a shape like a string, thin and two-dimensional, anchored somehow to a spool. She had no discernible hands, but she could move things; no distinct feet yet she could walk. What remained as full of electrical impulses as before was her heart, which though she could no longer hear or feel beating, she nonetheless knew was there.

She missed things. Finger painting. The feel of her teeth on her tongue. Toenails and fingernails. Furry animals, especially squirrels. Water, which she could see but no longer touch or drink or smell. Dirt between her toes. The warmth of someone's skin pressed to hers. She was so terribly cold. She missed chewing, the dissolving of chocolate against her throat, the flesh of hamburger in her teeth. She did not sleep, so she did not wake. She did not laugh, so she did not cry, and she did not know one year from the next except by the changes in cars and music. The people, it seemed to her, if she was even a she anymore, remained much the same.

If she had woken that morning, she would have known what was approaching. But since she could not sleep, she did not wake, she only knew with an urgency previously un-experienced, she had to try again to be seen.

2007

Helen Connor had never believed in the spirit world, but that didn't mean she didn't experience it. When her mother died, and young Helen had lain in her rigamortifying arms for three days, she had seen more than her fair share of what she didn't understand, and now, as she stepped ever closer to the hotel's window, she still didn't believe what was clearly beckoning her.

She heard the San Francisco jokes in her head as she stretched the heavy drapes open as far as she could. The sidewalk below was smooth white. It could be soft, she thought, like sand. The jokes they would make wouldn't be true. She hadn't taken anything illegal into her body. She hadn't been reading Ferlinghetti for too many hours, followed by a nightcap of Hunter S. Thompson and Kerouac. She had simply hoped she and her soon-to-be-ex-husband would be able to state the Decision in a decidedly civil manner with a glass of Merlot in the ornate lobby, or in the line waiting for the cable car, or maybe in the Stockton Street Tunnel on a jaunt to Chinatown. She hadn't known the Stockton Street Tunnel existed until they arrived here and she squinted into its green fluorescence and almost-remembered having been here before. She stood now framed by the dusty olive floor-to-ceiling drapery and thought she would just put one foot in front of the other and walk quickly through the window toward the girl. They would land together, giggling, on the white sand.

"Helen, there is no girl," said her soon-to-be-ex-husband Frank when he returned to the room after wondering why she hadn't joined him in the cable car line. "There is no girl."

But what did he know? He didn't believe in anything, had never supported her in anything, had only ever once spoken to her after one of her dreams in such a way that conveyed anything besides pity.

Helen was curled on the floor in a knot, not unlike the knot she was found in by a neighbor who had come to check on why her mother hadn't been to work in the past three days. The mauve carpet was as dusty as the drapes, which were beginning to remind her of the kudzu green of Georgia. Funny, what the mind remembers as it's about to snap. She hoped that wherever it went off to would be a pleasant place. She wouldn't mind a few sunflowers or a bluebird or two. She had always been partial to bluebirds.

Would Frank be with her in the new place of her mind? The sun stabbed the center of her forehead and the intensity of it kept her from following the break she was certain her mind was making.

Frank tapped his foot beside her head, and even in this moment, the last moment of her sanity, he couldn't find it within him to touch her. This was not from lack of kindness or compassion. It was simply from lack of ability. She had long ago stopped expecting or judging him for it. She had not, however, stopped wishing for it. "I've called for help," he said.

"I'm fine," she said to the carpet mites and his tapping foot. "I just need to rest."

"The light probably just caught something strange in the Tunnel and bounced it back. The windows are dirty. You know how that can make things look odd."

"I'm fine."

"Someone will be here soon."

"Someone is already here."

He looked around the room. "Where?"

No where, she said inside herself, in that place he never heard.

Sirens wailed, but they were not for her. There was no need. So many others here with needs. So many needs. She unrolled from her knot and touched her left forearm. She felt hot, like she had a fever, but that was not possible. Nothing had ever seemed so clear before. Someone in the throes of a fever would not be so certain that she was about to go mad and that she was about to divorce her husband and that there was indeed a girl just on the other side of the window who looked just like—she was less sure here—like someone she did used to know, maybe back in Georgia, a playmate, or a school friend, only she couldn't remember having any playmates, especially after her mother had died and she returned to school a very different girl than when she had last been there. Even the muddy girl with the orange braids and missing teeth who had been willing to talk to her before turned her back when she walked by.

Locked in the arms of her mother.

Locked in the arms of her mother.

Locked in the arms of her mother.

That's what the newspapers had said. Her daughter, Helen, was found by a neighbor locked in the arms of her mother.

"I never seen anything like it in all my days," said the neighbor, Claire Williams. "That little girl was curled right up in her dead mama's arms and those arms got the rig'mortis and she couldn't get out anymore. When I got there, she was sleeping, just like the Madonna and Child, only there were flies and a stink I'll never get out of my brain."

That's what the newspapers had said, so that's what Helen became. Locked in the arms of her mother.

"Like she was an animal in the zoo," the neighbor lady had said when the police arrived. "That little girl was just penned up in that cage of arms."

A knock, more of a pounding really, on the hotel door.

"I'm fine, Frank," she said, sitting up fully.

"Someone is here now," he said.

When he let the paramedics in, the man with thick black hair pulled back in a ponytail and reflective sunglasses perched on top of his head, placed an oxygen mask over her nose and mouth. The other one, a woman with an unfortunate mole between her right eye and her nose, wrapped a blood pressure cuff around her left bicep. "Just breathe regular, darlin'," she said.

Helen had been breathing regular. She started to wonder what it meant to actually breathe irregularly, but then she was sidetracked again by the thought that she was losing her mind, and these two people in uniforms were not going to rescue her, but were going to escort her to a new place. That thought must have made her breathe irregularly, because the man with the ponytail placed his hand on her shoulder. "It's OK."

Frank stood away from the three of them. His foot had not stopped tapping.

"Ever notice how the sounds of the car engines change when they enter the Tunnel?" asked Helen. "It's like the Tunnel wraps them in one of those puffy vests. The kind that don't look good on anybody."

The mole-lady laughed. "You're fine." She ripped off the blood pressure cuff. "120 over 80. You drink enough water today? It's dry here today, even though we're right by the water."

"That is a strange phenomenon, isn't it?" said Frank. The paramedics looked over at him. Had he been there all along?

Mole-lady continued. "Lots of folks come here and don't think about water. Not so hot usually, so you don't notice. That's one thing that'll get a person quicker than just about anything else. Not enough water. Don't let our crazy August cold make you think you don't need to drink."

Mr. Ponytail was going to remove the oxygen mask, but she stopped him. She wanted him close by for a little longer. He smelled of loam.

She suddenly wanted to eat him.

He removed the oxygen mask anyway. "What's your name, pretty lady?"

"Helen."

"That was my mother's name," he said.

Mole-lady snapped her bag shut. Her clipboard was open. "Last name?"

"Connor."

"Address?"

As Mole-lady filled out the form, deja vu overtook Helen again. The whisper of the draperies. Frank's tapping foot. Where had she felt that before? The place was on the edge of her tongue, the lip of her mind, but not enough-there.

Frank handed over his insurance card. They both signed releases. They weren't going to take her away after all, and she was somewhat disappointed. Somewhat concerned that now that they were going to let her remain here at the Hotel Gladmore next to the Stockton Street Tunnel, she would have to somehow make sense of the girl on the other side of the window all on her own. She was not up to that at all and was about to say so, when Frank opened the door to escort the paramedics out. He didn't replace the chain lock. She was still on the floor, though now her legs were straight out in front of her, and she didn't smell Mr. Ponytail's earth-scent anymore.

"I will keep you on my insurance," he said, though they hadn't yet had the official We Are Getting Divorced conversation. "I'm going to go walk into Chinatown. I'll bring back some moo goo gai pan." And he was gone without touching her, and she knew in that moment that he did love her, as much as his broken little-boy heart was capable of, and that this leaving was the moment. He would not be back, not with moo goo gai pan, not with kung pao chicken, not with egg drop soup. He would not be back, and he had left as graciously as he was capable of, and Helen resolved to forgive him as graciously as she could; after all, he saved her the trouble of being the one to take action. For the first time in their fragile seventeen-year marriage he made the first move.

Thin fog had arrived, and with it, a moon. Helen thought it would be a fine time for a walk. And maybe that second glass of Merlot. After all, the paramedics said she was fine.

She remembered to take her key since she knew Frank would not be waiting for her, asleep hugging the left side of the mattress. His suitcase stood in the closet; everything still packed except for the toiletries in formation in the bathroom. Maybe he would be back for them. She also took a tiny bottle of vodka from the honor bar because she remembered that the room reservations were under Frank's VISA card. Sweater. Scarf. Room key. Vodka. It didn't take as much as she'd thought to have enough.

Past Life Reasserts Itself
A Hashbury Daily Times Exclusive Scoop from Remmy X

A forty-year-old woman visiting from Phoenix, Arizona, almost jumped to her death from the seventh floor of the Hotel Gladmore in the tourist-heavy Union Square area of San Francisco. The woman said she was pulled back from the window by her past life. When authorities arrived after her husband returned from sight-seeing and found her collapsed on the floor, no sign of another occupant, past or future, was found. The woman was left in the care of her husband.

The Hotel Gladmore is at the corner of Stockton and Pine, just on the edge of the Stockton Street Tunnel into Chinatown. Frequent hauntings have been claimed by past residents of the hotel, but to date, nothing has been proven. There's the usual jabberings of the homeless or the lost, but this woman belied the expected appearance of a haunting-sighter. And perhaps that is why the authorities were called and responded. Or perhaps it was just a slow Friday afternoon in San Francisco on this 40th anniversary of our Summer of Love.

Sometimes, the city opens itself up, and sometimes it remains closed. There have been those who claim the city holds many time periods in its grip and all it takes is a glitch, ala the Matrix, (really great flick, by the way—the first one, not so much the other two) to skew someone out of their current location. This reporter makes no guarantee as to the accuracy of these claims; only not to report them would be unprofessional, since there were indeed so unusually many on this most auspicious day.

Remmy X: Hashbury Daily Times

REMMY X

Oh man, I saw her tonight. I hadn't seen her in a long time, and I know if I tell anyone I saw her again, they're going to make me go back into that place I can't even name anymore I've pushed it so far out of my brain-house. I was doing my usual. Sitting in front of Ben and Jerry's on Haight and Ashbury so all the tourists would see me. My Remington's up on a plastic TV table, and I have a stack of real paper next to it. My sign: *You pick subject. You pick price. I write poem.* Sometimes I make a hundred bucks or so. It's fun to watch the kids who never seen anything like my old typewriter. They look at it like it's a fossil someone pulled out of the earth. One of them even jumped back a little when I typed. The noise, he said. How do you take the noise?

When I'm not making poems, I'm a journalist. I'm the unofficial self-designated reporter for Hashbury. I have a dog, Shep, sits with me under my plastic TV table. Sometimes people give him some food, but not usually me. They don't usually want to pay for a poem either, at any price. I should write an article about why that is one day. Except if I did, I'd have to figure out why that is and I don't know as I could come up with a headlining-type reason. For me, poetry makes my blood pump.

I wrote that little story about the crazy in Union Square at the Hotel Gladmore because my buddy Don—he used to be called Starburst back in the day—is on the official SFPD. He's not on that Union

Square tourist beat; he's off in the Tenderloin, but he still hears stuff and he drops by to share the cool info with me for my paper. Don and me, we were here then when it was all color and light and electric. He got yanked out by his parents and sent to Ohio for schooling around '69 or so. But he came back here to us anyway. I know it's because he remembers, and because he knew Ohio wouldn't ever give him anything even close to what this place give him, even when it takes every last soul-cell.

"Remmy," he says to me from time to time—that's what people call me, because of my typewriter. "Remmy. Don't you ever think about it all?"

And I scratch my dog's ears (he likes it better behind the right ear) and I nod. "I sure do, Don."

"Sometimes I feel like it was just day before yesterday. You and me. Elle."

I get surprised when he mentions Elle. We're not supposed to talk about her. It sends me back to that place in my brain-house I am not able to stay. He remembers.

"Sorry, Remmy." He touches my back. "Sorry."

I know he is, so I say OK. Don's my friend. He's just about the only one comes by to talk to me, actually me, and not the burned out hippie stuck in the sixties everybody else sees. Though for the record, I haven't had a drop of anything, a smoke of anything, since 1972. No one believes me, and that's all right. It's easier to be invisible if everyone thinks you're tripping. But man, I want to say sometimes to those folks who I know are just gawking at me and all up in my business judging me, man, don't you judge Remmy. You stuck somewhere too, rich boy. You just too damn blind to see it.

- X out.

2007

Helen hadn't figured herself to be a woman who would commit suicide, but all signs pointed to the fact that she didn't know herself as well as she thought she did. Mr. Ponytail and Mole-Lady didn't seem alarmed. They probably see things like that all the time. Crazy lady from out of town. Too much to drink. Not enough to drink. And then splat. It's over before anyone can ask anything. Even before she can ask anything of herself. Clean-up crew comes in and after a half an hour, no one is interrupted traveling into Macy's from North Beach in an Escalade.

The doorman who opened the door for her on the street level, which was street and not sand, wore a maroon and gold uniform with tassels on the shoulders. The Queen of Hearts mysteriously floated through her mind. "Can I hail you a cab, ma'am?"

She tightened her scarf, patted her room key snug in her jean pocket. "Thank you, but no."

He turned away from her to help another guest.

"I don't know where I'm going," she said.

He didn't hear her. He was talking to a woman who was simultaneously talking on her iPhone. "What did you say?" asked the woman.

"South of Market," said the doorman.

"He said *south* of Market," the woman said to her phone. She shook her head. Not one hair on her auburn head moved. "He says it's not south of Market."

The doorman put his hands up in the air. "It's south of Market. If he doesn't think it's south of Market, what do you want me to tell you? It's my job to tell you where it is. It's your job to believe me. If you don't believe me, then I can't do my job."

The woman had stopped talking, her iPhone held a few inches out from her head. "Can you hear what he's saying?" she shouted. A produce truck rattled down Stockton. The number 30 bus knelt, sighing, inhaled and drove off again. The cab driver in front of the Hotel honked. The driver raised his arms. *You need me or what?* The doorman shrugged. "He says he can't hear you!" said the woman to the doorman.

"It's south of Market!" he shouted. "South. Other side. Away from here."

"You don't have to be such an ass," she said, sliding the phone into her bag and stepping into the cab. The doorman opened his mouth, noticed Helen still standing on the single step leading into the hotel, and closed it. The cab drove away.

"I don't know where I'm going," Helen said, a little louder this time.

"Well then I sure as hell can't tell you how to get there," the doorman said. "I'm sorry."

Helen smiled. He had delicious brown eyes. Like Mr. Ponytail. "That woman—she's going—"

"South of Market."

Helen let a little laugh leak. "Then I think I'll stay north."

He extended his polyester clad arm. "I'm Omar."

"Helen."

"Why is it you don't know where you're going?"

"I—well, I am looking for—I am—"

"You got good shoes on your feet, Helen?"

They both looked at the ground. Sensible brown Naturalizer walking shoes. "It appears so."

"Then just start walking. You'll get where you're supposed to go."

"That sounds very New Agey."

"Do I look New Agey to you?" He smiled wide, his two canine teeth missing. "Ma'am, I live in Oakland."

"I don't know what that means."

"Don't matter. Just head out there."

Helen started to walk towards the Stockton Street Tunnel. "Maybe not there. It'll be dark. The Tunnel gets dangerous."

"You sound like my mother," she said and her voice caught in her throat when she realized she'd said something she didn't know for a fact was true.

"Then you've got to do what I tell you, right?" Omar was close enough to her she could smell the menthol on his uniform. "Go back that way. Turn right at Market. Stay on this side of the street, and then see where the city takes you."

"Where are you sending me?"

"How should I know?"

"Well, why not turn left at Market?"

"Because you'll end up in the Financial District, and it's too late for there to be anything going on. Even the bagel places close up at five."

"I'm hungry," she said.

"Then you better get yourself something to eat before you set out walking."

REMMY X

I am packing up my typewriter for the night and I see it again. There's this kind of flick of a shadow and then there's nothing, so I know, kind of know, that there's nothing there, in that way nothing is always something, and I know, really know, to keep my mouth shut about it, except maybe to Don. Don's what my grandmother used to call a Stuffer. That's somebody who can just take in all kinds of stuff without ever letting anything back out again. "Those people often go into law enforcement," she'd say. "They get their sadness out on bad people." I don't know as Don does that, but I also know enough to know that Don's got something moving through his own brain-house. He's been by to see me a bit too much lately since his wife left him and he says his apartment is too loud and quiet both at the same time, which he thinks is a little strange, but I know is just the way things are.

Shep and I, today, are going to go looking for what I see. He likes to think he's a hunting dog, so I get him all riled up to go seeking things by rubbing his fur the wrong way and playing around with his muzzle. He likes it, though he makes a ferocious noise. I know he likes it because he is all smiling in his eyes even though he's growling in his throat. I'm a man who understands contradictions. Dogs got 'em too. I know what you're thinking. What kind of poet am I if my dog's name is a cliché from a melodramatic country song? Well, if any of you out there are writers, you know you don't name anybody. They tell you their name, if you're lucky and Shep just showed up as Shep. Wasn't much I could do about it. I used to name all the things I saw—toasters, fire hydrants, windowpanes—until it got to be too much for one person to keep track of.

Today we got a cup of Chunky Monkey ice cream from a tourist. I made only $42, but that's enough for us. I wrote a really good poem for this kid from Seattle and his girlfriend who had piercings all up in her cheek. She had wild green eyes and it was clear to me that he was way more into her than she was into him, so I said so in the poem. He wouldn't pay me what he agreed to for it.

"I told you to write about love!" he said, after he read the last lines:
The morning you forget to lock the gate it creeps into the street
leaving you in your bathrobe, coffee cooling in your cup
the open door behind you gasping
"I did," I said.

She got it though, and for just a minute I didn't see any piercings or any wildness, just a little girl who got herself stuck. But I'm probably just projecting that shit. My counselor at the Free Clinic uses that word a lot. Like I'm some kind of old-fashioned slide projector just throwing images around of what I want to see. Pissed me off at first, but the more I got to thinking about it, the more it seemed like it would be really odd not to project anything. Like, how is it that one person can look at beautiful old Shep here and see what a fine specimen of a dog he is and somebody else just sees a wore out old mutt?

I think about that word—projecting—when I think I see what I think I see today. Do I really see anything at all? Or do I just want to see something bad enough that I put it there? A man can spend his whole life thinking about such questions and never be able to stretch apart one answer from another and just end up with a headache to beat the day.

My typewriter fits nice in a solid black box with a black handle. It's a sturdy thing, able to withstand all the kicks it gets. I don't have any stickers on the black box like so many people like to do on their computers. *Save the Whales* or *Keep Your Laws off My Body* or some such pronouncements. Would be disrespecting, I think, to try and smack down words on a word-making machine.

When Shep dies, I'll carry his ashes around in my black box, too. All of us go together good. I've got a bike with a banana seat and a basket where the Remington goes. Shep trots on along beside me, and I ride the bike. It's blue gray, like the ocean up at the Cliff House. I used to go up to the Cliff House a lot and just watch the water crash up against all those sharp rocks. There's the ruins of an old bathhouse up there too, from when it was a fancy rich people resort a hundred years ago. And there's a tunnel. I liked to shout in the tunnel and listen to my voice echo back. I haven't been up there in a long long time. Bet the bathhouse ruins still look the same though. That's the thing about San Francisco. When stuff falls into ruin, it doesn't change anymore. It just hangs around looking more modern and more part of what has always been here. There's another pondering question I might like to write about: why is it that when there's nobody around anymore who knew what a thing used to be and that thing just becomes what it is, it suddenly is perfect and complete? Is that a pondering question for a poem or an article?

Shep doesn't project. That's one really cool thing about dogs. They see exactly what's in front of them—lots of times with their noses—and they don't usually overreact. At least not once they're as old as Shep. I am babbling now, which I do when I get nervous. I could have had a pill for that, but I told you, I haven't had a drop of anything, a shot of anything, since 1972. No difference at all between the drugs that come from a pharmacy and the drugs that come from the corner. That's no Remmy slide-projecting. That's just truth.

- X out.

2007

Frank had left his unpacked luggage in the Hotel Gladmore on purpose. He was ready to take a walk, but not the whole walk. Not just yet. He needed a few more days to be sure, absolutely sure, that he was ready to walk away. And he knew he'd need a clean shave and a good mouthwash before it was all over. When Helen said she'd almost jumped from the window after that wild girl, he'd felt a disturbing excitement. Not that he wanted her dead, no, not at all—just that the action had seemed so deliberate, so full of purpose—he had been enthralled, wondering what that sort of purpose might look like within him. As for the girl, well, of course that was impossible as the man in the moon. But he knew Helen well enough to know she believed it. Her unusual combination of deliberateness and her ability to throw logic and rational thought out the window and move forward on intuition alone was both what he adored and loathed in her.

He was not certain anymore that he wanted to not be married. Could a person both want and not want the same thing? He was an accountant, not prone to enjoying conflicting concepts. He wanted a few more days to be sure. To weigh the pros and cons. To consult with his, well, he had no one to consult with, but he had felt sure that a few more days would have illuminated the appropriate decision. Yes, I will marry you. No, I will not. Yes, I love you. No, I do not. Yes, I want to get a divorce. No, I cannot bear my life without you. Could there be a mix? Frank had always believed he had the most unfortunate luck of loving Helen and not wanting to marry her. The logical step was to marry if one loved, so Frank moved in the direction of logic. Helen, on the other hand, had leaned over to him in the front seat of his Buick Century in 1990, when they were barely into their twenties, and told him that she would marry him, though he hadn't asked.

"Why?" he'd wondered.

"You are a reliable person," she said. "You will keep me steady."

That was as close to romance as Frank had ever gotten, the most sincere compliment he could remember being given, and she did have very straight teeth, with a slight gap between the front two that he suddenly wanted to see if he could slide his tongue through. There had to be worse reasons to get married. He could not remember his parents ever complimenting each other, and they were together forty-seven years before his mother died. "She made good scrambled eggs," his father said on the day of her funeral. "I can't seem to make them right, myself." Frank knew the secret was fresh basil, but he couldn't bring himself to share that part of his mother with his father. Let him try to figure it out himself.

The energy of the City slapped Frank hard. Seven different kinds of music, truck engines, bus engines, trolleys, limos, pedestrians speaking a rainbow of languages, the green sewage smell from the Tunnel, the sharp edged cologne of the man in Armani, the discarded wine bottle left too long in the sun. He unconsciously patted his wallet in his rear pocket, made sure the button was secure. He had gone too far from the hotel to go back and ask the doorman for guidance toward a destination. Besides, he couldn't risk running into Helen. Not just yet. She might make the decision for him before he was ready again, like she always did. Or worse, maybe she thought he already made the decision by leaving her in the room.

His socks were too thin for a very long walk. He had sensitive feet.

The arches were too high and the big toe on his right foot had been broken too many years ago to remember, and it had never healed properly. When he walked too long it sizzled inside like a pink neon sign. Was it a long or a short walk through the Tunnel into Chinatown? Was it safe to walk next to all that honking traffic? Under all those dark arches?

He needed to move into this City energy. He needed to stop fighting it. His therapist always told him that resistance caused suffering. He stopped going to see her after she told him he needed to embrace his failing marriage so he could let it go. Of course, she couldn't provide him with any tips on how exactly to do that, so that was the end of that relationship. Well, he didn't actually end the relationship. He just stopped showing up for his appointments. He didn't want to call her and tell her.

He tripped on a bit of raised sidewalk. He could see her face, hovering a few feet in front of him. "Doing the same thing to Helen that you did to me, aren't you, Franklin? Just walking away." He hated that she called him Franklin. Only his mother had called him that. Unlike with most parents who used full names only for anger, his mother used his when she was tucking him in for sleep, lightly pushing his hair off his face. "Good night, Franklin-boy. My sweet Franklin-boy." Those were times when his father had either already collapsed in the orange vinyl chair with a plastic bowl of corn chips and his seventh Pabst or hadn't made it back home yet from "business with the boys." An unfamiliar stillness settled in the house during those times, the edges of which seemed to stretch his mother outward. Her smile re-formed. Her arms opened up and out, and Frank, Franklin-boy, could move into them and let out a full exhale.

This was different, dear Dr. I-Forgot-Your-Name. Helen knew what was happening. They were the only couple in America to plan a vacation together to decide whether or not to divorce. No secrets. No passivity (oh, how many times had Helen accused him of that, in her own passive pronouncements). No one could play the martyr card on this trip. They were both finally growing up, he concluded, and that, at least, was something to be quite proud of.

He tripped again. Which way was he going? The sidewalk seemed to be taunting him, jerking up from the earth at unnatural angles. Maybe he would turn back and ask the doorman for directions to someplace to eat that was quiet, off the tourist track, so he could make his decision. He turned, watching his feet this time, only to find what was behind him didn't resemble where he thought he had come from. A bus barreled by, but he couldn't catch the number, as if it would have made any difference orienting him. The sight of a number, though, would have comforted him. Numbers had no shadows.

People talking to the air (he assumed they had ear pods), people rolling metal carts with laundry, vegetables, and bread, people texting on their iPhones—all moved around him in unison with the grace of water. All right then. Frank Connor, sweet Franklin-boy, would move forward, and forward at that moment, was into the Stockton Street Tunnel.

HER

She hadn't meant to pull the woman out the window onto the street at the Hotel Gladmore. She didn't think she did, anyway. She had just tried to make herself as small as possible and then as large as possible to see what would happen. She'd been so startled to be seen, even for a second. She didn't remember ever staying at the Hotel Gladmore, or even spending much time in Union Square, but she was pulled as if into a vacuum tube to that hotel, that window, that woman, and since she was only a string, and a thin one at that, she did not know how to prevent being blown about by the fog and the winds. She threw her energy against the window when she saw the woman was about to jump, or perhaps more accurately, she could hear the woman's thoughts about the smooth sandy sidewalk and tried to send her own shriek back—*no, no, the sidewalk is not sand*—until the woman fell back into the room. She was undone by the shriek, shaking, jittery, all sparks and shorts, and fell, herself, the seven floors to the sidewalk. Only this time, no one noticed. She fell through Omar the doorman, who simply readjusted his cap. She quickly pushed herself away from the fast moving cabs and pressed into the stone wall of the hotel. Feral, she merged with the jagged stones until she felt invisible. The street was fast. The woman in the hotel room was real. She needed that woman. That specific woman. Today.

Hashbury Hauntings Increase
A *Spectre Speculation Scoop*

This reporter cannot be certain the time, since the clock on the corner of Haight and Ashbury has not worked since longer than even he can remember. But this reporter can be certain that for a moment, in the window of the People's Café, a flash of light occurred that had no discernible source. A flash of a strobe light from 1967? A glint from the sun hitting the #71 in just the right way? One of the slumped kids flashing a mirror or a lighter just out of boredom? Nothing can be said for certain, but this is the nature of a haunting. If everyone could agree on what it was, it would not be a haunting. It would be a fact.

Remmy's Reflection Moment: My dog Shep saw it, too. Most times he just goes with me where I go because that's what dogs do. But today, he saw it first, and I followed him. When I got to the windowpane, all I saw was my own scraggly self looking back. Well, in the interest of full disclosure, I also saw the employee with the pierced forehead who tries to keep me out of the café's bathroom when they're busy. But like all things worth reflecting upon, it wasn't what I saw that was all that important. It was what I didn't see. It was what I intuited. And what I intuited was that the Haight is just about ready to spew a little, like a volcano everyone thinks is long gone quiet. Except everyone knows volcanoes aren't ever for sure quiet. They're always just bubbling and hissing underneath the calm and everyone, even the scientists, act all surprised when a volcano does what a volcano does. What's funniest is when all the men in their science-suits act like they can put back in that volcano all it just spit out. And that's the close of this day's Remmy's Reflection Moment.

Remmy X: Hashbury Daily Times

P.S. Do you like the new Remmy's Reflection Moment? Drop by during regular business hours and let me know. I am working on making my voice stronger, not so formal and reporter-y. I'll give a free poem to the first five readers who come by with a comment!

REMMY X

I feel sad right now, and I feel like I should tell you a little what that's about. I didn't ever think my life was going to be like it has become. Don't get me wrong. I'm grateful for what I got, and maybe no one is more surprised than me that I'm still here, all things considering.

You'd never know it, not now, but I originally come from Mississippi, and in 1966 I had one of those moments where you know for absolute certain that God himself is knocking right at your heart. God said to me, "Remmy, get yourself out of Mississippi. Ain't going to end well for you here. Go to San Francisco and I'll take good care of you." You may think that's an awful lot of complete sentences for God to be saying to a nobody like me, but I got a pretty sophisticated relationship with him, even back then. Well, the draft was coming, and it was coming for guys like me faster than we could cut our hamstrings or enroll in college. Even if, on the off chance that it wasn't God made those sentences to me, it was a fine idea. I didn't need to be told twice. I'd gotten involved with the Civil Rights movement and the Klan was not too keen on white boys who helped out. I got marked in town one afternoon and figured that day was as good as any to take God's advice.

They were all saying a guy could disappear in San Francisco. Just go under. Be part of a new kind of civilization. I won't lie, not at this point in my life. I didn't have a lot of fire for a new kind of civilization or for fighting much of anything. I just wanted to stay out of 'Nam. Maybe that's why I stayed here so long after everybody else who come here is dead or long gone to some other kind of life that doesn't touch this one. Maybe that's why I'm sad today. I was left here to be the documentarian of a place that has become a cliché. I'm the one who has to witness what it is now, and that's really hard sometimes because I see not only what it was, but I see what it could have been, and both those things are long long in the past. Everything's been turned into retro-chic or modern hippie or worse. There's a shoe store right a few doors down selling sandals for $300. That's not what the Haight was about. But people buy them, act like they slumming here, stepping over me and my dog like we're made of dust. They buy them and go back to Pacific Heights or Sausalito or up to Marin County and show off what they found in the land of free love and ice cream. Those folks don't ever see this place right. Haight never lets those kinds of people see her heart.

I think about who's going to do the documenting after Shep and me are gone. I'm no fool. I know my paper's no *New York Times*, or even *USA Today*. I know it gets swept up on the street or the occasional tourist takes it home for a school project on *Hippies Hanging on to Hope* or some such nonsense. Don reads it. Some scattered raggedy folks who also can't leave, but I keep writing it because the neighborhood tells me to and that's always been enough. "Remmy," it says to me, not unlike the voice of God. "Remmy, don't forget me."

- X out.

1967

Elle dreamed of two black swans circling in a green pond. Lily pads dotted the surface of the water. She heard the murmur of frogs, but couldn't see them. At first she couldn't tell if the swans were chasing each other or dancing.

Each swan's golden beak jutted out like a warrior's chin. Each swan held to its swimming pattern, going round and round in concentric circles, passing each other at the same points on the circle but never touching, never getting close enough to slide feather against feather, never close enough to see underneath the blackness of the darting eyes or allow the wake of one to pull the other.

Elle woke. It was the morning she would leave. She looked down at her toes to make sure they had not webbed together in the night. She didn't notice the film of dampness just underneath her lower lip, or the way the blonde hair on her forearm felt that morning like feathers.

She stepped onto the sagging wooden porch in her bare feet, knowing exactly how to avoid the exposed nails and peeling paint. The rusted green chair where her aunt Sadie sat every night rubbing her callused feet had overturned in the night, probably from a raccoon hoping for some of the sunflower seeds always left scattered on the planks.

She took in everything as if she were being led to the gallows. This was the azalea that her third cousin John Junior tried to make come back from the dead by pouring his RC cola into the Georgia clay, as if that could counteract the months of neglect. This was the woodpecker hole that got as big as a half dollar before Uncle Sid managed to hit the bird with his BB. Aunt Sadie stuffed the hole with colored rags, which came in handy when someone sitting on the porch needed to blow his nose or wipe his tobacco-wet lips. This was the door handle that Elle carried as her first memory of life at Aunt Sadie and Uncle Sid's. The door handle was mounted crookedly; a top left to bottom right diagonal, and a tiny mouse head adorned the top of it. Sadie had found it used; at one time it had been a handle on a rich girl's dresser, now it had been left in the yard for trash pick up. Sadie loved mice and never could bring herself to set any of the traps that Sid kept bringing home from town.

"There's not going to be no Mousewitz in my house," she'd say, and shoo Sid back out the door. Sid set the traps in the shed, along the edge of the house, and around the garden, but he usually succeeded in trapping only the paws of stray dogs or the occasional garter snake that slithered over the top of one in search of bugs. Mice were blessed at Aunt Sadie's house, and Elle knew, with all of her eighteen-year-old soul, that this was significant—that this told her more about Aunt Sadie than any description could. Sid had no sympathy for mice, or rats, or garter snakes, or woodpeckers, or raccoons, or tomcats or wasps or any other creature that inadvertently set foot across his property line. This too, she thought solemnly, told her something deep and raw about Uncle Sid.

This was the spot under the porch behind a cement block where the kittens were born, all slippery and wiggly and mewling. She and Aunt Sadie had kept the kittens a secret from Uncle Sid, who would have been infuriated that they were wasting perfectly good table scraps on a stray mama cat. They managed, though, and Elle had found a home for every one of the seven kittens with kids from school. This was the spot on the driveway where the mama cat had been crushed by the back wheels of

Uncle Sid's pick up. He swore it was an accident, and Elle thought Aunt Sadie believed him, but she didn't. She knew what else Uncle Sid could do.

This was where she and John Junior made leaf piles to jump in every October, and this was where she, saltshaker in hand, saw a rainbow colored slug shimmering. She had been so captivated by it she couldn't pour the salt on it and missed her favorite dessert of yellow cake and cream staring at its glittering back.

The sun shot its rays through the base of the pine trees behind the house. This was the last sunrise she'd see in Georgia. The last time the Southern dew would cover her feet with kisses. The last time she'd see the kudzu running along the side of the house beside her bedroom window. She took these things in solemnly, severely, for she knew she had made a monumental choice during the night.

Aunt Sadie was already at work. She took the 5 a.m. bus into Atlanta proper to clean other people's houses. Uncle Sid was still snoring. Elle knew she should wake him up so he wouldn't miss his ride into town. John Junior had spent the night with his new friend Casey. There would never be a more perfect time for what she was about to do. She bowed her head.

"Dear God, please take care of Aunt Sadie and Uncle Sid and John Junior. Please keep the mice and the raccoons and the rabbits and the mama cats safe. Please keep me safe, God, and please bless Mommy every day all the days even though she went away from me, thank you God, Amen."

The prayer surfaced for her, even though she had, for the time being anyway, decided that God and Jesus and the Sweet By and By were for other people. Her brain might think that, but whenever she was about to make a big decision, or do something scary, she bowed her head and the words just tumbled out like seashells from a bucket. She knew the prayer was juvenile, much too simple for a young woman of eighteen, but it was what her heart knew.

Elle opened the screen door slowly to avoid the screech of the hinges.

She could put everything she owned into two paper grocery bags; she had set two aside last Tuesday after their weekly trip to the market, though she hadn't known why at the time. She had four changes of clothes, a toothbrush, a hairbrush, a barrette, a photograph of her mother taken when her mother was twenty-six, just two years before she ran off with that tent revivalist, and a fiddle. She had wanted a violin, but Aunt Sadie couldn't afford to buy one, and there was a perfectly good fiddle sitting up in the attic that Grandpa Clyde had played back in the day.

"Ain't nobody using it, hon," said Sadie. "Go on up there and take it down. Fiddlin's mostly the same as a violinin' anyway. Who would know?"

Elle couldn't tell her that she would know, and that her orchestra teacher would know, and that really, everybody knew the difference between a fiddle and a violin. She couldn't tell her because she knew Aunt Sadie didn't have any money, and she knew Aunt Sadie hadn't had enough money to take care of her after her mother ran off, but she took care of her anyway, as best she could. She couldn't tell her that nobody played fiddle anymore—that was hillbilly music—she couldn't tell her any of the truth that bubbled up in her, the largest truth being that she loved the wail of the violin, and imagined the violin could make the sounds she felt inside her when she had lain in bed with the realization her mother wasn't coming home. She had learned to make the fiddle wail, enough so that the orchestra teacher made room for a fiddle and gave her the school's first ever fiddling solo, the notes from which made even the dried-up principal dab his eyes with his yellowed handkerchief.

She'd rigged up a shoulder strap for the fiddle case from Aunt Sadie's old nylon hose. Ever since World War II, Sadie never threw anything away. Said you never know what you might need and God would be mad if He'd already given it to you and you let it slip through your fingers. The nylon hose was strong and didn't cut into the flesh of her shoulders.

And so she set out that early June morning in 1967, fiddle slung across her back, paper sack of clothing in each hand, down the dusty drive that had for the past nine years been the way home. She remembered a verse in the Bible about shaking the dust off of feet, so she did that at the end of the path, having to shake her right foot a little longer to dislodge a pebble that had gotten between her toes. "God bless Aunt Sadie," she whispered again. "Tell her I'm sorry."

Elle had left a note for Sadie in the kitchen above the sink, but she knew Sadie couldn't read, and she couldn't be sure that Sid would read it to her, or that he would read it accurately. So, she had kept it simple:

> *Dear Sadie,*
>
> *I have to leave. I'm going to San Francisco to play my music. Thank you for taking care of me.*
>
> *I love you.*
>
> *Your niece,*
> *Elle.*

Elle had just graduated high school, the proud class of 1967, and she knew in that way that bears know it's time to hibernate, that if she didn't get out of Georgia at this right moment in time, she never would, and she would find herself taking the 5 a.m. bus into Atlanta to clean other people's houses and bring home their leftovers. She'd read about San Francisco, about the music and the people and the kids. She'd caught glimpses of the color of the streets in an issue of *Life* magazine and on the radio, just once when she had been parked—only once—with Timothy Getz in his daddy's brand new shiny black Mustang, she heard the wailing of a woman called Janis Joplin. Her voice sounded just like Elle's fiddle, just like the wailing that Elle couldn't make when her mother left to follow Jesus and Reverend Jimmy Joe. She'd learned Janis was a Southern girl from Texas, who'd found her way into California and into singing the blues.

"She sounds like me," Elle had said to Timothy Getz as he inched his fingers down the back of her shirt.

"I didn't know you could sing," he said, breathy.

"I don't sing," she said, noticing the stiffness of the hair on the back of her neck. "My fiddle does."

"Uh-huh," said Timothy Getz, shifting on his seat. He traced the edge of her ear with his finger. She involuntarily shivered. "Come on, baby," he said, and Elle thought he almost whined. She turned her face to him, just the tail end of a tear in the corner of her left eye. He mistook the tear for joy, and she mistook his next move for love.

She hadn't thought far enough ahead to figure out how exactly she was going to get across three time zones into San Francisco, but she knew it would happen. She believed, like her mama had believed once upon a time in her daddy and then again in the tent revivalist, that if a person wants something bad enough, she can get it through sheer will.

It was 7 a.m. and already stifling. The air shimmered with humidity. The buzz of insects was a metronome. She'd taken three apples and two slices of bread from the cupboard, hoping Aunt Sadie would understand. It never occurred to her she might need more than two meals to get to California. It never occurred to her what sacrifices a person might make in the pursuit of will, or that the very act of pursuing could keep a person circling, circling, circling, with no time for a feather to brush against another's in the moonlight.

As she walked west, she imagined what Aunt Sadie would do when she got home and found her missing. Would she cry? She would, but quietly, in the way middle-aged women know how to do. She wouldn't share her tears with Uncle Sid, and she would spend longer than usual that night on the porch in the rusted green chair popping sunflower seeds into her mouth and spitting out the shells. She knew Aunt Sadie would be sad, but she also hoped she'd be relieved with only one child to take care of—if you didn't count Uncle Sid.

Elle wore denim jeans and a dark blue work shirt she'd stolen from Uncle Sid that she tied at the waist. She lamented forgetting a hat, but it was too late to turn back. If she went back, she'd never leave. She promised herself she'd write to Aunt Sadie just as soon as she got settled in San Francisco, even if Sadie couldn't read the letters. Elle imagined herself in a small apartment that looked out over the bay that she only knew in her mind—an apartment without rats or roaches—a place without her uncle's drinking—a place without her mother's ghost. She was young and strong and talented, and more than a little pretty, so it never occurred to her that she couldn't have that apartment overlooking the bay, that she couldn't find work within a few days playing in a band, that she couldn't leave her aunt behind in the same way her mother had left her. Surely, among all that color and all those people dancing she could find a place to belong.

She began to notice the cracks in the gray asphalt, the jaggedness of the white line that ran down the center of the two lane road, the litter—bottles, caps, cigarettes, a pair of pink socks—strewn along the side of the road. Her feet didn't know this road like they knew the wooden porch at Sadie's. Each step brought the fear of a nail or worse pushing through the soles of the ancient sandals she'd slipped on after stepping out of Aunt Sadie's yard for the last time. She was sure she'd been walking half a day, although the sun hadn't caught up with her. Her stomach growled, but she wanted to conserve her apple and bread, and, she realized a little later than she would like to admit, she hadn't brought any water. She'd need to find a creek.

It would have been easier to have run away from Aunt Sadie's when she was younger. She could have gone searching for her father, who her mother claimed was somewhere in Maryland taking care of his other children. About now, which she estimated at 10:30, though her aching legs thought it was much later, Aunt Sadie would be finishing up the kitchen in the Hurley's house. She'd be running blue cleaner over the large bay window, being careful not to knock over the jungle of plants

Mrs. Hurley kept on the windowsill "to bring more oxygen into the air" for her husband, who had TB and sat all day in a rocking chair with an Army blanket over his feet. She'd be getting ready for her lunch of cheese and an apple, maybe a little bit of cold bacon, before catching the bus to Mrs. Quimby's three story house. It was Friday, so she'd be washing curtains today, and she'd come home with her fingers wrinkled as figs. Maybe Elle should have left on a Thursday, which was an easier day for Aunt Sadie, a day of dusting and ironing and vacuuming. Friday was a day of scrubbing the week away.

Up ahead she saw a water moccasin crushed on the road. It was unusual for those snakes to ever be away from the water. A creek must be nearby, even if it was a creek with water moccasins. Her tongue was thick with thirst. She picked up a discarded beer bottle from the side of the road thinking she would rinse it out in the water and then fill it up for the afternoon, when a blue pick up truck pulled up beside her. She wrapped her arms around her chest, even as she cocked her hip to the right in a pose she hoped was grown up and unafraid.

"Do you need some help?" The man was a few years older—maybe twenty-one—and his eyes were the same pale blue as his truck. He held a cigarette in his left hand, his right hand draped casually over the steering wheel. A gray duffel bag lay in the truck bed and a clear jug of water perched enticingly on the seat next to him.

"I'm fine," she said, eyeing the water. "Just out for a walk."

"Where you walking to? I could take you." He slid a little closer to the passenger window and she thought of Timothy Getz.

"Just out walking."

He took a drag off the cigarette, then flicked the burning tip into the street. "Never known anyone to be out walking with bags of clothes and a fiddle unless they got themselves someplace to go."

"How do you know I have clothes?"

He shrugged. "It's in your walk." He turned off the engine. "Want some water?"

She said yes before she meant to, causing him to smile again. "Name's Brian. I'm not dangerous or anything. You can look under the seat if you want to." He held out a paper cup of water through the passenger window. Why would looking under the seat convince her he wasn't dangerous?

She drank it down in one gulp. "Thank you."

"You're welcome. Did I tell you my name's Brian?"

She nodded.

"And your name would be?"

She uncocked her hip. "Elle," and before she could close her lips, "I'm a fiddle player."

"I reckoned that from the fiddle on your back. How about you set that down in here? You've got to be hot and tired."

She held out the paper cup, which he refilled promptly.

"What do you say, Elle? Come ride awhile with me?"

"I'm going far," she said.

A look of sadness, brief as the twitch of a cat's whisker, crossed his face. "Me too. All the way to Chicago." He pulled out a large map of the United States and touched Georgia. "We're here. " He traced his way north and west to Chicago. "I'm going here."

She opened the door and took her fiddle off her back. "I'm going to San Francisco," she said. "I'm going to find Janis Joplin."

"She a relative of yours?"

"Not exactly. She's a singer."

"Well, I'm sure when you get there, you could just ask around and find her. I read the City's only about ten miles big. How hard can it be to find somebody?"

"I don't know." She held out the cup again.

"Help yourself," he said this time, pointing at the jug.

"I'll ride with you," she said, as if she had been the one making the decision. "Just until you get to Chicago. Then I'll find my way."

His top row of teeth was crooked, like falling fence posts. "I'm glad you'll ride with me, Elle. Just until we get to Chicago."

She closed the door behind her, and he started the engine.

"Think we can make it out of Georgia by sunset?" he asked.

"Let's go," she said, and leaned back in the seat, letting the wind slap her hair across her cheeks. She was alive and no longer thirsty, and she was going to San Francisco to play with Janis Joplin. Going, going, gone.

Elle worked at the apple skin between her teeth with the pine needle. It worked all right, but she had to be very careful not to tear the pine needle. She rather enjoyed the taste of the tree. Aunt Sadie still wouldn't know she had left. Uncle Sid probably knew, but he would be relieved. He'd likely already begun turning her room into a tool shed. What would happen if more kittens were found under the porch steps? She thought of the warm, wriggling babies—gray and white and brown and orange—speckled like someone had just thrown paint at them. Her head leaned slightly back on the seat, even as her body moved forward. Her thoughts had weight. They were pulling her back to Aunt Sadie's and were just about as strong as the 250 horses that powered the truck. She wanted to know for a fact that Sadie would be missing her.

This was a moment she would remember her entire life—a moment when she could have made a multitude of decisions—and she had chosen to travel west with a strange, yet sweet man who did not appear to be going to kill her. She already saw the colors of San Francisco in her mind. She'd seen some black and white images on the television, and even through the grainy feed, she could imagine the purples and the yellows and the glitter. The City seemed to be plastered with glitter, but it could have been just the snow on the screen from the bad reception.

She knew from the TV coverage that the Vietnam War was a disaster, even though Uncle Sid thought it was necessary and important and that America had lost its manhood and was now a bunch of long-haired baby-boys. A young man who lived down the street and was just a few years ahead of Elle in school had been killed over there in a place she couldn't pronounce. The boy's name had been Kirk. He had jade green eyes and he had once given her a piece of spearmint gum. He had enlisted after graduation in 1965 and was dead before the first year was over. His mama hung a black flag in front of her house that she never took down. She stopped going to church and even stopped working in her garden, which had once been one of the most colorful in the neighborhood. Elle remembered the black car no one had ever seen before driving down the street and stopping for its few, long minutes, in front of her house.

"Damn shame," Aunt Sadie had said. Uncle Sid had only grunted.

"Hero's death," he'd said. "Not many men get lucky enough to die a hero."

Sadie shoved her hands into the dishwater so hard the hot water splashed all over the counter. "Still dead."

Elle watched the road move outside the window. Nothing looked any different. She thought for some inexplicable reason when she left Aunt Sadie's that morning that she'd be in San Francisco by dinner. The City was so full of magic it could transcend the laws of space and time. "Ain't got the sense God give ya," she heard Uncle Sid saying. Now that she felt the length of each mile beneath the truck, she wondered how she imagined she'd get to San Francisco with two apples, a slice of bread, and no money. How was she going to get more food?

"I can play you a song!"

Brian laughed. "You don't have to fiddle for food!"

"I want to," she said quickly. "Let me. I–I'm really good."

"So you say."

"I am. I'm better than good." She knew that truth deeper than any other in her life. Mr. McPhereson, her orchestra teacher, had given her a five-minute slot in the senior concert to play a solo she'd written. When she told him she had no idea how to write music, he told her just to listen for it and the fiddle would take her where she was supposed to go. Mr. McPhereson hadn't even given Emily Patterson a flute solo, and everyone knew he had the hots for her, so she took the fiddle to the front porch and the man was right—the fiddle took her back to a place she'd never visited.

In 1958, Elle's mother, Millie, should have been pretty, but she wasn't. Her yellow blonde hair had gone dishwater, and her nose was a bit too long, one blue eye a touch larger than the other. She worked ten hours a day, six days a week, at the textile factory in Lumberton, North Carolina, where she stitched and cut and glued bolts of cloth for other people's fancy clothes. Her eyebrows arched like Betty Page's, but on Millie, they only looked like lost caterpillars. Twelve years of tobacco took the youth from her skin before she was thirty. Elle's father, according to her mother, was living with his other family in Maryland. According to her grandmother, he was a no-account Marine in Camp Lejeune. Elle didn't care where he was—Maryland, Camp Lejeune, or the land of missing fathers—she only knew that if he was with them, her mother might not be almost-pretty.

While Elle was in third grade learning long division, she didn't know her mother didn't go to the factory after she dropped her off for school. She didn't know anything about the tent revivalist, Reverend Jimmie Joe. She didn't know if her mother had been planning all along to leave her that morning, or if it had just struck her, like lightning from above, and she never looked back.

Brian turned the truck off the road into a dirt parking lot. A diner tucked behind a large metal pink man holding a silver tray stood next to a seven-unit motel. A sign reading NO COLOREDS was in the window next to an advertisement for Coca-Cola with a smiling blonde woman, her lips almost touching the neck of the Coke bottle. "How about here? I know it's not very nice, but I haven't seen anything else."

She had no money. She'd heard about boys who took things from girls who didn't have enough money. "I don't need to eat."

"We've been through this."

Elle pulled her fiddle case closed with her legs. "I'm not going in there."

"We've got to eat somewhere."

"Not there." The parking lot seemed sad. "Where are we?"

"Alabama."

"It'll be different in San Francisco," she said, eyeing the NO COL-OREDS sign. "People there are different. This is just a stupid Southern thing."

"It's a stupid people thing Elle. And people don't change."

She turned to the window. "Anyone who believes that has to be the saddest person on earth. If I believed that, I'd cry every day." She picked up the apple core and took another nibble on the brown fruit before placing it back on the seat. "Besides, what about you? I didn't even know you before today, but I bet you never thought you'd be here with me right now."

He grinned and nodded. "Got me there."

The NO COLOREDS sign was angry, jagged and black. Elle's stomach rumbled again. "OK. Let's go in." Even though Jim Crow was supposedly over in '65, and Atlanta had taken down most of its NO COLORED signs, Alabama and Mississippi were two places black people still didn't want to be, and she knew enough to be ashamed she was grateful to be white.

She was disappointed that Alabama wasn't any different from Georgia. If Brian hadn't told her they'd crossed the state line, she wouldn't have known they weren't still in the Peachtree state. There were still the same sad ancient trees, the same kudzu inching up the sides of gray-white clapboard houses, and those same signs.

The word Alabama was almost a palindrome. Almost. That seemed significant to her. Alabala or Amabama. One letter off from a miracle of language.

Brian hopped out of the truck, swiping the apple core off the seat into the dirt. He tried to help her get out, but she'd already opened the door and closed it behind her. She almost reached for his hand as they walked toward the smudged glass door, but retracted just in time.

The diner was dirty. Torn pink vinyl booths sat on black and white tile. Two of the eleven tables hadn't been cleared, and flies hovered over the bits of cube steak and potatoes. There were no other customers. A bald man in a white shirt and apron stood behind the counter, his gaze lingering longer on Elle than Brian.

"Ya'll want something to eat?"

"Yes, please," said Brian, and Elle was pleased by Brian's attempt to be polite. Uncle Sid was wrong about today's kids. They were polite. They were nice. They weren't all druggie Commie hippies. Whatever that was.

"What?"

Elle summoned her best adult voice. "Can I see a menu please?"

"No menu. You want it, I can cook it."

Elle caught a glimpse into the greasy kitchen through the open order window. "I'll just have bread."

The bald man laughed. "That's no food. You need to eat you something. You're way too skinny. I bet your—" He paused a bit too long. "—husband there would love it if you put on a little bit of meat."

"He's not my—"

Brian cut her off. "I like her fine just the way she is."

The bald man chuckled. "Suit yourself. What'll it be?"

"Two patty melts," said Brian.

"Fries?"

"No," said Elle, eyeing the oil in the kitchen.

"Suit yourself. Sit wherever. If ya'll need a place to stay tonight, I own the motel too. Got plenty of rooms."

"Maybe," said Brian. "We were, um, hoping to get on to Birmingham tonight."

"Suit yourself."

"I'm going to Chicago," said Brian. "She's going to San Francisco." Elle noticed his shoulders rolling down his back, his spine straightening a bit, an adult pride that made her smile.

"'Course she is," said the bald man, and disappeared into the dark kitchen.

Elle led Brian to the table farthest away from the uncleaned ones. The table was set with four plastic placemats with Civil War scenes. Her placemat had a large Confederate flag as a background. "Don't use the silverware," she whispered. Elle shuddered at the thought of what kinds of people's lips had been on the knives, forks, and spoons. "I can eat with my fingers."

"You're full of surprises."

She thought he was picking on her, but his eyes shone.

The bald man took an hour making two patty melts, and by the time he brought it to them, Elle was ready to stay the night anywhere.

"I can sleep in the truck," Brian said.

She had thought that they both would sleep in the truck, like a tree house on wheels, but after riding in it for seven hours, that seemed like less than a good idea. Her other plan was to camp along the road, or maybe a little farther beyond the road so that people who had too much to drink or too little sleep didn't accidentally run them over. She'd never stayed in a motel before, and she didn't want this to be her first experience. But perhaps if she'd had a father she wouldn't have left Sadie's without even ten dollars in her pocket. Perhaps she'd have learned to read a map so she'd know she couldn't possibly get to San Francisco from Georgia in one afternoon. But she didn't have a father, and this strange, yet sweet man didn't seem like he was going to hurt her. For once, she had a knight—a Lancelot—and she was going to be Guinevere, if only for one night in a dirty roadside motel.

The No Talk Motel was only slightly cleaner than the restaurant. The draperies and bedding reeked with smoke. Cigarette burns dotted the bedspread, the carpet, even the solitary nightstand with its Gideon's Bible. The bedspread was a thin orange velvet worn through in the four corners. The sheets were the same pale orange, as was the lampshade on the only lamp. The bathroom had two towels, one washcloth, and a shower with no door or curtain. An unemptied ashtray rested precariously on the windowsill.

"Smoke?" asked Brian, pulling out a pack of Lucky Strikes.

"No. Never. Disgusting."

"You're the only woman I've met who doesn't smoke."

"No. Never. Disgusting." She smiled at him though, and stuck her tongue between the gap in her front teeth. "Sometimes it gets stuck there," she said, and he laughed. "You smoke?"

He quickly put his pack away. "No. Too expensive." He opened the door and dumped the ashes.

"You know I saw the pack in the truck." She paused for the dramatic effect. "And the one you just stashed. And the cigarette you were smoking when you picked me up."

They laughed as long as they could manage it before they had to address the matter of the bed. It was a full bed, but it took up almost the entire space in the small room. It had a brown headboard that was mounted to the wall.

"I can sleep on the floor," he said.

Elle looked down. The floor was the dirtiest part of the room, and even if there had been enough room for a full-grown man to lie down, heaven knew what things would crawl into his nostrils. She pretended to be Guinevere and sat lightly on the edge of the bed, her fiddle case next to her. "I can play you a song."

Her chin quivered when she drew the bow across the strings. Her eyes were closed and her mouth open just enough to let air in and out, her back was straight and her little toes twitched. Her nostrils flared as she crescendoed. When she finished, she bowed her head, a small prayer, and murmured something only she and the music could hear. She kept her eyes closed and lowered the fiddle to her lap.

"That was the most beautiful thing I've ever heard."

"Shhh…" She held a finger to her lips. "Can't you hear it still?"

"I can't."

"The music always comes a little before the song and then it lingers a little after. Kind of like an approaching storm. You can smell it before it comes and you can taste it after it leaves. After the storm is over, it's like there's just a little bit of mist. I have to stay with it all the way through to remind me I just got wet." She bowed her head, a bit embarrassed. "You can't hear it."

"No," he said, and reached his hand across the dirty velvet bedspread. "But I hear you."

Elle wasn't sure what Guinevere would do next. She put the fiddle into its case, snapped it shut, and held out her hand to this strange, yet sweet man. He turned her palm face up and began to trace the lines that ran horizontally across her skin. He moved so slowly. How could he bear to move so slowly? She swallowed, listening for the music to come again, but she only heard her jagged breath.

"I've never had a day like today," said Brian.

Aunt Sadie would be home by now. It was nine o'clock. She'd likely be in the kitchen, hands plunged in too-hot dishwater, letting the steam press against her cheeks so her tears wouldn't show. Who was Sadie going to talk to now?

"I've never had a day like today before either," she said. How had she not seen the dark stubble of beard that danced across his chin? How had she not noticed the small cuts on his knuckles? She no longer wondered what Guinevere would do. She wondered what Elle would do. And then. "I think I should change my name."

"What?"

"Elle. It's too boring. I'm not going to live the life of an Elle."

He let her hand fall to the bedspread. "I've never heard of a girl named Elle. Is it short for anything?"

She wrinkled her nose. "Elena Mae."

"What about Carlotta? That's fancy."

She shook her head.

"Petunia!"

She laughed. Aunt Sadie always made fun of girls named after flowers. Just on their block there was a Rose, an Oleander, an Iris, and a Violet. "Maybe my name is OK. Maybe I just need to make my life match it."

"You're a brave girl, Elle," he said. "You don't seem to have fear."

"I got plenty of fear. That's why I have to act like it's not there at all."

2007

The sounds of Chinatown pulled Frank deeper into the Tunnel. He followed his feet forward in the fluorescent dark, moving quickly to the side as a boy on a bicycle whooshed past him. He held to a promise of green tea to quench his now shouting thirst, maybe a fortune cookie to tell him what to do next. When he popped out the other side of the Tunnel, the first thing he noticed was the mural documenting the Chinese railroad workers. The sidewalk was packed with people moving in both directions. Rows of white undershirts and socks hung from tiny window balconies above him. As he moved deeper into Chinatown, the store windows became filled with skinned animals—pigs, chickens, and a few he couldn't recognize by skeleton. The signs were in Chinese with only the price in splotches he could read. Spices from the other side of the world hung in the air like confetti snow. The sweet and sour spicy air hooked him deeper. Next came the stores of plastic—plastic shoes, plastic toys, plastic jewelry stamped with knock off Hello Kitty, Ninja Turtles, and Pirates of the Caribbean logos. A few nicer stores selling jade, amber and silver jewelry and statues of laughing Buddhas and Ganeshes were slipped in between.

He lost track of his feet for what seemed to be only a moment and found himself at a four-table restaurant in a neon orange booth ordering jasmine tea, a fortune cookie, and a plate of pot stickers. The table was still sticky from the last order placed and eaten there. "Anything else for you today?" the elder Chinese woman asked when she brought his food. "You'll like pot stickers. I make them fresh today." She put the plate in front of him, along with the ticket.

"Thanks. I'm fine with this."

She nodded and turned to go back behind the counter.

"Wait."

She looked over her shoulder at him, and Frank imagined what she saw—a lonely middle-aged white man, coming to gawk at the Chinese. "What?"

"I'm looking for something."

"North Beach right over there through the alley. City Lights Bookstore right there. Golden Gate Park other direction. Japanese Tea Garden in Golden Gate Park, not here. This is Chinatown. Not the same thing as Japanese. Get on bus number 71 from Market—"

"No, no," he laughed around sips of tea. "I know all that," he said, though he didn't.

She walked back to the table. He was pleased to have piqued her interest. She slid her blue Bic ballpoint into the bun of gray-black hair.

"What you look for?"

"My brother." The words slipped past his lips before he knew he was thinking them. Benjamin? Frank was not a man who shared. He wondered how to put the words back.

"Why you think I know where your brother is?"

"I don't. Never mind. It's been an unusual day."

"Where he live?"

"He's dead."

The wrinkles on the edges of her eyes turned up enough to let him know he'd said the right thing.

"My name is Frank. I am about to divorce my wife, or she is about to divorce me, or maybe we're just going to continue on, but I went for a walk after she almost jumped out of our hotel window."

Those clauses did not strike the woman as odd at all. Shortly, another even older woman joined them at the table. Her eyes were only lights beneath the weight of the skin of her eyelids. She was shorter than the first woman, but the first woman gave power to her. They spoke to each other, and though Frank tried to open and understand the signals of the language, it only sounded like crows speaking to each other high in a tree above the rest of the world. The oldest woman looked directly at him and spoke.

"What makes you so sure you need to see him?"

The tea grew cold in his cup. He thought he saw a hint of blue in her eyes.

"I'm not sure, at all. I don't even know why I said that. I need to be going. It's just—"

"Eyes are not to be trusted," she said. "The mind tells you what your eyes see. So mind decides. Never see with eyes. See with here." She slid her hand between her breasts over her solar plexus. "Here doesn't talk to mind."

He hadn't yet taken a bite of the pot stickers. He swallowed the cold tea, which would have been better hot. The women kept looking at him. He felt both invisible and completely present beneath their stares.

"Eat your pot sticker," said the youngest one with the pen in her hair. "We'll come back."

He took a bite. It was good. Why had he stopped eating pot stickers? What was it, actually, that he'd been eating lately? He needed to get back to the hotel. This was ridiculous. Frank Connor was an adult male. He needed to take care of business, have the conversation with his wife, or not, brush his teeth, and start again.

He broke open his fortune cookie, just for kicks, and slid the white piece of paper through its lips. *You will have a new addition to your life.* He turned the paper over. Chinese characters and lucky numbers 27, 10, 6, 19, 70. Benjamin? He was born in 1970. Folly and foolishness.

He was trying too hard to make a connection. He started to tear the fortune in half, but felt the gazes of the two women on his hands. He laughed. Foolishness. Folly and foolishness. But still he placed the fortune in his pocket.

"You through now?" asked the youngest one. "We have something to tell you."

"You do? I mean, yes, I'm through. Thank you. It was delicious."

The youngest one smiled. "I make."

He nodded.

The elder sat next to him on the orange vinyl booth. She sat close enough her thighs touched his and he could smell the garlic on her exhales. "You brought here today by no accident. I not know how to give you brother back. But I supposed to tell you this. You have unfinished business with him. That's why he not at peace. He not able to wait any longer for you talk to him, so he talk to you now. Does that make sense?" She paused long enough for him to acknowledge yes with his eyes. "Good. You have to make peace with him. Ghosts must be kept in peace. Something you need to do."

"What?" Though he knew, he knew, he knew.

"I not know what. Listen with here." She tapped her solar plexus again. "Listen from here. It tell you what you need to do. Pay very close attention now. This very important." He lowered his head so he could catch every word. "If you not do what you need to do, ghost become very angry. When that happens, there's no way to fix. You understand?"

He suppressed a laugh as he imagined a B horror film unfolding in front of him. This was too much a caricature. He was a silly middle-aged man. The kind everyone made fun of. But when he looked back at the woman, he knew she was not at all joking, so he only said, "Yes, yes. I understand."

She grabbed his wrist and he was surprised by the strength of her grip. "No way to fix."

"No way to fix," he said.

She relaxed, appearing satisfied that he heard her.

That third Saturday of July 1978, Frank and his younger brother Benjamin had each eaten a breakfast of corn flakes and toast. Frank had used grape jelly, while Benjamin had used the last of the strawberry jam. Frank knew their father would be angry about that when he came out of the bedroom for breakfast, but he didn't say anything, secretly hoping his younger brother would for once be the one to get into trouble for something, even something as trivial as eating the last of their father's favorite strawberry jam.

Their father, Hal, came into the kitchen and went straight to the refrigerator as he had done every morning that summer. Ben had put the jar of jam back on the exact same shelf, the second one from the bottom on the door, to keep his father from becoming suspicious. Hal opened the jar, stuck a butter knife in, and pulled it out without a swash of jam. Ben began kicking his chair.

"Frank!" Hal forced the glass jar onto the kitchen table, breaking it. Shards of glass splattered Frank and the two plates the boys were using.

Frank sat up as tall as his eleven-year-old body would let him. "It wasn't me."

Ben had crawled under the table, already crying, choking on the gasps of his breath.

"Benjamin!" Hal rarely got angry with Benjamin. He saved most of his rage for his oldest, the one who looked least like him. Benjamin inched closer to Frank's legs under the table, wrapping his arms around them and pressing his mouth to Frank's bare legs, biting to keep from making any noise. Later that evening, Frank would find those bite marks on his legs and cry.

"Benjamin! Get out from under the table!"

Frank managed to sit up even taller. "It wasn't him." The words weren't even a whisper.

"What?"

Hal turned to face his oldest son, the rage snapping in his eyes. Just as Hal was reaching for his son's shirt, their mother appeared in the doorway, a pile of sheets in her arms.

"Hal! That's enough." She didn't raise her voice, but all three males stopped what they were doing to stare at her. Frank had often wondered if his mother had any voice at all, so often had she let things go on far too long.

Hal turned to face her, a look of both surprise and anger on his face, like a bear who had been caught rummaging in the garbage.

"There's another jar of jam in the pantry." She dropped the sheets on the floor and stepped toward him. Frank was speechless. "Come on, now."

Hal moved toward her with force in his steps, but Frank could see from the forward tip of his shoulders that the moment of danger had passed.

"Come on, now."

Hal followed his wife past the pantry into the bedroom. Frank heard the soft click of the door shut, followed by the waiting. He wasn't sure if he wanted the inevitable punch to the side of his mother's ribs to come quickly so it would be over, or if he dared to hope that today it might not happen. Ben released his jaws from Frank's legs. When Frank heard the bedspring squeak, he exhaled louder than he meant to.

"It's OK, Ben. You can come out."

Ben's face was mottled red—a swirl of watercolor—but he looked at his brother with awe.

"What do you say we go to the lake?"

Ben nodded, allowing himself the smallest edge of a smile.

"Let me clean this up first. Don't eat the rest of that toast. There's glass in it."

"I'm not hungry."

Frank slid the chair back from the table as quietly as possible. He took an envelope from the stack of mail on the counter and began to scrape the glass shards on the table into a neat pile. Then, he removed the metal wastebasket from underneath the sink and pushed the glass into the can. The bits of broken glass tinkled the sides of the can like hail. Frank carried the plates to the sink and watched the remaining breadcrumbs and glass swirl into the drain.

"There," said Frank. "Let's go."

"Race ya!" Ben already had a head start to the screen door. Frank reached for the tail of his shirt, a blue and gold one he'd handed down to his brother last year. The shirt was still too big for Ben, and he looked a little like a mini-sailboat in it.

"OK!"

The boys ran across the yard as the clap of the screen door echoed behind them. The "lake" was really nothing more than one of many glorified swamps throughout central Georgia. Boys used the swamp as a swimming hole, except for the years when polio swam in its waters. Their swamp was about fifteen feet deep, and housed all types of wild-life—water moccasins, crawdads and crayfish, pelicans, osprey, frogs of all kinds, and bugs that skated on the water. Ben called those bugs skaters, but Frank was sure that couldn't be the scientific name.

"I'm gonna win!" Ben shouted, looking back at his brother. Frank had already decided to let him win, knowing Ben would want to race on the way back, and that he would most surely lose, being hungry, tired and thirsty. He pretended, nonetheless, to try to catch him. Ben reached the muddy shore first, and slid, laughing in the mud. "I won! I won!"

Ben's face was no longer splotched with fear. Frank wondered if he had ever been as carefree as Ben, if he'd ever been able to let things roll off his shoulders as if they didn't happen. "Help me get the boat down."

Their boat was a raft made from found pieces of wood. The boys had waterproofed it together the previous summer, and Frank had found a roll of aluminum siding that he attached to the edges of the raft, making it more of a box than a boat, but it floated, and it gave the boys enough room to pretend they were Huck and Tom floating down the Mississippi on their way to find a different home. They christened her the *Marilyn*, after Marilyn Monroe, a woman the likes of whom they'd never seen in real life, only in the pin-up world of their father's garage, but the boys figured she must have some connection to their tiny town of Monroe, Georgia, otherwise surely she'd have changed her name to something more exotic.

Sometimes, if the water level was too high, they couldn't get the raft down from its hiding place in a cove along the shore. The boys had to find other ways to occupy their time while they waited for the water level to recede and release the fangs of mud that held their sanctuary in place. They were able to dislodge it that day without any problems.

"Don't forget the oar!" said Ben.

Frank had found a broken piece of a telephone pole floating in the swamp one day and decided it would make a good oar. It was useless for steering, but it was able to help push them out of corners when they got stuck. Frank thought the sky was exceptionally blue, smiling on them, if he believed in such personifications, so they would have a good experience on the water.

"Ready?" asked Frank.

"Ready!" Ben jumped in the raft and Frank pushed it away from the shoreline with the oar. He leapt onto the wobbly planks before the raft got too far away from him. They floated for a while in silence. Frank scouted the water's edges for alligators. Once, they'd seen one's hovering onyx eyes just beneath the water's surface.

"Do you think there are panthers in the woods here?" asked Ben. Ben loved cats that year. As far as he was concerned, nothing was a more amazing specimen in the natural world than a cat—the bigger the cat, the better.

"No. Not anymore, anyway. Opossums maybe."

Ben scrunched his nose. "Opossums aren't cool." He poked Frank's arm with a twig. "Do you think Dad's getting meaner?"

Frank was surprised by the question. For the last few years, neither one would speak about their father. Neither son had a good enough reason to start up a conversation, and neither son wanted to know the real depth of the scars their father had inflicted on the other. "Hard to tell." There had been a period this summer when he had seemed almost normal, wanting to hear a story or two from his sons about how they spent their summer days, but today wasn't one of them.

"I don't think I love him, Frank. Is that a sin?"

Frank hated the talk of sin that permeated their town. How could it be a sin not to love a father who doesn't love you? But Ben took sin and the church seriously. He always knelt on the hard wooden kneeling benches at St. John the Baptist Baptist Church a few moments longer than anyone else. Frank knew he wasn't trying to show anybody up, either. He was genuinely trying to find a way to talk to God. "I don't think it's a sin, Ben."

"The Bible says to honor thy father and mother."

"Yeah, maybe, but the Bible doesn't say the father and mother must honor thy children. How fair is that?"

Ben lay back on the raft and folded his arms under his head. "Bible's not about fair, Frank. It's like a teacher at school. Sometimes it makes sense and sometimes it doesn't, but as long as you do what it says, you won't have to miss recess."

Frank nodded. The sun sliced his eyes, so he couldn't tell if Ben was serious or making a joke. He didn't usually joke about religion. He loved the ceremony and costume of the worship service. Frank thought it was a glorified circus with a lot of guilt thrown in instead of elephant dung.

"I'm going to try harder to love him," said Ben.

When Frank was younger, he had tried to imagine what his father had been like as a boy so he could maybe find a way to like him a little bit. He'd never let himself think about the word love. Ben rolled onto his side, signaling to Frank that he was going to take a nap. Frank lay down in the raft as well, looking forward to seeing what pictures he could make from the clouds.

The explosion of thunder woke him up. How long had he been asleep? He sat up and saw the sky had turned from clear blue to charcoal, and that the wind was beginning to toss the tops of the reeds. Lightning followed before he could count to three.

"Ben! Get up!"

The sky's mouth opened and released sheets of rain. Ben slowly sat, rubbing his eyes.

"Storm! Help me turn it around!"

Ben staggered to his feet when a sudden, severe gust of wind pushed him to the edge of the raft. The eyes of his knees lined up perfectly with the top of the siding and he tumbled over the edge before Frank could catch his blue and gold shirttail. Ben bobbed, grinning in the water.

"Give me your hand, Ben! Get out of the water!"

"Come make me!" he said, but he was laughing, a laughter from behind his belly button that Frank hadn't heard in a long time. Thunder cracked again.

"No time, Ben! Lightning!"

Ben kept laughing, then held his nose with two fingers and dove under the water.

"Ben!"

Twenty seconds.

"Ben! It's not funny!" The rain and the wind swept Frank's words out of his mouth toward the sky.

Sixty-five seconds.

"Ben!"

Seventy-nine seconds.

Frank dove into the water, aiming for the place he'd last seen Ben's head. He couldn't be far. He kicked his arms and legs, trying not to think about hungry alligators, but he came in contact with nothing. "Ben!"

One-hundred-twenty-five seconds.

Frank dove under again, pretending his feet were flippers, trying to reach the bottom, or as close to the bottom as he dared. He didn't want to admit he was afraid of what might be living down there. His lungs shrieked louder than the wind, though underwater all he heard was a hollow echo. When he reached the surface, he was sure he'd see Ben dog-paddling next to him. But he didn't. The *Marilyn* was buoying away from him. The oar had fallen overboard as well, and it floated near Frank's arms. He reached for it, and slid it underneath his armpits. "Ben!"

Four-hundred-sixty-two seconds.

The raft. He had to be in the *Marilyn*. He must have popped out of the water and didn't see Frank so he swam to the boat. It was logical. What wasn't logical was that an eight-year-old boy was here and now he wasn't. The rain was the fiercest he'd seen since the last hurricane hit the Georgia coast. Where had it come from? The sky couldn't have been more blue.

Six-hundred-nine seconds.

Frank gathered all his strength in his belly and began kicking toward the raft. Surely Ben would be on there, panting, laughing, all splotches and smiles. Eight-year-old boys don't die. Especially not eight-year-old boys who read the Bible. Not eight-year-old boys who want to love their rotten fathers more.

Nine-hundred-two seconds.

The wind had shifted to his back, and he soon flopped along the swamp's edge, a few yards from where the *Marilyn* hovered. "Ben!" He stood and fell twice on wobbly legs as he ran toward the raft.

No Ben.

One thousand thirty-six seconds.

"Ben!" The rain kept him from seeing out onto the swamp's surface. Reeds circled around an eddy like the breadcrumbs had done that morning in the kitchen sink. The thunder was so loud and close he fell to the earth as if to pray.

One thousand thirty-six seconds was all it took. Frank stood, hooked the oar under the raft and began the steep climb back to the house. He would have cried out to God if he had any words at all, but since he didn't, his throat simply closed, and his feet pushed hard into the mud, eyes steeled against the wind.

Frank stepped back into the pulse that was Chinatown. He thought of the fortune snug in his pocket. *No way to fix.* Helen would be wondering where he was. Suddenly, he was overwhelmed by a memory he would never have—her face at 70. His belly told him what he needed to do. His belly turned him away from Union Square, toward Fisherman's Wharf. Night was lapping at the edges of the buildings. The buses hissed as they spit passengers out. Cabbies honked, swore, and skidded through the narrow streets. The night's song was more fierce than the day's song he was accustomed to hearing during his morning ride to work. The night's song switched into neon quarter notes, staccato glints of teeth and long nails, the ghetto bass of rage. How had he missed the seductiveness of night?

If he were Benjamin, where would he have gone? He didn't think he would recognize him now, after so many years. Would he still look as he had as a boy? Red-blonde curly hair, a single dimple in his left cheek, eyes so blue they were the color of cartoon tears. What, exactly, was he doing—this sensible man with sensible shoes and a steady, stable job—what was he doing, after all these years, hoping?

REMMY X

I wrote a fine poem today. Wrote it for free too and gave it to Shep, who ate it, which is as good a thing as any to do to a poem, I suppose. I was writing about this nagging thought been dancing up in my brain-house that maybe it's time to move on. I sometimes can't tell what is my smart-voice in my brain-house and what is my 'don't-be-a-fool-Remmy-and-go-do-this-thing' voice. Sometimes the voices trick me. The one that seems like it should be the smart voice is actually the fool voice and the one that seems like it'd be the dumbest thing I could possibly do is sometimes exactly what it is I am supposed to be doing. I can't get a read on this voice, so I did what I do when I'm trying to figure stuff out. I ask it and sometimes it answers me in a poem. Never an article. Voices like this aren't prone to articles. I'd share that poem with you here, but like I say, Shep ate it. Just as well. The voice didn't tell me whether it was the smart voice or the fool voice. Tricky. Must be the fool voice. Then again, that's exactly what the fool voice does, makes me think I know what it is.

Let me start again. Try and make some new-sense. I wrote a fine poem today. Nobody asked me for it. Nobody paid me five dollars for it. Nobody was even around. That's why I could hear the voices so loud. I thought at first there really was somebody behind me whispering to me. "Remmy! Time to move along. Maybe go on back to Mississippi.

Might find you got you some family left there." Now, you got to admit, that's a pretty direct and specific statement from a thought. I don't know about you, but most times my thoughts are just floating by, like ducks on a big dark lake. If I look at one too hard, it quacks, but mostly they just float on by not paying any attention to me if I'm not paying any attention to them. But every once in awhile you get a quack like that. Makes you stop and ask yourself some of those hard life kinds of questions. I hadn't thought about going back to Mississippi in this lifetime ever again. You can't go home again is one of the truest things I've ever heard. Haight here's been my home for over forty years, but try as I might, I stand on the same sidewalks I been on all this time, but I can't make my way back to her.

I asked that voice in my head was it the good voice or the fool voice and it told me nothing. Just clammed right up and acted like I hadn't asked it a direct question. So my poem took it head on and wrestled around with it.

No firm answer showed up, but I got one good line I can remember.

I dance the waltz while you dance the salsa.
What music should we put on?

Think on that.

- X out.

2007

Helen ducked into a Middle Eastern café near Civic Center just to rest her feet and maybe get a little food. She felt light-headed.

"Pita bread and some grilled vegetables," she said to the man behind the counter. His dark moustache was longer on the left side than the right. He didn't make eye contact. "And just a water." He pointed to the do-it-yourself beverage bar. She nodded her thanks. Maybe Frank had returned to their room with the moo goo gai pan. Maybe right now he was running his fingers over her nightgown and wishing he'd have said something different when he left. Maybe he was remembering their wedding day and the strange black and white scruffy dog that had crashed the reception, slapping the lower tier of the yellow cake with his tail. She pressed the paper Pepsi cup against the ice dispenser.

Stop it. Just stop it. If she knew anything about Frank, she knew he wasn't doing much thinking about her. If he went back to the hotel at all it was to retrieve his precious toiletries. He'd always been difficult to explain to people. She could never sufficiently explain why she married him, why he married her, and how she felt that even though he was likely halfway back to Phoenix by now, he did love her and she did love him. Why, and that's the biggest question indeed, love wasn't enough. Why, even knowing he might well have already left the state, she wasn't angry about that, or even especially pouty or put out. He was predictable, which served them well in parts of their lives together, tore them apart in others. She couldn't fault a person's nature. That's just what you get. And, if she were being honest, and now was about as good a time as any for that, her nature wasn't particularly conducive to traditional touchy-feely huggy-muggy sorts of relationships anyway. As easy as it would be to fault Frank for everything, she knew nothing was further from the truth.

The sky was dark, but the City's streets were bright. Frank toyed with the idea of putting on sunglasses just to be—well, he didn't know what. A foolish middle-aged guy wearing sunglasses at night. He hadn't gotten used to the noise yet. Nowhere was quiet. Not the alleys. Not the bus stops. Not inside the restaurants. And the noise was a babble. Languages layering upon languages, some of them even variations of English, all designed to make him feel even more alien than he did every day. When he was a kid, after Benjamin died, he used to pretend he was an alien. It was the only explanation that made sense—the only explanation that accounted for his ability to keep on going to school, turning in homework, getting somewhat interested in the way Becky Fletcher's pony tail moved when she walked. He managed to think about his brother only in that moment when it was too dark to sleep and he could lay on top of the cotton coverlet and even with his eyes wide open see nothing.

REMMY X

Shep and I go back to our apartment in the lower Haight we'd been (or at least I'd been) living in for well on thirty-some years now. Rent's way out of my price range, poetry not paying so good these days and all, but I stay on anyway. The building manager, Pop Rocket, is from the days. The building is kind of the Chelsea Hotel of San Francisco, and I guess the new yuppy-duppy-guppies pay so much for rent for their big windows overlooking the Street that Shep and I can stay in the basement apartment as sort of local color. A curiosity. A walking piece of his-stor-ee. We don't mind. We know a good thing when we got it, and we also know times are gonna circle around again like they always do and Shep and I won't be needing anymore places to sleep, least not on this earth anyway.

One great thing about our room is the boiler is right down here with us so we get the hottest showers of anyone in the building. It's also underneath everybody, being as it's in the basement, so no matter how much noise I make pacing around trying to find the right words, I don't disturb anybody. That's important, because as soon as you start worrying about how all your carryings on are affecting other people, it gets harder to keep connected to the things you're supposed to focus on.

I'm not stupid. I know people look at me and my dog and my TV table and my typewriter and they feel the pity for me. They feel like they know me and what I'm about just because of where I am and what I look like. They feel the pity—not because I'm pitiful, but because they can feel powerful. They can think of the good things they got— the student loan debt, the car loan debt, the house loan debt, the job that don't see them but gives them an office where, I might add if you would allow, they have their own expensive version of a TV table and a typewriter, and, might I add once again, they don't got a dog sitting underneath that table pressing his nose up against their knee just to remind them there's something still alive in the world.

They think my life is some kind of failing because it doesn't look like theirs, but I ask them, can you hear the whispers of your neighborhood? Can you see the ripples at the edges of the buildings that are visible only at dawn and dusk? Can you see the layers and layers of things that have happened on a single square block? I tried to explain it once. I got so frustrated with all the ways people looking at me, I finally said to the couple who'd tried to barter a poem from me with a measly dollar, Look, I know it's peculiar, but I think of it as a blessing, being able to hear the heart of the neighborhood, being the one to be trusted with all her history and all her stories. Someone's got to be the documentarian and I didn't apply for this position, more like I got appointed and there weren't nothing I could do to refuse that calling. It's sacred work to be the one who carries the stories.

But I could see the more I kept talking, the more they turned away from me or stuffed a dollar or two in my milk carton (without even getting their poem! Remmy does not accept charity!) The more I kept talking, the crazier I sounded until I knew I just better shut up because I was somehow betraying my neighborhood even as I was trying to defend it. I'm not sure how that happened. Sometimes things in my brain-house don't make a lot of sense, but what I thought was clear as day became cloudy once I started speaking too much. I watched their pity turn to fear and that's worse—much worse—so I sat back down, waited for another group to pass by, and played the part of the stuck-in-the-60s-hippie in my tie-dyed shirt wearing my mala beads eating my pint of Cherry Garcia ice cream. People feel safer around clichés, I guess. It turns out if people think they know who you are and what you're about, they may let their guard down a bit and tell you something real.

"I used to smoke the dope," one guy said to me after his wife and kids had moved on towards the swanky shoe store. He leaned in real close like he really wanted me to see him.

"That so?" I said.

He smiled real big, the hopeful kind of smile that masks a lie. "I followed The Dead."

"That so?"

"Some kind of time," he said. "Some kind of time it was."

And he gave me a fiver, which I didn't consider to be charity since I had to bear witness not only to his lie but now I had to carry his longing for a few hours till I could shake it free. He looked back over his shoulder once before he followed his family of blondes into the swank. He flashed the peace sign, real quick before anyone else saw, and that time it was me that felt the pity. I didn't follow The Dead around the country. They came right here to me and set up house. Weren't any need to go wandering in somebody else's dream. I wrote a poem for that man anyway, even though he didn't ask for it, but I only wrote it in my head. It was too sad to put on paper.

- X out.

2007

Brian worked at the Boudin sourdough factory down at the wharf. He'd worked there since the fifth day after Elle died. The work was easier for him then. The bending and lifting and kneading of the dough made him feel like he was making something from nothing, like he thought Elle did when she played the fiddle. Where did it come from? Her music. Where? And why didn't he have anything like that? So he made bread and fed people and went to work and went home every single day, never once calling in sick, for forty years, not even on the forty separate anniversaries of the day she died.

Unlike many of his coworkers, he liked the tourists, liked the way they stared at him through the big glass windows on Jefferson Street, liked the way the sons tugged at their fathers' arms as he pressed the bread flat, then twisted it and flattened it again. He liked thinking the boys thought his job was much more important and exciting than their fathers' jobs. He had a product the boys could see—not a stock or a bond, not a real estate deal or a hedge fund. And even better than that, they could eat his product, literally not metaphorically, and at the end of every day he could count accurately what he had done, how many people he had fed with his elbows and knees and lower back, and it made him feel useful and needed. Now, he didn't make bread too much anymore. It was too hard on his body. The younger men, with tattoos and piercings in places he wasn't sure he even had on his own body, were much faster and more efficient than he was, though he doubted they loved the dough like he did. He doubted they felt each ingredient under their fingerprints as they blended them together. But what could he do now?

He was the old man to these kids, and most days he felt it. Sixty-one. Now, he wore a white apron and took groups of tourists through the plant, showing them the important places along the way. He posed with uninterested children holding up bread sculptures while parents fumbled with their new digital cameras. He told the "I could tell you when" stories about the glory days of San Francisco, snuck in stories about the 1906 quake and the fire, snuck in stories about the opium dens and the human trafficking. He'd never tell Elle, even if he could still tell Elle anything, but he loved San Francisco as much as she had, only he loved its past, the wooden sidewalks and early trolleys and the potential of this port city long before he and Elle had been born. He spent hours in the archives at the public library on Larkin, peering through a loop at the photographs from one hundred years ago, his white gloved hands touching the people in the photos, everyone surely now long dead, and thought about their stories. Who they loved. What they drank. If he might have passed them on Haight one day while he was walking with Elle, stars still squarely centered in his eyes.

Brian knew immediately something had happened. He was taking a tour group of twelve—four from Germany, two from Japan, one from Florida, and five from Minnesota visiting the City with their Lutheran church group—past the young men working the bread with their young hands when he glanced out the window at the traffic heading west toward Van Ness. It was probably just a flash from a car headlight catching the sun just right. Or maybe a sea gull that flew a little too close to the glass. It was probably nothing, but he couldn't shake it. In fact, it shook him so much that he forgot how to make the bread, and thus forgot to tell the twelve how to make the bread, resulting in a strange and unwelcome silence.

He thought of Elle. The silence of her body on the shiny, splashing streets. The caves of her eyes, tide pools of licking marsh grasses. He had to stop the tour, something he had never done before, and leave work early, squinting without sunglasses over the bay, past the seals and the one hour tourist boats, past the red and white fleet, and over and beyond Alcatraz island until everything blurred together into sky.

No one was more surprised than Brian to find himself outside of Boudin in the middle of the day walking in a direction away from the 19 line at Polk. For forty years he left work, turned right, and walked to Polk Street to board the bus. He tried to always sit in one of the single seats by the middle doors. That was usually possible since he was picking up the route at the beginning. He'd become overtly agitated if someone got to the seat before him. Once he stared at a dark skinned teenage boy long and fierce enough to get him to move with a toss of his hand and a "whatever, old man." Brian had settled in the seat quickly, not minding in the least the warmth the boy had left behind.

At first he thought he'd walk a ways along the wharf, get past the tourist section and maybe even make it to the Ferry Building before he got on a different bus and meandered home. Then, in a thought that took him by complete surprise, he thought that was too predictable. Too safe. He needed to try and find some place he'd never seen before. Was there anything left in this City he hadn't seen?

He walked east now, toward Chinatown. Elle had been waiting for him on the side of I-40, wearing a denim jacket with patches shaped like roses, or that's what he remembered. She stood as tall and confident along that dust covered highway as any self-respecting oak tree might do. He watched her let an 18-wheeler go by without a glance, though the driver slowed down long enough for her to jump in if she'd been so inclined. He liked to think she was waiting for him—or if she didn't know she was waiting for him, waiting for someone in particular, who she'd know when she saw. How else could he explain the way she jumped up and down when his Chevy came into full view? How else could he explain the way she all but leaped into the cab, her fiddle case snug between her ankles, and smiled at him as if he were her finally resurrected savior?

It was the way of things then—people hitchhiked all the time. Nobody was really worried that anything truly bad would happen. The entire country was coming out of a long, dark sleep, like when you turn a heavy rock over and all the bugs run around in circles, unsure of what to do in sunlight. Folks were like those bugs—spinning like the pinwheels you can get at the fair for a quarter. Some people spun as fast as they could, while other folks held on, trying with all their might to stop the dizziness. But no one could have stopped that spinning. Not Jesus himself. Not Bobby Kennedy, not Martin King. Nobody could keep the colors from mixing on that pinwheel.

Just five years before he picked up Elle for the first time, it would have been unusual to see a woman by herself on the side of the road holding a musical instrument, but soon it happened all the time—women packing up and moving somewhere, anywhere, but where they'd come from. A man who was willing to take the time to stop and pick one of these women up might find himself in a most unexpected place. Brian knew he'd found himself in that unexpected place. Then, he'd have said he'd pay any price to have picked her up. She was so magical. And he recognized himself in her a little. He was running from someplace too, and he'd seen stories from the west where people lived in school buses painted with huge flowers and peace symbols, and it looked like everywhere you went you could find a friend, somewhere to sleep, someplace to eat. It had only taken that first night together in Alabama for him to forget about Chicago and point himself toward the farthest edge of America.

He wanted that because she did. He didn't know he couldn't "turn on, tune in, drop out" and fall into oblivion like so many seemed to be able to do. But he did want to try. He didn't know the ways of ghosts then. He didn't know the woman in the denim jacket would teach him more than anyone should know about the ways of ghosts. He'd promised his mother he would not get himself killed. Would not become a ghost. No card; no draft; no getting killed. It all seemed simple, but of course, it was anything but.

She told him her name, and that she'd go as far west as he was heading, if that would be all right. She'd been walking long enough to sweat, but the oils on her skin seemed natural, like seal's skin, and she smelled like the earth mother, and she smiled wide, a pinch of collards stuck between the gap in her teeth, and assured him she was a good girl—woman. A good woman. She drank from his water bottle without asking, or so he remembered, and the sheer brazenness of that act turned him on.

The face of the woman of the 60s was unlike the face of his mother and aunts. It was unlike the faces of the women in his church, or in his high school. The 60s woman was a feral cat, bra tossed to the flames, hanging loose, limp, and free. Anyone who'd ever tried to feed a feral cat could have told him what was in store for all of them. His rulebook said one thing; their rulebook said another. As much as he wanted the wild thing in his house, he couldn't find a way to make her think she was still in the wild when she was in his bed or in his yard. She said just a few months later he had wanted to tame her, take away her screams, but he didn't, truly, he didn't. He just wanted her to be comfortable curled up in front of the fire with him, and she never could be. She peeked out from time to time, a wild cat, and he would get a glimpse of her hunting eyes, but most days, she was too far gone.

He should have brought a bottle of water. He had actually thought someone from Boudin would have come looking for him. Maybe one of the young men with their young arms and legs would come chasing him down. He might surprise them all. He might shock the young men with their young arms and young legs and dart into an alley and become swallowed by the City. It happens to people. Average people, just like Brian, walking home from work one day on a different route find themselves an offering to the City's ruthless god.

He reached for the top of his head but found his white hat missing. He must have shed it somewhere along the walk. He was almost bald, but not quite. He had the unfortunate curse of too much hair from his ears back, and not enough from his ears forward. The thick strip of white hair at the base of his skull looked more like an old-fashioned hand muff than respectable hair. His mustache, in contrast, was thin, a worn carpet to shade his upper lip. The top of his head shone in the sun. He needed some water. When was the last thing he drank? Coffee that morning in the automatic drip machine he'd bought a year ago so he could wake up to fresh coffee and maybe, he'd hoped, still foolishly, share it with her.

He'd left his entire lunch back at Boudin, a pimento cheese sandwich with a golden delicious apple and a handful of organic trail mix he'd been picking up from the new market towards Union Square. He imagined the raisins and cashews, the pale chewy granola and Newman's chocolate.

He needed more than water. The Powell-Mason cable car line was nearby. He hadn't ridden a cable car in nearly twenty years. He wasn't comfortable with the tourists there. He couldn't quite articulate why the cable car tourists were different from the Boudin Sourdough tourists, but they were. Cable car tourists wanted snapshots and the outer facade of his City. Boudin Sourdough tourists wanted the process of life. Bread was inner life. Without bread, there'd be no Coit Tower, no crookedest street, no Grace Cathedral to look at.

He boarded on Columbus, surprising himself for at least the third time that day. He stood on the running board, right hand holding the brass post. The cable car was a cheerful red and dark brown. The operator loved the bell, and Brian soon found himself looking forward to hearing its song as they entered each intersection. Only a few people were on the cable car. It was still mid morning. A weekday. Past the peak of summer traffic. A little girl, maybe three or four, wearing lacy pink socks and black buckled shoes held a red lollipop in her hand. Her mother had one too. He watched the woman's mouth around the circle of the hard candy for a moment too long.

The cable car merged right onto Mason Street, heading downhill. Even though the car wasn't going terribly fast, he enjoyed the feel of the air pushing past his face. Dogs feel like this, he thought, when they hang their heads out of cars, enthralled, absolutely, with the dew of life. The girl and the woman with lollipops got off the car on Pacific Avenue. He almost followed them. His hand left the safety rail, but he remembered who he was, a man of routine, and though his body yearned and wriggled in ways he'd no longer thought possible, he resumed his grip on the safety rail. Maybe he'd get off at California Street. He needed to eat.

REMMY X

Shep kept old Remmy awake all last night. He only does that when something extraordinary is about to happen. He only does that when it's real important that I pay attention.

- X out.

2007

The pepper seasoning on the vegetables scratched Helen's throat. She tried a swallow of water, but the tickle wouldn't go away.

"Can I have some butter?" she asked the bearded man behind the counter. The café was empty except for a petite woman in a maroon headscarf reading a newspaper at a corner table.

"You don't like the food?" asked the man.

"I do." She cleared her throat. "I just need something softer."

His lip, which she hadn't noticed before since it was covered with bushy dark hair, curled. "Hear that?" he said. The woman in the headscarf looked up. "Lady here wants something softer." She smiled, resumed her reading.

"I didn't mean to offend you," Helen said. "It's just that—"

The man behind the counter stopped chopping lamb. The woman in the headscarf put her paper down. No one else had entered the café. The sidewalk out front was a mass of moving people—Armani suits and stiletto heels, dropped jeans and Keds, briefcased and Blackberried and cart-pushing—all on their way *to from towards away.*

The woman spoke. "It's just that what?" Her voice was a distant church bell. Helen wasn't sure she heard it until the reverberations hit her bones.

"Pepper's good for you," said the man. "Clears you out." He touched his chest with the cleaver handle. "Starts a fire right here."

Helen felt the water welling inside her belly first. "I don't need fire—"

"Nonsense! No fire, no life." He chopped a leg off a chicken. "You Americans run away from pain. That's what makes you weak."

The woman cleared her throat. "Khaleef."

"It's true."

Helen sat back down, unsure of what had just happened. Khaleef resumed his chopping. She took a sip of water, but the tickle only grew. She covered her mouth with a paper napkin and coughed, surprised that something solid, like a seed or a pit, had been discharged.

"See?" said Khaleef. "Pepper."

Helen hadn't noticed the headscarfed woman had come to her table until she was sitting down.

"Forgive my husband," she said. "He has a good heart, but he has trouble sometimes with the way things are in America. He is not able to give people what they ask for if he thinks it is not good for them. He put too much pepper on your vegetables. Should you like, I will give you a refund. He did not want to give you butter because the butter would neutralize the pepper and you would not cough. Please forgive him. His ways are different."

Helen opened the napkin slowly. A pit, like a peach pit, slightly larger, stained a blue black like octopus ink, was inside. She did not know why she showed it to the woman. "What is it?"

The woman held the napkin gently, then set it on the table between them. "It is heavy."

"But what is it?"

Khaleef shook his head slightly. The woman pushed the pit across the table closer to Helen. "I cannot say. You should carry it with you. It may have something to offer you now that you've released it."

Helen was both appalled and intrigued by carrying a disgorged peach pit around with her. Wait until Frank heard.

"You are sad," she said. "I will leave you so you can feel your sadness."

And just as invisibly, she returned to her corner and picked up the newspaper.

Helen forced herself to finish the pita and vegetables—a child swallowing a bitter medicine. Each bite raised heat in her belly, her throat, her eyes. The tears that fell were not the cold tears of loss, but the jagged ones of birth. When she finished, she took her trash to the orange can, placed the wrapped pit in her handbag, and refilled her water from the beverage bar. "Thank you." No one else had entered the restaurant. The headscarfed woman did not look up from her paper. Khaleef beckoned her closer with his index finger.

"Don't throw it away."

"What?"

"What is in your napkin."

"Forever?"

"Nothing is forever. Just until it is time for you to do the next thing with it."

The woman put down her paper, shook her head.

"Come back sometime," Khaleef said. "I make you what you need."

She wrapped her hand around the napkin in her purse and backed toward the door. The chiming of the doorbell startled her, but the movement of the people on the sidewalk pulled at her and she was swept away.

Frank was not a man to be bound by introspection. Too much thinking made a man question everything, and Frank had learned that questioning leads to uncertainty, and uncertainty leads to mistakes. This kind of thinking made him excel at his job at Steinhart, Schlink, and Sons, where he had been just a few short days before, pencil resting between his teeth. His suit had been too hot for the Arizona day, and the sweat danced down his back, making him afraid to take off the heavy suit coat for fear of stains. Most of the office team didn't wear the suit coat, not in Phoenix, not unless clients were coming in, but Frank didn't feel like he was properly ready for work if he wasn't dressed up.

His office had no window, but he had been promised one, soon, just as soon as old man Steinhart retired and everyone shuffled offices. He had an assistant named Rose, a frumpy girl with large black-framed glasses that would have been fashionable on someone else, who could not spell, but was nonetheless funny, and he appreciated the jokes she told him every morning when she handed him his messages. He liked her to take them down, write them on pink slips of paper, and give them to him when he walked in. He didn't like the intimacy of e-mail or voice mail. It frightened him to be so accosted by his own technology.

He appreciated the methodical way Rose ate her daily tuna fish sandwich, carefully wiping her lips on a cloth napkin that she saved throughout the entire week and then took home on Fridays to wash. She didn't intimidate him, like so many of the other women who worked there, with their long legs and even longer fingers. They spoke in tones that made him turn away as much from embarrassment as insecurity. He needn't have worried. They never looked at him except to say "good morning" in the hall, and they never, of this he could be certain, entertained the idea of going out with him after work to a corner bar.

He emerged from his office just before noon. Rose, wearing a pink dress with a single strand of faux pearls, was rummaging through her desk drawer. He could see down the front of her dress, and he surprised himself by not looking away. He surprised himself even further by noticing a mole that kissed the top curve of her right breast.

"Mr. Connor! My goodness, I didn't see you standing there." Rose quickly straightened up and Frank looked away. "Can I help you with something, sir?"

He held his briefcase in front of his waist. "No, Rose, no. You go ahead and have a nice lunch. Why don't you take an extra hour today."

Her hand rose to her lips. "Really? Thank you, sir. Are you sure? Where are you going?"

For a moment he thought she asked him where he was going so she could accompany him, but he quickly realized she was curious only so she could tell people who asked where he had gone.

"Just going to meet a friend," he said. "I'll be back around two."

He still stood in front of her desk.

"Is there anything else, Mr. Connor?" Rose already had her purse, a black shiny one with a gold clasp, out on her desk.

"No, no, Rose. Nothing else." He put his hat on his head. "Have a good lunch, Rose. Thank you."

"For what, Mr. Connor?"

"What?"

"You said thank you. Thank you for what?"

"Oh." He hadn't noticed her eyes were the green of his favorite boyhood marble. "Just thank you, Rose. You've done a wonderful job for me."

She nodded, seeming to accept the explanation. "I'll see you at two then."

"Yes, Rose. Two."

She picked up her purse. "Have a good lunch then, Mr. Connor."

He stepped out of her way, watching her walk down the hallway, her legs wobbling just a little bit in heels too high for her. After Rose left, he got in the elevator. He noticed for the first time the dinginess of the elevator buttons. The carpet, which he had once thought was a cheerful orange, now appeared dirty, like it had been out in the sun and trampled on by dogs.

He was in the elevator by himself, which was unusual for lunchtime. Where would he go? Why didn't he ask her to join him? He suddenly didn't want to go to Cheryl's Place, where he knew Donna, the lunchtime waitress, would have already put in his order of a patty melt and fries, paired with a glass of sweet tea, which she made up special just for him because he once said he was from Georgia. She would have already set his favorite table, in the back left corner, and put out a several-times read copy of that day's *Arizona Republic*. He had eaten a patty melt at Cheryl's every weekday the entire thirteen years he'd been employed by Steinhart, Schlink and Sons. It was practical, inexpensive, and close to the office. And Donna never once made a remark about his dining alone. But somehow he knew that if he walked in today and had another patty melt, he'd be eating patty melts at Cheryl's until he was older than his father, older than his brother Benjamin would never be.

He started the Prius' engine, rolled down the windows and sat idling in the parking lot through twenty minutes of Talk of the Nation on NPR. A few cars passed on the street in front of him. A blue jay perched on the power line. He took off his suit coat, took off his tie (his second-best one), unbuttoned the top two buttons on his white dress shirt, kicked the car into reverse, and backed out of the parking lot for the last time.

Numbers were reliable, maybe not the ones on the tiny piece of paper in his pocket, but one could at least agree on the *rules* of numbers, and because of that, one could have a civilized conversation about numbers without risking offending someone, a most distasteful trait Frank had been horrified to see proliferating in recent years. No one could say anything anymore. No one could express an opinion without risking the wrath of this group or that group. Sure, accountants had spirited conversations, but it was all in good fun and no one ever complained to HR or committed suicide as a result. Feelings were messy and were impossible to hurt if one kept one's distance from them.

"This is no longer the age of reason," he said aloud to the moving San Francisco street, and much to his surprise, no one paid attention to him. The City's hum had its own rhythm, and the people walking and biking and honking through Chinatown paid him no more mind than the flies that settled on the open mouths of the fish in the windows of the street markets. He spoke louder. "This is no longer the age of reason!" A blond German tourist handed him a buck. Frank tried to give it back. "But I'm not—"The man kept walking, his traveling shorts a little too short and his support knee socks a little too high. He pocketed the bill, which he hadn't yet noticed was a euro, and thought maybe he'd try to claim a corner. The shouting had felt strange in his mouth, like a surprise present he hadn't yet experienced. He should start with a small corner. But then he worried he'd get mugged and murdered and no one would even know he'd been there. That could happen on any corner. He moved across Waverly toward Grant, trying to determine the flow of traffic, but it seemed like everyone moved in whatever direction they wanted. The arrows and walk signs and stop signs were merely suggestions. Frank stepped into a side alley with a graffiti-ed cat pedaling in the air. Invisible Bike! it read.

Frank cleared his throat. He tingled; his flesh actually tingled. He had thought that hyperbole whenever Helen used the phrase.

"This is no longer the age of reason! We have allowed our emotions to get the better of us!"

He realized, a few minutes too late, that he was dangerously close to the First Chinese Baptist Church, which might be like the Baptist churches he grew up with ready at a moment's notice to rise up and crusade against science. He was afraid he might be stirring up conflict when he only wanted to scratch the back of his throat with sound.

But no one approached him. Shopkeepers on neighboring streets began pulling closed the iron curtains. The trolley car rattled down Sacramento Street. The #30 Stockton bus kneeled and hissed. This place was otherworldly. The hills sloped too high. On one side, a steep drop into water, on another, the lights of the Financial District, and the moon, the moon was not at all where it was supposed to be. The moon should have been in the east, but here it shimmered over the Bay, which had to be west because the Pacific Ocean was as west as you could get and wasn't the Bay somehow connected to the Ocean? But here, this City turned his internal compass upside down.

He'd left his phone in the hotel. He could have asked someone, one of these kids with ear buds, to show him how to use the GPS feature on his phone. A map would show this place. San Francisco could be mapped, and ordered and explained. Google had done it so it must be able to be done. It would show him why the moon or the Bay were in the wrong place.

The moon was too full. When they'd left Phoenix three days ago, the moon was barely half awake. How could it have grown so much so fast? An orange pumpkin belly mocking him from the wrong side of the sky.

No More Dead in San Francisco
A Hashbury Times History Lesson

In 1902, the San Francisco Board of Supervisors outlawed burials within the City limits. By 1942, all the bodies that had been resting, except for those in the San Francisco National Cemetery at the Presidio and the Mission Dolores Cemetery, were moved to the 2-1/2 square mile town of Colma, California. Even today, it is illegal to be buried in San Francisco's City limits.

Can you imagine the chaos? You're in your earthly repository and you suddenly get interrupted by the government who decided the land of your eternal slumber was better suited to a golf course. They didn't even manage to rebury everybody. Some graves just got plowed over. Others got mismarked. Imagine the hullabaloo that must have gone on, and maybe, if you dare, the screams of all those dead trying to come back home. Is it any wonder, really, that San Francisco is such a spooky place? All those dead folks can make a lot of ruckus trying to find their way back home.

Remmy's Reflective Moment: Elle was sent back to Georgia on a train. There weren't a thing we could do about that. Brian wasn't her husband, and he was hiding anyway. To the coppers, she was just another kid who wasted her life in the Summer of Love. The straights had so many ways of letting us know how much we were throwing away, how much we were wasting all our parents had fought so hard for us to have. Ungrateful! They said to us. Ungrateful! And that somehow gave them the right to pack Elle in a case of ice and ship her back away from us. We weren't family, they told us. We didn't love her, what with all our smoking of the marijuana and dropping out of college and evading our patriotic duty

to be cannon fodder. They hated us, yes they did, and that
hatred made them send Elle away from us and we have never,
and I do mean never, gotten over that.

Remmy X: Hashbury Daily Times

2007

Frank promised himself this would be the last time. He would stand solid and stable in this alley in front of the Invisible Bike graffiti in this crazy City that refused to align itself on a grid and he would speak his truth clearly and loudly and then he would regain his composure and return to the Hotel Gladmore and explain to Helen he had been unable to procure any moo goo gai pan in Chinatown (she would not understand, but she would not say anything) and they would get into the king-sized bed and hold hands in the dark and he would say, "I have to go," and she would say, "I know," and they would lie there together holding hands until the sunrise washed the room.

"Everyone has lost their minds!" he shouted. "This is not the time for stories! This is the time for reason! For proof! For science!" No one had stopped walking. No one applauded him or threw fruit at him. He'd shouted his loudest, spoken his truth, and it had made no difference. Well, he thought, such were the workings of the universe.

He stepped off his corner and raised his arms to the backwards moon. What a peculiar day. He needed to find a restroom. He thought he remembered one in Woh Hei Yuen Park where the women gathered to play mahjong in a place that used to be a mortuary. He was right, and when he finished he stepped into the center of the park, its boxed trees and precarious angles notwithstanding, to try again and figure out the moon.

"Beautiful, isn't it?"

Frank hadn't heard anyone approach. He touched his hip pocket to make sure his wallet was still there. He should have put it in his front pocket like all the travel guides advise. The man next to him was older than Frank by maybe twenty years. His stripe of white hair looked blue under the streetlamp. Both of the old man's hands were in his pockets. Frank assumed he was referring to the moon.

"It is. Quite an unusual shade of orange."

That should have been that. Frank was proud of himself for sustaining that small bit of conversation. Helen would have been surprised.

"My name is Brian."

"Frank."

The two men resumed staring at the moon. A verbal fight broke out at the mahjong game to their left. One woman stood, spit on the tiles, and stomped off into the dark. The remaining women looked at the ground. Brian didn't move and this made Frank uncomfortable. The pleasantries and then some were over. The man should move on to wherever he was going and let Frank do the same. That was what happened in polite society. Frank could have turned away and walked back toward the Stockton Street Tunnel. He could have let himself be absorbed by its dampness and green fluorescence, and who knows, perhaps he would get mugged, or worse, and he wouldn't actually have to tell Helen he was leaving. A small gift that would be. But Frank recognized something in the man's eyes—a sadness that men didn't seem to be able to talk about.

"It's a Harvest Moon," said Brian. "They make me feel young."

Frank didn't know what to say to that. He didn't want to explain why it was astronomically impossible for the Harvest Moon to be out tonight, so he murmured a non-committal assent.

"Which way you headed?" asked Brian.

Frank almost said Union Square, but he suddenly didn't want to be a tourist in this strange town with a backwards moon. He wanted to belong here, somehow, if just for one night. He didn't know another neighborhood to tell the man, though, so he made another grunting noise that he hoped translated into someplace special. Brian nodded and Frank at once felt a deep affinity for this sad old man.

"What about you?" he asked.

"I don't know," said Brian.

Brian turned to Frank, and in the strange night light Frank noticed the unusual length of Brian's earlobes, how they appeared almost feminine, how they somehow made him more lost. "I know where we can go," said Brian, and before Frank could weigh his response against the laws of safety and restraint, the two men were walking toward Jack Kerouac Alley, a turquoise and red lamppost lined with golden dragons lighting the way.

Helen was surprised to be surprised by the movement of the street. The people were a river, and if she didn't step in and start moving, she would be stomped on, kicked to the curb, washed down the drain. No one would know she had been swept away. Frank would have mocked the headscarfed woman. Would have said something crass about no one minding their own business anymore. When she disgorged the pit, he would have shaken his head, speechless once again at her strangeness, her inability to be a normal wife. She thought of his index finger on his right hand, broken from a childhood fight with someone whose name he never revealed. Helen had always assumed it was with his father.

She was at the corner of Cyril Magnin and Ellis. The crowd was waiting, pulsing, for the light to change. She was mesmerized by this place, by being a part of an organism but not recognized by the organism. She needed to be somewhere where she could be the heart of the creature she was inhabiting. She'd thought as a girl when she lay against her dead mother that maybe her mother just needed her heartbeat. That she would come back if she pressed herself closer to her, but her mother had only grown colder and stiffer, and then Helen hadn't known what to do.

The light changed and the cars and pedestrians crowded each other out of the crosswalk. She chose a spot in the middle of the throng and hoped to be pulled along. It was night, but the lights from the buildings made it as bright as noon.

She couldn't have seen a girl in the window. She couldn't have seen a girl in the crosswalk. She was just suffering from over-stimulation and the weight of the eternal "ing-ness" of divorcing. The trip had seemed like a grand idea when they were in Phoenix. They'll go on a trip. Be civilized. They'll have a drink together, a nice meal, maybe Indian or Mexican in the Mission. They would say nice things about one another, recount good memories (the trip, six years ago, to Yosemite). They would do this as they had done everything, with precision and common sense. Helen had even packed a blank greeting card in her luggage. She thought she might write him a note after they had the conversation that told him nice things, wished him well, hoped he could find love. He would save it, because even though he did not want to save her, he would save the objects of her. Her effects. He would place them in a drawer and pull them out occasionally and remember.

But what would he remember? The odd angle of her nose, an inheritance of her Irish DNA, the way her left eye was smaller than her right, the way she placed drops of essential oils on her collarbone? She felt suddenly tired, the clanging and neon and honking and pushing no longer a seduction, but a drain. She wanted to go back to the hotel. Frank would surely be there. They could fall asleep to the sounds of the television and in the morning finalize everything. He'd probably been waiting for her already. The room was paid for. It would be illogical for him to go anywhere else, contrary to his nature.

Omar, the doorman, was busy with a well-shod couple when Helen approached the hotel. He caught her eye and winked; she raised her hand in a small wave, feeling for a moment she had come home to family, albeit family in a very large house with dripping chandeliers and bright red lobby carpet. In Phoenix, her neighbors drove in and out of their garages, entering their houses unseen by anyone, the tall cinder-block fences between them enough to ensure privacy. No waves. No smiles. Tinted windows. Air conditioning. A box, just like the layout of the city. Perfect angles. Straight edges. No surprises.

She pulled the gate closed across the elevator's open door and the lurch of its ascension pushed her off center. The inside of the elevator had mirrors on two sides. She tried to look at herself as if she were a stranger. The wrinkles under her eyes were not yet deep, more like scratchboard art than heavy engraving. She needed a haircut, but she'd thought she would wait until after the conversation so she could try something new. Maybe she'd dye it darker, or blonder, or maybe she'd cut it shorter, or perm it. She was a cliché. A middle-aged divorcee getting the requisite makeover so she could reinvent herself for the next phase of her life. She'd just buy a fancy barrette from one of the accessory stores on Powell. She could even buy a fake tiara. A perfect fortieth birthday present for a newly single woman.

When Helen first started wearing makeup, she would look at her eyes in the mirror of her powder compact. She would try to imagine her eyes through the eyes of someone else—how they would look to someone who loved her. She'd practiced flirting with her newly mas-cara-ed lashes.

The elevator slammed to a stop. She sunk into the carpet in the hall-way, so much so she took off her shoes and stood, in the mauve plush, letting each toe press the fibers. How is it possible that public carpet could be so fluffy? Strange day. She hadn't drunk enough water. She ate too much pepper. She threw up a pit and was carrying it in her purse like it was a gold doubloon. She swiped her keycard, amazed that it was a clean swipe the first time. The room was dark and cold, too cold. Had she left the air conditioner on? She didn't remember even turning it on.

"Frank? It's me."

Nothing.

She turned the light on. The room was just as she'd left it, paperwork from the paramedics on the nightstand, her open suitcase on the bed. "Frank?" The air conditioner was off. She turned on the tap and filled a glass with water. It was icy cold. The tap water in Phoenix never came out cold, even in December. She drank quickly, enjoying the burning cold down her throat. Frank hadn't come back for his toiletries. Maybe he was lost. He didn't do well in an unfamiliar landscape. His phone was still on the bathroom counter.

She set the empty water glass on top of the paramedics' paperwork and lay down on top of the coverlet. She was getting used to the cold, but she wished she'd turned the lights off before lying down, stretching her feet to the foot of the empty king. This was not how she'd imagined her life would be at forty. She had thought there might be children, or a cabin in the mountains, or some magic something that she believed adults had figured out. Her job was nothing spectacular, graphic design for a soap company, but it wasn't awful. Maybe the mistake was believing there was more than just living. She remembered reading somewhere, Wikipedia probably, that vacations didn't come into people's lives until the 1930s. People just worked, farmed, slept. When did the expectation arrive that something full of fireworks was supposed to happen in a life? When nothing was actually wrong, how was it possible that things were wrong?

Frank would want her to make another chart to address and analyze this problem. He would help her see, linearly, that there was no cause for dissatisfaction. And then he would run out of things to say. What had she dreamed of as a girl? Those dreams were nebulous, floating just beyond her memory. Her childhood house was near a grove of peach trees. She could run just a few short steps across the grass and pick the fruit, eating way too many most days. No place on earth has peaches like Georgia, her mother used to say.

Helen got out of bed and pulled the napkin-wrapped peach pit from her purse. She ran her fingers over its bumpy edges. Peach pits had always reminded her of ancient tree trunks, and as a girl she'd tried to find faces in the patterns. She took the pit back to bed, slipped it under her pillow, and thought about the girl in the window. She looked a little like Helen imagined herself looking as a girl. Desperate and beautiful at the same time, reaching into the world for anything that would hold her up.

Throw the Bums Out
Draft Dodgers in Vietnam

This reporter feels the need to clear up some common mis-
understandings about the Vietnam Draft. The actual lottery
that most people think of when they think of the draft was
drawn on December 1, 1969. The first number drawn was 257,
which corresponded to lucky birthday September 14. So all
those folks who were born on September 14 between 1944 and
1950 were assigned number 1. Then, it got even more compli-
cated. The letters of your name were also assigned a number
and then it got even more convoluted, government-style.

Statistics, charts, graphs, and the promised randomness
of death didn't go over so well with the kids who were being assigned numbers like lab rats. This lottery system
was supposed to help clear up the previous quota system
used to snatch bodies up from '65-'69. The quota system was
anything but random, and all a person had to do, assuming
he had the money and the means, was to go to a more crowded draft board and get himself eased on down the road to
freedom. It didn't take long for cries of "foul" to surface
regarding the randomness of the draft numbers, and in December of 1969, shortly after the first lottery number was
drawn, Senator Edward Kennedy asked the National Sciences
Academy to analyze the "apparent lack of randomness" in
the selection. Well, the wheels of government turn slowly,
especially if those involved are in no danger of turning
into dead.

America's youth got creative here. While many did believe the war in Vietnam to be unjust, quite a few just
wanted to stay alive. This reporter feels that is not an
unreasonable thing to expect of one's life. People went to

great lengths to avoid the draft, and draft offices were increasingly vandalized. On October 27, 1967, Reverend Philip Berrigan, a Catholic priest, walked his holy self right into a Baltimore draft board office and poured blood from Polish ducks all over the draft records. This reporter would have loved to have seen that.

All over the country, boys were burning their draft cards, getting married to the wrong girls, or hurrying to get themselves into a PhD program. Getting that coveted 4-F deferment was a full-time job. Phil Ochs's popular 1965 song "Draft Dodger Rag" gave a handy list of ailments one could parlay to try and get out of the grip of Uncle Sam.

The Vietnam era was very different from World War II. People often think there was no draft until Vietnam, but that was not true. The draft has been a part of America since its birth-pangs. It didn't work so well in our Civil War, but by World War I, the Selective Service Act had been signed by Woodrow Wilson in 1917, and there were very few protests concerning conscription. The shame of not serving in World War I and World War II was a powerful cross to bear, so just about everybody sucked it up and bore it.

Perhaps by the time Vietnam rolled around, the kids had seen what the wars had done to their daddies and granddaddies. Perhaps they didn't see patriotism as blind adherence to someone else's ideas. Who's to say for sure. This reporter, though he did not go to Vietnam, has some regret about it. Not about not going to fight, but about sneaking out of it while other boys went.

But this reporter is not alone. Lots of men came to San Francisco to disappear. They couldn't be tracked like we can today. They could hide, and by that point, the Haight was turning colors. It was darkening at the edges like overdone crust. It held more fear than it held hope and that difference turned it upside down. In 1974, President Ford offered a conditional pardon to draft dodgers, but in January 1977, on his very first day in office, President Jimmy Carter

fulfilled one of his campaign promises and offered uncondi-
tional amnesty to hundreds of thousands of men who fled the
country or refused to register for the Vietnam draft. It
was a glorious day. Not because lives hadn't already been
ruined. Not because lives weren't going to continue to be
ruined. But because someone in the White House noticed that
things weren't right and did his humble best to turn that
train back around.

Remmy's Reflective Moment: I guess I just don't understand
the notion of country. America seems so crazy big, so much
a machine, that it's hard to believe that my tiny life makes
one bit of difference for her foreign policy success. I don't
know if men from previous generations asked those questions.
Those generations were so quiet. What does it say about a
person if there's nothing you're willing to die for? I'd
die for Shep. I'd step right in front of a bus to save him,
that's how much I love this dog. And I guess there's one
other person I'd have died for, but I didn't get the chance.
She went first.

Remmy X: Hashbury Daily Times

1967

The first thing Elle noticed at Golden Gate Park that Solstice, 1967, were the smells. In Georgia, unwashed flesh was unhappy, miserable even, the stench of hog farms, dirt farms, lye soap—here, the unwashed flesh held patchouli and sage, wood fire smoke, clove and dope sweetness. This unwashed flesh clawed itself a space—see me—dance, laugh, sweat, breathe—see *me*. The flesh in Georgia hid behind woodsheds, dissolved into groves of trees, sank, unnoticed, into church cemeteries lined with stone lambs.

Brian held her elbow—the two of them side by side at the top of the last hill at the end of Haight Street before it eased into the park. Everywhere was color. From the bright oranges and reds of Guatemalan fabrics to the daffodils and violets and unreachable moss of ancient trees. They stood side by side at the top of the last hill, unsure of how to enter all that color. Underneath the smells of skin and smoke were the sharp notes of pepper and curry, BBQ and fish. She held her fiddle case with her left hand, the nylon strap left in a hotel room in Oklahoma. Her right hand was open, grasping air. A chubby girl with a white patch of zinc sun block on her nose ran in front of them, trailing a pair of lavender balloons.

"She's going to get hurt, wearing no shoes like that," said Brian.

Elle was startled; surprised he saw her feet at all. She had been so captured by the lightness of lavender.

"We can go on home if you want," he said.

She looked at the ground, his work boots heavy, solid, planted. Home, where? Back to Georgia where maybe she'd notice a different set of smells, now that she'd been away? Home to their futon mattress on the floor of the fourth floor flat on Waller, which at first had felt like sky diving, but soon began to seem a crowded lifeboat.

"Let's stay awhile," she said, unable to imagine ever leaving this kaleidoscope. She eased her elbow away from his open fist and bent down to unbuckle the straps on her beige, sensible, low-heeled sandals. The grass was wet, even though it was long past dawn.

"You'll cut your feet," he said.

"Perhaps."

The next thing Elle noticed were the dogs—Labradors and poodles, Dobermans and Dalmatians, German Shepherds and beagles. Dogs chasing lavender balloons and dogs dancing on two hind legs. She saw boys with no legs back from Vietnam, boys with eyes a wet jungle. The Grateful Dead were here today, but she had come for Janis. She'd been playing the Fillmore lately, and in her photographs her eyes were as wild as the legless boys'. Elle understood why Brian didn't want to be here. His biggest risk had been picking her up in Georgia. Now he confined his activities to: "Let's try the new Thai place on Jones," and "Let's take the N car to the end and watch the sunset over the ocean." His basic sweetness coated in a sour safety. Brian's wildness had sprung to life when he picked her up on the side of the road, but it had been cowering in the back seat ever since, with the ghost of someone Elle did not recognize.

The first time Elle heard Janis was on the radio. She heard her shriek from the wombs of all the women—and she wept in an unexpected gasp. She gasped as if she could swallow that voice—take it back inside her and find a way to explode it out her own throat—a way to shower herself with the sparks that flung themselves, unchecked, from her belly.

The moment she stepped into Golden Gate Park, she knew being with Brian was a mistake. She looked around and saw all that life—maybe the kids were screwed up or irresponsible or high, but no one could accuse them of not being *alive*—and they were alive in a way she'd never seen before. She was the right age chronologically to be topless with them, to be wearing daisies and twirling her dirty hair between her fingers. She was the right age to be having an orgasm right there on the grass right under a 200-year-old tree—the right age to have the passion to shout down Lyndon Johnson, to cheer with Abbie Hoffman and to wear round purple sunglasses. But she did none of those things. Not yet. She slid her sensible sandals off and felt the grass peek up between her toes, still wet and cool from the morning, and heard an almost-whisper: "This is the only piece of freedom you will have," and she looked at Brian because she thought he might have said that, but he was quiet, stiff, feet still in his boots, and she tasted his fear in the air between them and knew in that instant she could swallow his fear into her or put up a wall between them and that the rest of her life would unfold based on that swallowing or that refusing, but before she had time to absorb the magnitude of that choice, she swallowed, her female reflex, and the lead taste filled her mouth.

"You'll cut your feet on glass," he said, looking squarely forward.

"Yes," and she slid her shoes back on, not thinking until much much later how nice it would have been that Saturday summer Solstice to bleed.

She was wearing those sensible sandals when she first saw Janis. She had a sensible man beside her who was content with the same breakfast every day, even on the road—two hardboiled eggs, coffee (one cup only, no sugar) from the same tan mug every day. This sensible man looked at Janis and saw a loud, drunk woman—a woman who could have benefitted from the same meal every day, clean laundry folded and put away in drawers, a sensible four-door tan car to take her safely to the grocery store and back. He looked at her and saw what happened when a woman was left alone to go wild. Elle looked at her and saw the goddess incarnate, the tug between creation and destruction, the power of a talent too fierce to be contained in flesh. She saw the alcohol. She saw the drugs, but she knew what Brian could never know—she was painfully lonely in that way only a woman could know—painfully lonely because she knew no man could ever give her what singing gave her—that no man was strong enough to stand beside her and let her sing. Elle's fiddle case was heavy, a burden suddenly, like her shoes, on this summer day when all the world seemed to be dancing, feet and chests bare to the sun, convinced a revolution was on its way.

"Let me carry that for you," said Brian, taking the fiddle case from her. "That's too heavy for you here in the hot sun." He surveyed the crowd. In front of them a black man and white woman dancing barefoot, eyes rooted into each other's. Two thousand miles away civil rights workers were still "disappearing"; Strom Thurman ran for Senate as a member of the Klan; Elvis was in Germany, MLK about to die for, in some ways, the right of this man and this woman to dance together, half naked in the sun, a part of all the world.

"Someone might bump into you and steal it," he said. His hand was cold as it closed over hers. She released the handle of the fiddle case into his. Janis made noises Elle knew were inside her too. She was turned inside out. Janis was a wound that never had a chance to scab over. She picked it open every night and blew air on it and everyone watched while she screamed.

The smell of hash was overpowering, of perspiration, pepper, and patchouli, and Elle began to dance in spite of her sensible sandals. She wanted to be wearing one of those long flowing cotton skirts and she wanted a flower in her hair. She so wanted a flower in her hair—a yellow one, the color of the sun that day—not orange, the color of war dropped from the sky on straw villages, not red, the color of the fires in Detroit, not white, the color of the sheets in the South, a simple yellow for the sun, for the hope she felt on that magic day.

But Elle wasn't part of that shout. She stood at the edge of Golden Gate Park, the youth she should have been experiencing dancing in front of her, this man beside her she didn't need, the roadmap of her life charted before she knew the pen was in her hand.

Janis saw her that day. She saw Brian take the fiddle case from her. Her arm was covered in bracelets, a fuchsia boa tied in her hair. She saw and she said, "You gonna use that or are you gonna let him take it?" Brian didn't hear that. Janis was in the middle of telling a story, he said many times later, not singling people out of a crowd. But Elle didn't expect that he would hear; after all, she wasn't talking to him.

They'd landed in Hashbury like so many others, penniless with no prospects, frustrated with the world they'd come from, and hoping that a new culture would show them what was next. Time opened its mouth and held them all suspended on its tongue as long as it could bear them. Occasionally, it swallowed one of them, or bit off an arm or leg, but most of them survived, holding tight to its taste buds, lulled by the steam of its breath.

Elle knew from the first inhale that San Francisco wasn't Brian's place. He did things right. He followed the rules and he believed that the rules would hold up their end of the bargain. Hashbury had no rules, no order, no "system", as Brian said often. But it did have those things—he just didn't know how to look for them because they wore leather fringe jackets and carried mimeographed fliers on the benefits of LSD or just because they smiled more than they shouted, even if they didn't know what they were smiling about.

The Haight was one long afternoon of blooms and seeds and hummingbirds. One long afternoon of light shows, of smelling your own armpits long enough to no longer notice, of reading about risk takers who were sprouting up in gardens all across the country—activists for abortion rights, activists for the Equal Rights Amendment, anti-war activists, Civil Rights activists. It was as if the whole country suddenly woke up from its thousand-year slumber and tried to right everything in a single decade. Everything was urgent, as frenetic and frantic as the electric light shows they held in basements, and everything mattered now. And since she didn't know what she didn't know, it was easy to follow the drumbeat wherever it led her. It led her to Janis, which led her to a place she still couldn't name.

She didn't know where it led Brian. He liked his shower every day, his three squares, his clean shoes. She liked the feel of her feet as they hardened from the concrete of the sidewalks beneath them. She liked waking up every day as if she had slept inside a kaleidoscope. Wake up facing north and she saw a smear of reds and golds. Wake up facing south and she saw blues, greens and white. When she tried to hold them both in her vision, she stopped, mesmerized, waiting, until someone reminded her she had to move because she was standing on their skirt.

Brian wrote a letter that he slipped into Elle's jeans' pocket before the undertakers took her. He didn't know if anyone would ever read it, but it was important that there be some words from him with her wherever she went. Elle would never have thought he would do such a thing, seemingly romantic and sentimental.

Since she died, he had grown out his beard and stopped washing his hair. He hoped to be caught by the draft board, so much so that he even used his own last name, Richardson, when he went looking for a job; a job he could have gotten before Elle died, before he stopped shaving his beard and washing his hair and became one of the men no one wanted to hire; they only wanted to kill.

2007

The short alley was speckled with poetry etched in English and Chinese in the stone. Frank's eyes were too old to read them in the dusk.

"You weren't born then," said Brian, "but this place was something else once."

"This alley?"

"This alley. This corner." The Vesuvio mural overtook them on their left. People milled about, waiting to get in to the famous bar that once kicked out Jack Kerouac. They stopped at the triangle shaped building at the end of the alley. "I was born, but I wasn't here in San Francisco then."

"When?"

"When this place changed the world."

REMMY X

There's something coming. Shep won't stop barking no matter how much I scratch under his chin or rub his spotty-belly. I decide I need to go find Don over at the official SFPD station where he works. Don got the Tenderloin beat, the beat nobody wants, but he's walked it for twenty years now. He likes the people, and he knows how to talk to the desperate, and he never hurt any citizen ever in all his years on the force. I always thought he was a Stuffer, but maybe I'm wrong because he can take it all in and not turn it back out on folks. Maybe he turns it in on himself. He's on tonight because it's Friday night and he likes to be the one out on the night when there's going to be the most to do. His precinct looks out at Father Alfred E. Boeddeker Park, and it's just a short walk over toward the Glide Foundation on Ellis Street, which, I have to tell you, is some kind of place.

Don didn't always walk the beat, nossir. When Don was Starburst, he was on the other side with us—with me and Brian and her. He was one of those folks got himself re-ha-bi-li-ta-ted to much fanfare by his folks. He says he's glad they did it now. Who is Remmy to say how the direction of another man's life should go?

Don came back to us, though. That's the part that matters. He loves the Tenderloin. Loves its people like I love the Haight. I think he sees what the Tenderloin could be too, but more important, he sees who the people, the lost ones, could be, and that's something powerful valuable. Not many people can look underneath the crazy-ness—not Remmy-crazy, I feel like I should add, but the kind of crazy that you've been living with so long, been fighting so long with whatever kind of drug or person or ideology you got right at your bony fingertips— and see something beautiful. Sees the faces of God in them people, he does, and for that, whether Don's a Pig or some militant conservative jerk-off, he's still Don from back in the day, and he sees these people, so Remmy can let the rest of everything sort of hang on in the back shadows. I got me a certain kind of grace, yes I do.

Don tries to get me to go to Glide, get me a meal or two, sing a song, but I tell him I'm OK. I'm not starving. That food's for folks who got nothing. I got plenty. Got my typewriter. Got my dog. Got my poems. Most days I am a very rich man. I tell him thanks, but no, Remmy's good, then I tell him how much I made with my poems that day, or maybe how much ice cream I got to eat, and I tell him that God and I, we get along fair enough, but I don't feel the need to go visiting him in a building. No need, I say, no need, when He shows up plain as day in everything I write.

I find Don just as the sun is sinking behind us and the streets of the Tenderloin— Larkin, Jones, Eddy—are turning into a different kind of wonderland, a kind with that other Alice. I think of a forest when I walk through here, and how there could be any sort of animal waiting in the branches of the tree to swoop down on you. Not because the animals are mean, but because it's what they do. Once, a lady (well, I think it was a lady) wearing a purple velvet jumpsuit and white plat-form heels tried to take Shep from me. She got on the sidewalk with him and tickled under his chin, and boy did he love it, and when she smiled I saw she only had the three teeth, right there in the front, like a jack-o-lantern. I couldn't let Shep go with her of course, but that moment where she was loving on him and he was loving on her will forever be a Polaroid in my brain-house.

Don's leaning up against a streetlight watching the park across the street from the station. He mostly watches, makes sure nothing really awful happens.

"Hey," he says to me, and I can tell he is jonesing for a cig.

"Hey yourself."

We stand together apart—I do keep a respectful distance. I don't want people to think I'm an informant or worse—and I feel the fog-damp rising up from the streets. In the Tenderloin, the damp rises up from the streets, not down from the sky like it does a few blocks over in Union Square. Can't figure out the physics of that one.

"I know you don't like me to mention this, Don, but—"

He surprises me. "I know it, Remmy. I do."

"Think an earthquake is coming?"

"Always an earthquake coming."

We hear the rattle of the 38 Geary. Don rests his right hand on his nightstick, a habit I suppose.

"I have to tell you, the Haight ain't talking. She's like that moment before a hurricane when it's all quiet and then oh-sweet-Jesus look at all that water."

"Got your mind on natural disaster today, Remmy?"

"Got my mind on things I don't understand. Makes my brain-house hurt."

He laughs. "Your brain-house is always hurting."

"Maybe so."

"It's funny," Don says. "That tourist—that woman who almost jumped out of the Gladmore? She said she saw a girl in the window calling for her. Said she forgot she was way up in the air in the hotel and thought she could just go on out the glass and have a regular conversation."

I don't want to jump to my usual too-fast conclusions, so I wait, then decide to play the devil's advocate awhile. "You know, everybody's crazy. The tourist-lady, she probably just got tired of her life and had a momentary lapse of control. It happens."

Don nods. He knows it happens. He sees all those police reports. He sees the stuff that doesn't get police reporting, too. The stuff that gets all up in your body and doesn't get dislodged, no matter how many times you cough up the blackness. "Just got under my skin, that one. I mean, it's probably just all this crazy fortieth anniversary shit of the Summer of Love. All the strangers coming to get a taste of what they think it was. The City here capitalizing on what it wasn't. Just probably got me thinking more than usual about it all."

"That's probably it."

Don's partner, Officer Peter Frye, comes out of the station doors. "C'mon, Don. Got a call."

Don pets Shep right behind his ear like he likes it. "Maybe I'll come on over one of these nights."

"That'd be good, Don. Shep and me'll get the Ramen ready."

I watch Don assume his police-posture and slip into formation with Officer Peter. He's got many skins, that one. Many skins indeed. Shep is nosing in a wadded up old Burger King bag that still had a few fries left in it. That dog sure does love him the french fries. I don't feel too much like going back home right now, don't much want to go back through the forest. This is its most dangerous time, the time between end of day and dark. Nobody sees quite right in that kind of light. All sorts of things play tricks on you. Maybe we'll head down to Market Street for a time. Maybe someone there is in urgent need of a poem.

- X out.

2007

It seemed to Frank that City Lights was open way too late for a bookstore. People who read were supposed to be quiet, demure, uninterested in the late night goings on at Vesuvio or one of the other clubs of various persuasions Frank was too tired to attempt to understand. But that did not seem to be the case for this bookstore, with its strange triangle shape jutting out into Chinatown and toward North Beach. Brian didn't seem surprised that people still crowded into its doors, although it was close to nine o'clock. This strange City with its strange moon also kept unnatural hours. Dinner wasn't at six for everyone. Frank noticed Brian's gait sped up as he approached the open doors. Carts of books lined the street. Inside, the store felt more like a cramped airplane than a bookstore, but Brian moved easily among the stacks and people, nodding at the hipster behind the counter, who looked up from his iPhone to say hello.

"Do you like books?" asked Brian.

"Sure. I mean, everybody likes books."

"Not everybody. Some people think they're dangerous."

This concept of danger contained within the hard arms of a book had always amused Frank. People were far more dangerous than books. Life was far more dangerous than any story even the best writer could create. "I like essays."

Brian smiled. "Really. Not many people say that these days."

Frank wasn't sure if Brian was making fun of him; people frequently did. He decided his new friend was genuinely curious, and he found himself wanting to talk about it. "I like science writing. I like to understand how things work."

"That's why I like a good poem."

"Poems don't tell you how things work."

"They do indeed," said Brian. He led Frank past a handwritten sign that read, "Have a seat. Read a book," past the Via Ferlinghetti sign to the Poetry Upstairs sign. A bright red banister led people up the staircase; poems and archived photos lined the wall on their right. At the top, two large windows reflected them back at themselves and shelf upon shelf of poetry books were held together, a family, with a special shelf for poetry published by City Lights. Sirens wailed outside, honking, shouting, but inside the store, the potential energy of all the silent books shouted loudest. Every type of book, every binding, every topic under the sun had a home on the shelves. Brian bee-lined for the City Lights publishing section and held out a copy of Kerouac.

Frank quoted his father. "A drunken bum."

"Possibly," said Brian. "Drunken, hard to dispute." He held out Ferlinghetti. "Still kicking, this guy."

The book was *Poetry as Insurgent Art*. Insurgent. That's a claim. Frank held the tiny black hardcover, its splash of red on the front evoking urgency. He flipped it open and read aloud. "'If you would be a poet, write living newspapers. Be a reporter from outer space, filing dispatches to some supreme managing editor who believes in full disclosure and has a low tolerance for bullshit.'" He closed the book. "Deep, man," he laughed at himself. Brian didn't laugh. He took the book back, placed it carefully on the shelf. "Sorry," said Frank.

"I need to smoke," said Brian. Frank stopped himself before explaining all the various ways that cigarette smoke, first and second hand, could kill him. "I'm going outside."

Somehow Frank had done to Brian what he did to everyone. He tried to be funny, tried to be one of the guys, tried to be a husband, and he ended up making people hate him. Helen always told him he wasn't funny. He never quite understood what made a line funny in another man's mouth, but in his turned to toxic dust. He'd only known Brian an hour, but he knew he didn't want to make him sad, knew that there was something already quite sad enough hanging on Brian's shoulders. Helen would be pleased at his perception. He wished he'd brought his phone. She may be worried about him, out way past his usual hour in a hippie bookstore on a dark side of town. Strange, how this City had pulled him somewhere new. Strange, how this City had taken his black-and-white spreadsheets and painted them neon.

He thumbed through the Ferlinghetti book, watching for Brian to come back up the stairs. Five others were in the room with him; two appeared to be a couple, three others browsed alone together in this house of poems. A woman with rhinestone cat's-eye glasses browsed the greeting card tree. Her lips were bright red and she seemed, to Frank, dangerously thin. An angular man wearing a beret and smelling of cloves hung onto a copy of *Dharma Bums* like it was the Bible. He glanced around the room furtively, waiting for someone, perhaps. He stroked the cover of the book, slid it into the front pocket of his trench coat. Maybe it was already his. Laughter floated up the staircase, but the poet-browsers, too serious for that, remained as silent as the books they held so close. Brian probably went home. He had no obligation to remain with Frank. They were just two strangers who met on the way out of something. Nothing more random than that.

Helen turned the television on. She was surprised to find she was waiting for her own story to be on the news. The strange almost-jump. She laughed at her arrogance. The City certainly had more than enough actual news. A tourist's mid-life crazy-crisis wasn't going to be the lead in. Had she jumped, she might have made a thirty second clip before the dog food commercials. The bed was big. Very clean. The sheets very white and very pressed. She would never have such a bed in her own house. Certainly, she would never have such pressed and white sheets. It was a shame that Frank was missing them. He would have appreciated the precision of the bedclothes. She was so small underneath them, she would barely make an indention on the pillow top. So light she wouldn't leave a mark at all.

The news usually put them both to sleep. They'd make it through the headlines and midway through the first commercial break at ten past the hour. She made it all the way through the 11:00 news. The final story was a human interest story on the fortieth anniversary of the Summer of Love. It was filled with the clips you always saw—race riots, the Monterrey Pop Festival, the hippies on Haight with their dogs and their ferrets, Timothy Leary saying once again, "Turn on, tune in and drop out." The bubbling newscaster flicked her eyes after the footage ended. "This Sunday, thousands of hippies, young and old, will gather once again in Golden Gate Park to reminisce, to celebrate the fortieth anniversary of the Summer of Love, and to commemorate a time that was supposed to change the world." She turned to look at her older colleague. "It didn't really change anything, did it?" The colleague, a balding man, gave a weak smile and shook his head.

Never one to wallow in her memory, Helen turned the television up louder. When she was younger, before she met Frank, she would fall asleep on her Salvation Army flower-print sofa in front of the television, waking up around four to the exuberance of an infomercial for an ab cruncher. She would try instead to reconstruct what she thought she saw in the window. Frank would be proud that she was seeking a logical conclusion rather than her favorite magical answers. She'd put her mind to work trying to solve the problem of what had happened that afternoon. If the television news didn't put her to sleep, surely attempting to use reason at midnight would do so. Frank would make a list. He would say, "Write down all the things you remember about the afternoon and then we'll figure out what caused the hallucination." He would, of course, assume it had been a hallucination, which he should know would skew his interpretation of what she remembered. Maybe she should write down a list of why they were getting divorced. It had seemed so clear in Phoenix.

She rummaged through the hotel's nightstand drawer. Next to the Gideon Bible was a pad of paper. First, she had been drinking. That was important information. She was hardly drunk, but she had been drinking and a person never really knows how much that affects perception. She was thinking a little like a scientist now, observing herself in the third person. She turned the volume on the TV down. She felt instantly sad because the room was so dark. She almost thought she would cry, but there would be plenty of time for that after she and Frank had their conversation. She crossed the room to the heavy drapes and opened them with her hands. A voile panel danced beneath them. No girl. The room was very still; she distinctly remembered that. "Alcohol," she heard Frank's voice in her head. "You can't distinctly remember anything when there's alcohol in your system." A drink of red. She almost spoke aloud, "Get out of my head, Frank!" but the room once again was very still and quiet and his voice, even static from her memory-tape, was welcome. Maybe she didn't *distinctly* remember the stillness of the room, but she felt something empty, as if the emptiness was its own entity and had grown from a tiny box in her heart to a being that filled and pressed up against the edges of the hotel room. She'd sat on the edge of the bed, noticing its fanciness, its satin duvet cover, its two extra sleeping pillows and an additional red velvet throw pillow with the letters "HG" for Hotel Gladmore embossed in gold on its front panel.

Their suitcases stood side by side in the open closet. Frank had not unpacked his clothes—two button down shirts and a pair of dark denim pants. Helen had not taken anything out of her suitcase yet, either.

That was a different pattern. Usually she took over the closets and the bathroom. Why had she not unpacked the clothes yet? Why had she somehow behaved as if she were only a visitor while Frank had at least partially moved in? She'd crossed the room to open her suitcase, a fun pink polka dot one she'd gotten on sale at Ross, when she saw the woman in the window. Yes, it could have been a flash of light from outside. They were right above one of the busiest intersections in the City. The light was the strange twilight light, where street lamps start popping on but the sun hadn't yet let go of its responsibilities. Shadows looked different in twilight. Everything looked softer, as the world moved from daylight to dark.

She closed her eyes. The drone of the television, which had become a late night comedy show, floated through her ears, not taking root. What exactly had she seen? The girl's hair was stringy, like her own had been when she was a girl and refused to wash it, the oils tainting the color a mouse brown. She wore no glasses, but her jacket was fringed and too big for her. She saw the girl's whole body, oversized fringed jacket, light denim jeans with a hole over the right thigh, boots with the same fringe as the jacket. Helen wanted to remember that her arms were outstretched, calling her forward, and that's why she kept walking, but (alcohol, alcohol) she could not be sure. Why would she walk toward a window, open it, and start to jump if she hadn't believed someone would catch her?

1967

Elle clutched her fiddle case. No, Brian would not carry it for her. He could not carry it for her. Janis had asked her a direct question and she'd be damned if she wasn't going to pay attention to that. She thought of the kittens under the porch in Georgia. She had written a postcard to Sadie, but she figured it would be intercepted. There would have been a fight, a shout about how ungrateful she was after they took her in when her mama ran off to the holy life, but it wouldn't be Sadie shouting, it would be Sid. And the floorboards would rattle, and the cans would pop open and pile up along side his porch swing, and he would fall asleep, or more accurately, be slammed asleep by the liquor and the anger, and her beautiful Aunt Sadie would creep upstairs and lie on top of the covers and cry silently, as she had well-learned how to do. Elle couldn't think about that too much or she'd hitch a ride on the next truck she saw heading back east. It took all she had, more than she knew she had, to get out, and she couldn't, not without giving this life more of a chance, turn tail and run back home, no matter how haunted she was by the sounds of Sadie's sobbing.

Elle and Brian stayed close to each other. Everywhere they looked was a new sight, a shout from a bearded young man to buy *The Oracle*, the official hippie paper, a smell from an unwashed group of kids or from the soup offered up by the Diggers in the Panhandle every day.

There were isolated ghosts of fog on one street, and then one street over claimed bright sun and clear skies. There were tour buses, people from all over the country coming to gawk at the hippies, to tsk tsk at them, or snap Polaroids, or sneak off the bus and join them. There were dogs, all colors, all kinds, leashed and loose, floppy eared and droopy eyed, walking along with the crowd. Never before had Elle seen so many colors of people, all walking together, all singing together, all seeking together. She saw the shimmer of it all, and whenever Brian pointed out a young girl or boy, younger than even they, who was actually starving, or strung out, or muttering to herself under a torn blanket, she looked away, as she had been taught to do in Georgia when a white man shouted, or worse, at a black man until the black one bowed his head, "yes, suh, suh" or fell to his knees after a club found the backs of them. She knew well how to turn away. The world was big and dark, but here there were rainbows and collectives and co-livelies and posters of neon color. Here was a place that could never exist in Georgia. Not for a single day.

"Don't look down," she said to Brian. "Look how pretty the sky is!"

Brian held on to her because he had to, because she'd climbed into his truck and now she was his responsibility, but even more than that, she was under his skin. Never before had anyone told him to look at the sky. Never before had he looked, and since he did, there was no way he could not have seen it, the bright sky, the blue, the tops of the skyscrapers, and the clouds billowing over the sea, darker than those over the Haight, but moving inland just the same.

2007

Frank could think of nothing else to do in the poetry room. The couple, arms entwined like vines, had left; the cat's-eye-glassed girl still perused greeting cards. He felt old. No one had ever mentioned that middle age felt so old. No one had told him that there was really no place to belong when you were in the middle. The young people had their fire and their potential and their energy. The old ones, the lucky ones anyway, had a modicum of freedom, a chance for the things they'd put off while they were young and chasing, and middle-aged and holding. As life took things and people from them, the old ones grew lighter, both of body and of heart, and walked among the City streets looking at buildings, fire escapes, bus stops, remembering what used to be there.

Frank felt his irrelevance whenever he tried to talk to the younger employees at work, or when he tried to use technology. He knew technology shouldn't be so difficult for him, but it confounded him. It knew things he didn't understand and that was unnatural for objects that didn't breathe. He hadn't told Helen he had decided not to go back to work, so there was still time to un-decide it.

He grasped the red banister and made his way down the stairs to the main room. He spotted Brian through the front window having a smoke. He hadn't left him after all. He toyed with the idea of going back upstairs. He could sit in one of the chairs beside the floor to ceiling windows and try to read one of the books. He would really try this time. He wouldn't make a joke about it, even if he didn't understand what he was reading. Maybe he would ask the cat's-eye-glassed woman what a verse meant. It was possible. He had already done so many things this day that were previously impossible. Before he could make up his mind, Brian had come back inside.

"Getting chilly out there," Brian said.

"Not like Phoenix, that's for sure."

"That where you're from?"

Frank nodded. "Well, sort of. I've been there a long time."

"I come here just about every day. When I walk through the alley and the world opens up to this place, I feel twenty again, and I guess what's even better is I feel like people treat me different. I feel like, even though I know most of them think I'm an ancient man, I have a mind."

Frank was awed by the sheer amount of words Brian had uttered together. He couldn't even let himself think about how personal the words were. If he said something, he was going to say the wrong thing, so he kept his mouth shut, except for a small grunt to say he'd heard him.

"This place saved my life."

Oh goodness. Surely that was a sentence that was going to require a response. "A bookstore?" Frank asked, knowing it was the wrong thing but he had nothing else to offer.

Brian smiled wanly. "*The* bookstore."

Frank should know what that meant. He scanned his history classes in his mind. City Lights, City Lights, City Lights. He couldn't remember anything significant. He was failing again.

1967

Brian's brother had already gone to Vietnam. He'd already come home, too, though not in the same state as when he left. Quick tour. It took the Army only three months to turn his brother dead. They'd always called his brother the lucky one, so Brian didn't feel like he had much of a chance at all. His mama broke when her oldest boy turned to mulch, and his father grew more rigid, always half-building things in the garage, the whine of the saw drowning out whatever other sounds he might have felt he needed to make. When Brian wondered how he got to San Francisco, he remembered the buzz saw, the bottles of vodka his mother kept in the refrigerator, the frozen shrine of his brother's room. He wouldn't go. He. Would. Not. Go. So in order not to go, he left, and though he was thinking he'd try to disappear in Chicago and then make his way to the Canadian border, Elle had different dreams, and Brian, never one to force his way on someone else, had gone along. Elle had that kind of magic about her. She made you want to do what she wanted, no matter how bad it might have been for you.

It seemed to Brian that the whole world was moving that year, like when the continents first broke apart from one another and went on their ways, apart, yet always yearning to be reconnected with that part of earth that once had been a second limb. In 1967, the epidermal layer of America was peeling up, redistributing itself in hand painted

German buses and migrating west. The once impenetrable edges of neighborhoods were beginning to erode and slip into one another. The barbershop quartets had become electric shrieks and the whole country, whether they were willing to act or not, heard the howl. The band-aid was slipping off the wounds of World War II and anyone paying the slightest bit of attention knew the blood was going to run in the streets.

The day he left home, he sat with his mother at the green plastic breakfast table. The orange and brown curtains she'd made years ago that hung in permanent open arms on the kitchen window held spider's nests. He listened to the percolating coffee as he stirred his cereal.

"Want I could make you an egg?" his mother asked.

Her gray hair was loosely wrapped in a bath towel. Her cigarette burned in the ashtray on the stove. She wore bright red lipstick.

"Nah, thanks." He was supposed to go to work at Fancy's Diner, where he'd been a line cook for two years. He worked the lunch shift that day. It was Friday, so the special would be grilled ham and cheese with a pickle for a buck and a quarter. He hated Fridays.

"Could make you some bacon?"

"Nah."

She picked up her cigarette and sat next to him. Her cigarette rested in her right fingers; her left fingers picked at the edges of the plastic placemat. "Go on then," she said, then took a drag longer than Brian thought possible. She blew the smoke up at the ceiling. "It's OK."

At first Brian thought she meant go on to work, but he caught the redness popping in her eyes that he knew was not from alcohol. "Make sure you say good-bye to Stevie a-fore you go. Tell him I'll be by directly." She pulled the towel from her head, causing her tightly permed hair to spring to attention. "Ever' day I plan to go, but it seems something always comes up gets in my way." She grabbed Brian's hands, which had long since stopped stirring his cereal. "Tell him I'll be by. Tell him."

Brian nodded fiercely. His throat was too hot to speak. "I'll tell him, Mama. Tell Daddy I— " His throat burned.

"I'll tell him, son."

They stood up at the same time, and when Brian pulled her to him, he felt the fragility of her bones underneath the housedress.

"Don't get yourself dead, boy," she said.

"I promise."

She pushed out of his embrace, turned toward the sink and waved him off with the back of her hand. "Go on now, get."

He closed the kitchen door as quietly as he could, started up the truck and pointed toward the cemetery.

Ezekiah Baptist Church's cemetery sat back a ways from the street and from the main church sanctuary. Huge oaks and pines covered the gravestones with their arms, cradling them with their leaves and needles. The sun didn't shine directly on the cemetery, so it always stayed a bit cooler than the rest of the world. Iron arches welcomed visitors with the words Jesus Wept. Brian stayed in the truck, idling the engine for a bit. The truck used to belong to Stevie, who stopped wanting to be called Stevie when he enlisted in '65. "What else am I going to do, bro?" he'd asked Brian the night they drove this truck out to Hag's Hill, the overlook that had seen the loss of many of the town's youth's virginity over the decades. "What other kind of work can I do?" Brian didn't know, didn't know what kind of work he was going to be doing after he graduated the next year. The world didn't seem to have too many opportunities for guys like them.

"Say something," Stevie had said.

"I don't know what to say."

"You think it's stupid."

"No."

They passed a cigarette between them. It was late, or early, depending on your view of things, close to four a.m., and the overlook was empty except for a few owls and some stray cats. They'd already had more than a few Schlitz; the empty cans crushed to the floorboards. There was no moon, or if there had been, it had already eased on into the next phase.

"So you go tomorrow," Brian finally said.

"Yep." Stevie reached his hand in the dark toward Brian's cheek, then pulled it back, cracked a joke. "Going off to see the world courtesy of Mr. Uncle Sam!" He tooted a drunken version of Reveille, then belched. "Going to save America from gooks."

Brian was going to speak, but Stevie cut him off. "Don't get all serious, man. Like you always do. This is our last night." He crushed the cigarette into the overflowing ashtray, then tossed the butt out the window. "Don't get all serious."

Brian smiled. "Gook killer."

"Damn right!"

They laughed a hollow laugh together.

"You take good care of this truck, Brian. She's been good." He lit another smoke, offered the pack to Brian. He took another, though he was starting to feel sick.

"I will. I'll be careful with her."

"Yeah," said Stevie.

"Yeah," said Brian.

They said nothing for the next hour. Brian got out to relieve himself in the bushes and as he walked back to the truck he saw the silhouette of his brother in the driver's seat, chin sharp and proud, shoulders slumped, right hand resting on the steering wheel. He paused there in the new dawn, promising himself he would always remember this moment. He was old enough to know that this kind of night was never going to happen again for them, no matter what happened in Southeast Asia. No matter who came back.

He turned off the engine, rested his hand on the wheel where he remembered Stevie's had been, then opened the door.

He was ashamed to admit he hadn't been here since the funeral. Folks'll think he forgot, but nothing could be further from the truth. Every time he got in the pick up, every time he placed his hands on that steering wheel, he was with Stevie. Even with all the trees and moss and red birds, the cemetery was dead for him. A line up of the lost. He hadn't been here since the stone was laid, and he was surprised that his feet knew where to find it. The marker was dark granite, his brother's name etched deep. "Beloved son, brother, soldier" it read beneath the dates. Stevie would have hated that word "beloved"; now he's got to be with it forever. Brian crouched down, brushed a leaf off the stone, coughed a sudden sob and whispered, "I'm leaving, man. I just can't stay." He thought of his mother's hand waving him out, setting him free. His love for her in that moment almost rooted him back to his childhood house, to his job at the Diner, to his, as the preacher at Ezekiah Baptist like to shout, "predestination."

They had not been allowed to see the body. Brian didn't know if any part would have been recognizable. Dog tags came home, which his mother now had hanging in the kitchen on a hook above the stove, and boots, and a picture of a girl Brian had never seen before. They hadn't known how to find her. Hadn't known if she would even want to know. The Army sent a flag back too, which his mother had thrown in the trash, poured her glass of Vodka on it and tossed in a match. When it burned out, she sat in front of the ashes for hours making soft bird noises. Many nights Brian had tried to imagine what had happened to Stevie. "He died a hero," said the man who came to the door. But what does that mean? What does that look like?

"I just can't stay, man." He imagined Stevie's right hand slapping his back, pulling him into a quick hug, rubbing his knuckles on his scalp. He imagined him saying, "I understand, Bry, I do." But of course he only imagined it, could never know if it would have been real. If his brother would have been OK with him leaving his mother alone in that house with the orange and yellow curtains and dog tags and their father. He stood, brushed the dirt from his pants' knees, and tried to pray but couldn't. "I miss you," croaked out. "Mom said she'll be by soon." And softer, "Just because she doesn't come here doesn't mean she doesn't care." He couldn't reconstruct Stevie from scalp to sole anymore. He couldn't conjure back his voice, not for sure. He listened a moment longer but heard only the birds' feet on the dried leaves. When he started up the truck, he waited again, for a surprise visit, perhaps, for Stevie to leap from the trees, "Gotcha, bro! That was a good one! I really had you."

REMMY X

Chatty, chatty, chatty, that's what everything is tonight. Way too chatty. I can't get me a read on any of it. I even entertain the idea of going into Glide, just to find me some peace and quiet and maybe a bit of water for Shep, but I can't bring myself to do it. Shep and me walk past a man as angled and white as Jack Skellington, who asks us for a quarter. I give him one and he asks for another. "Don't got another," I say. "Shi-i-i-t," he says, but moves on past us. The windows we walk past have thick iron bars on them. I head west back toward my apartment when I see the commotion at the Motel 6. Don's there, with his partner and another copper I don't know. There's a woman, rasta-braids flying, wrapped in a blanket. A man in dark beehive shaped sunglasses and a loincloth is holding an ax. "I told her!" he shouts. "I done told her this was gonna happen!" Don sees me, shakes his head, but I stay on a bit anyway. He's trying to keep me safe, trying, I think, to keep me from seeing what he really has to do every day. Shep barks and I shush him. The man wielding the ax spins around. Guns are trained on him.

"Put down the ax," says Don, and I'm surprised by how authoritative he sounds. He, who in my brain-house memory banks, used to call the cops pigs. "We will shoot."

"I told her! I told that woman."

"I'm sure you did," says Don. "Put down the ax and we'll talk."

Motel 6 employees are watching through their barred window. I see one of them snapping a picture. The woman is carrying on in a tongue I can't recognize. The blanket slips a little and I can see she's naked underneath. An ambulance pulls up and waits, lights flashing, siren off.

"Put down the ax," says Don again, and the man, now wild as a dervish, starts jumping and slashing at the air. Jack Skellington has appeared beside me again.

"Can I have a quarter?"

"No," I say.

"Shi-i-i-t," he says. Then, "That's Jimmy Dean! Jimmy Dean! Jimmy Dean!" He leaps like he's on a pogo stick. "It's me, man, Shelby! What you doing?"

A cop I hadn't even spotted before comes over. He's big and black, four of my legs could fit in his biceps, and I am most sincerely hoping he's coming for Shelby.

"Sir, step back, please," he says, and I do, and Shep does, but Shelby keeps leaping.

"Jimmy Dean! Jimmy Dean! What you got you an ax for?"

Jimmy Dean stops slashing the air. Don's gun barrel has not left its target. Jimmy Dean lifts his sunglasses. "Shelby?"

"Yeah, man! Me!"

Shep wants to go. Right. Now. Go. Not just-one-more-minute go. But I can't seem to move my feet. I can see they aren't stuck to the sidewalk, but I feel like someone nailed them down, without the nail and all the pain, of course. Shep moves behind my legs, sticks his nose between my calves. I feel him shaking. My Shep would be a very bad police dog. He got all the sweetness of a German shepherd and not so much of the fierceness. Guess when you get you a mutt-Shepherd you don't get to pick which parts you get.

"Shelby, man!" Jimmy Dean makes the mistake of letting his arm with the ax fall to his side, and then faster than I knew Don could move, he zip-a-dee-do-da-ed in, grabbed the ax, and wound Jimmy

Dean's arms behind his back. That was some kind of impressive.

The woman stops jammering and speaks, clear as day all of a sudden. "Don't hurt him!"

A female cop emerges from somewhere behind the building carrying another blanket. The woman pushes her away and she runs, naked, toward Jimmy Dean.

"Baby! Baby! I'm so sorry!"

Jimmy Dean laughs a little. Shelby is still bouncing; Shep is still shaking. "You know I'd a never hurt you," he says.

"I know, baby, I know." She only has a few teeth and her arms are tracked.

Don and his partner take Jimmy Dean to the patrol car. Don nods at me. The big black cop has disappeared and my feet become unstuck.

"Can I have a quarter?" asks Shelby.

I reach into my pocket and hand him my honest and true last one.

"I knew you had another," he says.

"Yeah," I say.

"Jimmy Dean used to be a medic. He healed me my leg from the shrapnel." Shelby stops his bouncing and Shep finally wags his stick of a tail. "Long time ago that was."

I nod, reach back into my pocket and hand him a dollar.

"You holding out on Shelby," he says, but he's laughing, and I see his rotten teeth and wonder how much they hurt him all the time.

"Maybe a little."

He reaches down from the skyscraper of his height and pets Shep, who lets him. "I had a dog like him once. Name was Rover. I said, Rover, Rover, get yo ass over, and he did for awhile. And then he didn't." Shep licks his hand. "Man, Jimmy Dean? Stitched up a thousand men in one day, he did, all the time the fire raging all around him. He didn't even seem scared. Just stitched him one man after another. We called him the Tailor for awhile, but after a time he quit answering to it, said he wanted to be called Jimmy Dean now, cause all night every night he only dreams of sausages. What you think that could mean? Why a man who used to stitch people back together want to chop them back apart?"

Shelby's eyes have a glimmer of the boy he'd been and I almost think I can tell him what the dreams meant, but I can't really see much point. It was pretty obvious, and if he don't want to see it, then some part of his own brain-house don't want him to understand it. It ain't none of Remmy's affair to start messing around up in other people's brain-houses. I got enough crazy up in my own head.

I got to get out of here and go back to my Street. Every time I come down here to wander—though I know it's not just wandering-wandering, but avoiding-wandering—I think it'll be the time I tell Don. I think: Remmy, you can't keep letting this go on. He's breaking apart, old Don. But then that coward-part of my soul that I'm sorry to say sometimes still wins starts shouting and banging pots and pans and I just say pretty much, "Hey, Don, good to see you old friend," and leave him be.

"We best be going," I say to Shelby.

Shelby pats Shep again. "Can I keep your dog?"

"Nah."

"That's cool." He turns abruptly away and starts hopping down the street. Shep's beside me again, the leash loose between us.

- X out.

2007

Helen had fallen into a restless sleep. The television droned on all night, the room stayed too cold, and Frank never came back. She half-woke, several times, to a song she couldn't quite grasp whispering from the walls. On the fifth awakening, she went to the bathroom, scooped Frank's toiletries to one side of the sink, and began to run a bath. She poured in the vanilla scented complimentary bubble bath. She hadn't taken a bath in years. Showers were faster, more efficient, or so Frank said. A bath was decadent. The complimentary bubble bath did not produce a great amount of bubbles, but the bathroom lights had a dimmer switch, so she lowered the lights to what she thought was a soothing level and slipped into the hot water.

The tub was big enough for her to be comfortable, even to sink down a little so her head was just above the water. She closed her eyes, the pressure of the water heavy against her skin. She remembered floating in the warm Atlantic Ocean on an inner tube one summer when she was a teenager. The water was so warm and so calm and the waves just held her, carrying her farther and farther away from shore. She'd closed her eyes then and dreamed briefly of mermaids and fantastical sea creatures with long green tentacles and friendly hearts. She didn't know quite how long she'd dozed, but when she opened her eyes, she could tell without touching that her exposed skin was burned. The shore looked miles away, but at least she could still see it. She tried to pinpoint the red and white umbrella that marked her beach bag and beach towel's location, but she could not see that far. She suddenly worried about sharks and jellyfish and the sea creatures of her dreams began to grow teeth and stingers. She would wash up on the shore one day; a foot, a hand, maybe a torso, and residents would wonder who she was and how she had come to meet such a grisly end. Had she gone to the beach alone? Foolish, foolish girl, they would say, as the seagulls circled. She relaxed and resigned herself to a melodramatic death when the tide shifted and the waves that had carried her away from shore began to slowly pull her back. Well, she'd thought, it must not have been my time.

The bathwater grew cold faster than it should. She opened her eyes. She couldn't tell if the sun was up yet through the blackout drapes. Her skin had wrinkled, her tailbone grown sore. She reached for the oversized towel she'd placed on the toilet lid and eased herself out of the water, imagining for a moment Botticelli's Venus, herself as a voluptuous, sea-goddess emerging from her clam-sized home.

HER

She had realized something was wrong right away. Remmy had put his hand on her body and she felt it at the same time she watched him touch her. She heard the gasps of the crowd, even wondered why she hadn't had the luck of falling on the backs of one of them. Maybe she would have lived. She saw the blood start to pool on the sidewalk and she had the fortitude to look up and take notice of where this had happened. The corner of Waller and Downey. She could read the street signs at eye level. From this height, the crowd was a sea of scalps, center-parted, straight and stringy. The cacophony of music coming from the open windows of the Victorians hadn't stopped. The buses kept to their routes. The shouts to get your copy of *The Oracle* didn't soften. The world had at once expanded to unbearable proportions and contracted to two squares of sidewalk and the face of Remmy, green eyes filled, his own brown stringy hair shivering, and she knew what she had not previously noticed. He loved her.

She thought she could breathe, but didn't feel the rising and falling of her chest. She thought she could cry; she felt the heat, the water inside, but nothing manifested. Brian came running; someone must have found him where he'd been working down at the Free Store. He lifted her head, then dropped it back quickly when he saw the river of blood. She didn't feel the pain, just felt the thunk. Remmy stepped back when

Brian arrived, giving him the place of honor next to her.

"Help! Somebody get help!" Brian shouted.

Remmy touched the back of Brian's neck. "Someone called, man. They're coming."

She floated up to the window, the edges of the frame fringed with shards of glass. The curtain, a single panel of imported fabric, hung by a single bracket. The record player still played, her favorite 45, Buffalo Springfield's "For What It's Worth". The candles in the snake-shaped candelabra that they'd traded just yesterday for a song and a smile hadn't yet melted down. The flames flicked in the breeze from outside the window. She could see the music in colors lifting off the turntable—a green daisy with a flexible stem, dust of royal blue, gold, and silver, a chocolate brown when he sang—and she had wanted more than anything to stop and watch what was going down, and maybe she had finally stopped, but surely stopping was final, and this, wherever or whatever this was, was not the end. The coffee grounds were still in the sink from that morning's remake of the coffee from the day before. The socks she had worn yesterday were deflated on the scratched wood floor. She couldn't bear to be in the room anymore, and she couldn't look at the paraphernalia on the coffee table, a 4 x 8 raised up on two bricks.

Brian was wailing, actually wailing, and she wished that he'd have made that kind of noise just yesterday. He had gotten out of their nest on the floor, told her she was no longer making any sense, and begged her to stop taking drugs. Downer, he was, bad energy. No one talked about getting off drugs, and LSD was perfectly safe, and everyone was doing it, and oh! How it made her feel. When she played her fiddle it shook. She breathed music. She was going to play with Janis and with Big Brother and the Holding Company, and people were going to move to her music in the darkness and she would show them sparks from each string and together they would form a rainbow cloud that everyone could elevate to. She felt she was getting younger here, and

Brian was getting old, and she was here to live and to be and to feel and if he couldn't feel or wouldn't feel then what was he doing hanging around her anyway?

"You're so beautiful," he'd said in the dark, but she pushed him away, wrapped herself in the dirty sheet, and said he knew nothing of beauty. He only saw lines.

"That's not true," he'd said, but she said it was and he left her there and went out of the apartment into the swarm of people that never stopped coming, never stopped pulsing, and disappeared.

"I don't need you!" she'd said, or thought she remembered she'd said; now it was becoming more difficult to remember as the wind seemed to blow her from side to side in the room. Now, he's wailing and he's cradling her head that he'd dropped and he's touching her hair and she wondered why he hadn't thought to do that just yesterday. Just eleven hours ago.

She lost track of Remmy in the crowd, but Starburst had come, eyes glazed from too much something. "Dude," he said, but Brian just kept wailing. "Dude, calm down. Calm down. It's all groovy."

Brian pushed at Starburst, who fell back and started laughing until he threw up. He was quiet for a minute before erupting once again.

"What did you give her?" asked Brian.

"Hey, chill. I don't know man, I'm fine." He threw up again. "Some cat from the show last night handed me—" Brian rested her head, softly this time, on the sidewalk and punched Starburst so hard three teeth flew out. Sirens moved closer and the crowd began to disperse, moving toward the Park or the Panhandle. The inside of her mouth felt cold, her tongue fat. *Brian! Don't hurt him!* But her swollen tongue could not form words, and without breath they could not take flight.

"Pigs!" someone shouted and the crowd got even thinner. She watched her body, bent backwards, shrink as well, as if being absorbed by the sidewalk on the corner of Waller and Downey. Without her breath, her body fell in on itself sooner than she'd thought possible.

Without breath, she was only pieces of a girl. She saw Remmy far away, almost at the ocean's edge. He was screaming too, only no one was around to tell him to stop or keep going. The ocean's voice swallowed his; the ocean's wind took his breath. *Remmy!*

The uniformed men were not gentle with her. They took some notes, looked four stories up to her window, took more notes. They put numbers at the points her body hit the ground and when the coroner arrived, he rolled her onto a gurney and with the help of a medic took her to the back of the waiting ambulance. Men moved through her apartment scooping up the paraphernalia with gloved fingers. One of them stepped on their tangled nest on the floor. One of them washed her coffee grounds down the drain. They moved with jerking motions, mechanical dolls following procedures. She was a case number, and she would soon be gone and they could add another statistic to their files. One of them, who had taken care to step over their makeshift bed, went to the turntable and lifted the needle off the record and stopped the chocolate sounds that had carried her away.

Starburst lay puking and bleeding on the sidewalk. Remmy ran and screamed along the surf, and Brian pressed his fists into his eyes and shook, making no sound at all. The uniformed men didn't ask them any questions. No one offered them a blanket, or some water, or even a touch on the back. No one was sorry. She realized she was no one to them. No one's niece. No one's daughter. No one's friend. She was not a musician. She could not change people's lives with her notes. She could not stand on a stage and elevate them to the stars. She was on the sidewalk, pieces of a girl, her fiddle silent, the case's hinges burst, an open mouth beside her.

The uniformed men did not care about her fiddle. They did not care if it made chocolate sounds or sparks, and they did not care that she had jumped, only that her jumping was going to cause them to be late, again, for dinner.

Tender Moments in the Tenderloin
A Sociological Study in Serenity

This reporter had the privilege yesterday to take a stroll
through one of the City's best-kept secrets: The Tenderloin. Many folks are afraid to go in this neighborhood,
which is bordered by Geary and Market, Mason and Larkin.
Our City's fine government establishments are just to the
west of the Tenderloin and our upscale shopping and dining
establishments are just to the east of it. It was said that
officers used to get a hazard pay bonus to work her streets.

The Tenderloin is full of hungriness. Transsexuals, trans-
vestites, prostitutes, drug dealers, imported drug gangs,
petty theft, gambling, pornography, graffiti art, you name
it, the Tenderloin has it now or has had it before. The
neighborhood sees some gang shootings, some trafficking of
all sorts, and boasts some darn fine Vietnamese food. (This
is in no way an indication that the Vietnamese are responsible for the crime in the neighborhood.)

Tourists find themselves lost here. They take one step
south from their $300 seats in the Theatre District and
they find the shadows have shifted. Shoppers step one block
too far west and they can no longer buy Manolo Blahniks but
condoms, needles, and blow.

For purposes of researching this article, this reporter
looked up maps of San Francisco and was shocked to learn
that the Tenderloin is actually left off of several tourist
maps of San Francisco neighborhoods. This reporter thinks
that is indicative of a larger concern, which he will address in his Reflective Moment immediately following this
dispatch.

Today, several of San Francisco's finest, including this

reporter's friend, helped stop a potentially violent act at the Motel 6. It is to everyone's credit that no one was hurt or killed, though the ramifications of the situation will likely linger on.

Remmy's Reflection Moment: Shep and me didn't know what we were going to see. Not much gets me, and to tell the honest truth, it wasn't the ax-swinging that got me, or the toothless track-marked woman who got me, it was Shelby and his story about Jimmy Dean. It was the knowledge that the ax-swinger was once a medic, and the crack-head Shelby was once a soldier, and it made me think once again about our War. When I see what the kids from my generation turned into because of it, and when I see how much the country that turned them into it don't care, it's hard to maintain my usual optimistic light on the world. I left the Tenderloin today wanting to apologize to someone, but I didn't know who that would be. The kids today got their own war that no one seems to care too much about, and I suspect in less years than people would like to think, the Tenderloin will be one of the only places to welcome those soldiers back home. American folks once again landing alone in a place left off an American map.

Remmy X: Hashbury Daily Times

2007

Brian couldn't get out of City Lights fast enough. Strange, since he'd considered the place to be his home for so many years. He found himself sounding like an old man in the Poetry Room, trying to convince some young kid, though Frank could hardly be considered a kid, of the value of his whole generation.

He remembered his grandfather doing that, going on and on and on about Germany before World War I, when it was the greatest county "in the world!" And his grandfather would slam his blue-veined fist on whatever surface was nearby and then his eyes would fill with tears and he would deflate like a balloon. His grandfather had come to America alone when he was thirteen and made his way through Ellis Island, through the docks and shipyards of New York City, and somehow chosen to go south, out of the throng of the city, into what he thought was America's heart. It didn't work for him. He was lonely. He missed people who could speak German. He missed people who ate foods other than grits, biscuits, and chicken. But he got by, because that's what you did, and then you told your children and your grandchildren stories of the way things used to be, and you told them with vitriol, and you told them with vigor, and you expected they would see, with just one telling of the story, the magic of the world you had known.

It was cold out on the street. He wished he had a warmer coat, or at least a scarf, but he was long supposed to be home, positioned in his olive green La-Z-boy rocker, white cat Anastasia (named for his great-grandmother) on his lap, watching nothing on the television but enjoying its noise nonetheless. He'd almost finished his cigarette when he decided to go back inside the store to find Frank. Certainly, he had no obligation to stay with the man. Two grown people could part in a bookstore in North Beach and never see one another again and all would be fine. No one would think the other rude or unaccommodating. They were strangers, after all. But Brian was not trying to convince Frank of the glory of his generation. He was trying to convince Frank that he had once mattered. That he had once been *relevant.* And that awareness was harder to push into the silences of his chest. Brian wished he could speak to his grandfather today. He would listen better, ask questions, touch his hand before he slammed it onto the table and tell him that he understood now.

He should go home, feed Anastasia, pull out a Stouffer's and go back to work in the morning. They would understand. They all thought he was ancient. They thought he was cute, the guy with all the stories. The girls loved him. He wasn't threatening, so they told him things they would never tell their lovers. He wasn't threatening, so their lovers told him things they'd never tell their women. They probably wouldn't even dock his pay. He'd been there so long. Tomorrow everything could be ironed out, straightened, folded and put away as it was supposed to be. Instead, he went back in the bookstore. He needed Frank to understand with an urgency he hadn't felt since Elle died.

Brian had watched Elle go long before she went. There's a blurry quality a person gets when they're on their way away. Part of them is already in motion and part of them is still standing right in front of you. He knew his mother had felt it when she had breakfast with him the last morning he was in Georgia. He'd seen it sitting in the truck with Stevie the night before he shipped out. Most people don't actually say good-bye when they go. You just wake up one morning and their skin feels colder, their eyes looking past you at some place you know better than to ask if you can even visit.

San Francisco was eating Elle. From the second they found themselves in the bumper-to-bumper traffic on Haight, Elle was swept away. She stepped into the merry-go-round with both feet, holding on to nothing but her fiddle. He couldn't have stopped it. He knew that. He couldn't have kept her off the ride.

She smiled at him still, but the smile was teeth and lips, no eyes. She laughed with him, ate breakfast with him, but then she vanished into the street. She came back at night, or she didn't. She showered or she didn't. But he stayed, trying at first to act like he could be one of the kids dancing and chanting and running, but it wasn't in his nature. He rooted where he was planted, and although he'd have never chosen San Francisco, he was here. Had been here all this time. And she was here now too. No amount of reason could convince him otherwise.

The Howl that Woke the World

A Special Neighborhood Exclusive to Hashbury Daily Times

Every so often, this reporter likes to do a special interest piece to help enlighten readers of this fine paper of
the interesting and diverse history of the great City of
San Francisco. Today's piece, as indicated by the title,
will discuss City Lights Bookstore and the one and only Mr.
Allen Ginsberg. City Lights lives in the triangular-shaped
Artigues Building at the intersection of Columbus Avenue
and Broadway in North Beach. Now, San Francisco is a City of
many fine bookstores, many literary bars and activities, but
none quite as revelatory and revolutionary as City Lights.

As the Official Chronicler of the Haight, I would like to
offer a sister-city designation, as it were, to City Lights.
Since I empowered myself as the Official Chronicler of the
Haight, I am empowering myself with the power to offer this
honor to our compatriot in counterculture. City Lights was
the Haight of literary revolution; the Haight of the counterculture before even the Haight flowered into herself.
City Lights fostered and supported underground presses and
provided shelter and protection for people hiding from the
FBI infiltration of those presses.

In 1955, long before this reporter first set foot in this
grand City, the Venerable Mr. Laurence Ferlinghetti started
City Lights Publishers (and, of course, he used it to publish his own work, participating in the fine tradition of
self-publishing that this reporter is continuing to partic-
ipate in). He also published translations by the likes of
Kenneth Rexroth, early work from Denise Levertov and San
Francisco Grande Dame Diane di Prima. His press gave voice
to the Beat Generation writers, and more recently, political

writers such as Howard Zinn, Cindy Sheehan and Noam Chomsky.

But you're not convinced yet, I know, because I haven't mentioned the most influential, most stupendous, most unbelievable piece of literature ever to push America on its proverbial knees. Yes, *Howl*. Mr. Allen Ginsberg, with the help of Mr. Ferlinghetti, fired the shot heard round the world, setting off an obscenity trial, which, much to the E-stab-lish-ment's dismay, they won, launching an unprecedented poetry print run. Today, over one million copies of *Howl* are in circulation. Mr. Ginsberg put City Lights on the map, now and forever, as a place that shattered the stone ceiling of literature. City Lights made room for everyone, regardless of gender, regardless of race, regardless of sexual orientation. City Lights gave voice to the voiceless in a scenario not recreated since Gutenberg. (Remmy cannot be sure of this, since he was not alive when the Gutenberg press came to be, but he can imagine, a very important quality of any reporter.) City Lights Bookstore is a place where people can still go to discuss literature and the value and revolutionary potential of art. Mr. Ferlinghetti still walks its floors, giving the occasional reading, laughing at the folly of us all.

Remmy's Reflective Moment: We have us some anarchist bookstores on the Haight, and we have us some old used bookstores that have dusty tomes stacked and wedged up to the ceiling. We have a newer bookstore too, next to the co-op up the hill a ways closer to the Park. But we don't have us a City Lights. And perhaps that is for the best. Even a City as powerful as San Francisco could only hold one.

Remmy X: Hashbury Daily Times

HER

She was zipped into a plastic bag and her world fell under a screen. She wasn't in darkness, but the light filtered in through a sieve. Before Brian ran away, he'd scrawled a note on the back of a poster that had blown off a telephone pole. *Live! At the Fillmore! June 20, 1967. Jefferson Airplane with the Jimi Hendrix Experience!* He'd borrowed a pencil from one of the on-lookers, scribbled quickly, folded the poster into a small square, and slipped it in her jeans' pocket before the uniformed men came. The ride to the coroner's office was bumpy. The men riding in the back with her talked about their families, their conquests, their lives. She tried to wiggle inside the black plastic bag so they would pay attention to her. It was like they were transporting a mattress or a used piece of furniture. One of them rested his muddy feet on the bar of her gurney. She didn't know where she should go. Her world was shrouded, clouded, and her body was shrinking into the plastic. When they reached the morgue, they took no care in lowering her gurney to the street. It bounced and she slid to one side, almost falling off. They pushed her back on, continuing to talk about things she no longer could quite understand. They left her in a green room, and eventually someone pushed her off the gurney onto a metal slab and slid her into the freezer.

She lost the ability to recognize time. She waited. A man with thick glasses rimmed with black wrapped a tag around her big toe. A black rotary phone rang. He answered it. Wrote something down, returned to her toe and wrote "transport" on the tag. She continued to wait, perched on a cold shelf with instruments and jars. She thought she could smell mold. Days and nights must have passed, but she could not tell. Her body stayed in the freezer on the slab with a tag on its toe. Her world stayed cloudy, and she felt less and less connection to the pieces in the freezer, but as that connection dissolved, she had less and less idea where she was supposed to go.

REMMY X

I got to give you some bit of real important information. You've been reading a long time now, so you've earned this truth. I am not the most honest of reporters, for I have a lens that I see everything through. I am much more of a poet than a journalist, but these days, people like to read things only if they think it's true or that it really happened, as if somehow that makes it more valuable. I am not a liar, no not at all, but I have the things I carry too, just like everybody. I have the gift of a long life, which brings also the gift of a soft memory. I have more failings than many, but I feel like mostly I am an honest man, if not an honest reporter.

I make such a big deal out of this because I am getting the sense that you don't believe in the Haight. I get the sense that you look at those old film footages that have become archival and make up your mind that this was just a freaky moment in America's history, and that it could never happen again. That those "crazy kids" just got a little out of control. I get the sense that you then want to decide the kids were losers, drains on society, addicts and thieves, or that you then want to decide the kids were angels, little versions of Sister Teresa and Mahatma Gandhi wandering the streets, watching the light shows. I know it's easier to keep the lines very clear, to believe that there is a right side and a wrong side to things, a left side and a right, a black and a white.

Black men walked down the street with white women in the Haight in 1967. Black men kissed white women on the streets of the Haight in 1967. Black men killed each other in Detroit in 1968, and white men killed black men in Mississippi in 1968. It was a time of lines. Lines behave in ways that circles don't. I understand that. But I need you also to understand the lens I see the Haight through isn't one of those lines. I see it like a circle. I saw devils acting like angels and angels acting like Lucifer himself. The Haight shone so bright we needed sunglasses on all day long, but with any kind of light that bright comes a darkness of equal and opposite force. It is just the way of things, and the Haight did not disappoint. The Haight behaved according to the natural order of the world. You may think I didn't see that, eating my Cherry Garcia and chronicling the Street, but I did. I sure enough did.

- X out.

2007

Helen peeked around the edges of the drapes. It was not yet dawn on her first morning in San Francisco. It was a Saturday, the first of September, her fortieth birthday. When she was a girl, she loved September for its crackling colors, wooly sweaters and school-day familiarity. Most people, Frank included, dreaded the shrinking sunlight, but Helen welcomed it. She felt safest in the cool dark and damp of winter. She took a picture of the clock on the iPod station (4:32), then of her rumpled bed, then the bathroom, steam still on the mirrors. She quickly snapped a self-portrait, too, hoping the cheap camera wouldn't capture the gray under her eyes. She could call room service. It was supposed to be twenty-four hours. She craved eggs.

There was not a single crease on Frank's side of the bed. She'd slept, what little sleeping she did, decidedly on the right side of the bed. She hadn't even taken an extra pillow from his side to make herself a little more comfortable. She sat on the edge of the bed and stuck her legs straight out and took a picture of her bare feet, second toes on each foot longer and more crooked than the rest. The towel fell from her shoulders and she lay back, imagining her breasts still round and stable instead of banana-shaped and floppy. She was softer than she used to be. Everything seemed to roll, the skin under her bra strap, the pouch over her waistband, the little clusters of skin around her elbows.

She was not fat, but she had become stretchier, more elastic. Nothing stayed put anymore. To lie on the bed, exposed and unthreatened, unjudged and untouched, was a gift. When was the last time she'd done this? She raised her hands to her throat, warmed her vocal cords with her palms. She began to hum softly, enjoying the vibrations of her throat against her skin. The act of making sound was miraculous. The force of intention against breath made noise. Why had she not noticed that before? What else had slipped unseen under the edges of her life?

HER

The longer she stayed in the room with her body, the stiffer she became. She kept waiting for a sign, or a light, or a tunnel, or any of the
mythologies she'd heard about. Just last week (was it last week?) she'd
been learning about Hinduism and had marveled at how many gods
and goddesses, how many stories made up the way Hindus viewed the
world. But no one came. Not Jesus. Not Buddha. Not Krishna. Not
Yahweh. There was no gravitational pull that sucked her into a vortex
and sent her pummeling into her next life. There was no devil either,
thankfully, and she began to understand why there were so many elaborate stories about what came next. What actually came next was kind
of unbearable. As she grew stiffer, the shroud of gray that had covered
her vision began to dissolve enough so she could see some colors, sepia
tones of red, amber, blue. The world was a daguerreotype of shadow
and light, and it was very very cold. She was aware of its coldness but
not uncomfortable by it. How long was she supposed to wait? Maybe
this was all there was—just a lot of waiting and a lot of cold and a
lot lot lot of emptiness. That does not make a compelling after-life
mythology. Who could raise money for a church with that story? She
tried to force a sound, but couldn't locate her throat, so she imagined
speaking.

Hello? Is anyone out there?

She couldn't be sure she said anything, and she couldn't be sure anyone heard it, but it felt good to speak, even if it was silent. She couldn't see her body in the freezer, so she imagined what it looked like, turning blue and gray in the dark. Would her eyes coagulate or would they remain clear? She remembered that hair and nails kept growing for awhile, failing to instantly get the message that there would be no more need to keep the scalp warm, no more need to tear at pieces of paper or scratch an itch.

If you can hear me, say something.

The coroner walked in the room with another gurney with a black bag resting on it.

I'm here! I'm here!

The coroner unzipped the bag, flicked a toe tag on the boy, lit a cigarette. She saw his gold hair, dirty and caked with blood. His eyes were closed. He was wearing a paisley shirt. She couldn't see his legs. The coroner took a call.

"I'll be home around eight." Pause. "I'll grab something to eat on the way." Pause. "Yeah, sounds good." Pause. "Love you too."

He hung up, zipped the boy's bag, slid him into the freezer next to her. This time, when he left he turned out the lights and she felt afraid.

Hello? I'm here! I'm here!

The dead boy didn't make any noise, or if he did, she couldn't hear it. He was still in his bag in his slot in the freezer. She was in pieces.

I'm here, she tried again, with less enthusiasm, less force. *Hello?*

1967

Elle thought she should be forgiven for being young. Isn't that what all the old people said? Ah, the follies of youth, they'd say, and they'd smile, and remember mistakes with far greater fondness than things that worked out alright. She thought she should be forgiven for what she was about to do, and that there would come a day when she'd be able to look back on it with her husband, whoever that might be, in their breakfast nook overlooking the Pacific Ocean. They'd hold hands and he'd wish he would have known her then, when she was braver and more beautiful and more innocent, but he would never say that, because he was a nice man, the man she was supposed to marry, the man who would have never caught her eye in 1967 when she was braver and more beautiful and more innocent. Their wedding bands, a bit worse for wear, would shimmer in the morning sun, and they would pass the paper silently between them. One of their children, the boy perhaps, would have just gotten into a bit of trouble, but they would be progressive, they would be modern. "Kids," they'd say, and remember the follies of their own youth, pour a splash of vodka in their orange juices, and forgive him.

She liked Brian, she did. He was sweet and attentive and kind of freaky responsible. She was free now. Free of home. Free of jobs. Free of school. Free, free, free, but all he seemed to do was worry. All he seemed to do was ask boring adult questions that squished any ounce of fun out of anything they were doing. He smelled good, though, and he had carried her all the way across the country in a haunted truck, so she felt loyalty to him. So much so she hadn't told him the truck was haunted. At first she was sure he knew because it was so obvious. The seat she sat in had another whole body in it and she hated to be rude and sit on it, but there was no other place for her to be. The body was warm and taller than she was.

"Who's here?" she'd asked, somewhere around Nevada.

"What do you mean?"

They'd just had an amazing breakfast of cheesy eggs, thick fatty bacon, and bottomless cups of coffee and were back on the road. Brian seemed to have an endless amount of money with him and he didn't mind spending it on her.

"In the truck." He must not know, she thought.

Brian curled his lips under his confused face. "Is this a trick question?"

She decided to let it drop. "Just a game," she said. "For the road."

He was chewing on something in the very back of his heart. "What kind of game?"

"Never mind." She didn't want things to turn serious. This was just so much fun. Breakfast and motel rooms and fiddles and salty skin. This was being alive. This would have never happened on Sadie and Sid's front porch.

"No. You meant something." He sped up, passing a lumbering cattle truck.

The body underneath her kicked her. "Nothing. You know how I don't make sense all the time. It's alright." The body settled back down and she aligned her leg bones directly over his. He seemed to feed off her breathing.

"Sometimes you make a lot of sense," he whispered, shifting the truck into overdrive straight into the Sierras.

REMMY X

Sometimes when I walk past the old offices on Haight of the famous *San Francisco Oracle* at 1371, which is kind of where Recycled Records is now and a mega Muni stop for the 6, the 71, and the 71L, I want to have a do-over. Aren't so many indie papers now, or if they are, they're on the computers rather than on the streets. An old guy like me can't help but wonder if something that never actually exists in the hands of folks can have the kind of impact it should. But I know I'm older than I ever thought I'd be, so that makes me, at least if I hold on to what we believed then, pretty much irrelevant.

I thought I'd write for the *Oracle* one day. I thought they might want to do a Haight Beat column or some other kind of human interest thing—the kind of reporting I'm the best at. There were a lot of different underground papers slinging around back then, but the *Oracle* was the one that had the world talking. It had subscribers in South America! In Germany! All over the world people were waking up to our energy and I wanted to be a part of it. But as much as the *Oracle* claimed to be open to everyone, it was, at its heart, a group of friends who wanted to publish their friends and I guess that's no different today.

They made these beautiful papers though. The inks were purple and yellow and orange and the images were of us, only us broken apart into parts of myths, parts of legends, and parts of aliens. I sent them some of my poems but they didn't print them, not even in the Letters pages where it seemed like they'd print just about anything. Maybe now I think I wasn't good enough, but they were publishing Ferlinghetti and Ginsberg and Mark Sandburg and they were obsessed with yoga and Ganesha and Hare this and Hare that and they ran endless interviews and conversations with Timothy Leary and Carl Rogers and they pretended to be concerned about American Indians and the plight of the planet, and I guess I believe they believed it. We were all so earnest then. Lew Welch and Alan Watts and all sorts of smart people were trying to tell us something on the psychedelic pages, only they were telling us through a haze and the messages got blurry.

These days, I have found some compassion in my heart-house for them. I hated them then because I wasn't part of them. I didn't know how to slip into their club, the club that was supposed to be free and open, but it wasn't, it just wasn't, and they made a lot of us ache even more inside with a desire to transcend into the dodecahedron of consciousness melting and tripping, and when the thing we were chasing turned out to be getting farther and farther away the harder and more intently we chased it, we burned out, and a lot of those folks in the club burned out too.

But some are still alive and kicking. If I could talk to Alan Watts today, I'd buy him a cup of decaf coffee and say, "Man, you're real." I run into Ferlinghetti from time to time, but he doesn't know who I am. He's jolly. Santa-like, and I feel I must tip my hat to his superior genetic make up to have not only survived, but to have continued to make art and fight for art. See, Remmy's not all jealous and petty.

The *Oracle* wouldn't publish my poems before I met Elle, and after I met Elle, I lost interest in everything but her. She was both my muse and my succubus, but not at the same time. After Elle, I wrote a beautiful piece about her and her fiddle. I got poetic and I got deep. I drew a picture of her with my words and I even sketched out an image that could go with it, all light show colors and butterflies like the ones she drew on her face every morning. I made notes on what should be purple, what should be lime green, what should be orange. But they sent it back to me. Or maybe they didn't and they lost it. I just know it never showed up in their paper, the paper that traveled the farthest around the world. I wanted to send her out into every corner of the planet. I just wanted the world to love her too.

So when the *Oracle* went under in '68 a little part of me sang, only I was so far gone into the void at that time I couldn't do anything more than listen to some far far way-away voice inside my ribs that was nodding, still awake no matter how many blankets I'd tried to smother it with.

- X out.

A Birth Story
Hashbury Daily Times

This reporter feels like he spends a lot of his time telling
you, his loyal reader, (dare he say readers?) about the past
and about what has died. In the spirit of balanced journalism, he is now going to tell you how this humble paper, one
of countless that have been hawked on Haight, came to be.
It is a story of the past, but because this paper is still
here and the others aren't, this reporter feels he can claim
a small corner of the history of the Street.

By 1972, the dreams of Haight had darkened. This reporter was part of that darkness, living his life in paranoid
shadows, jumping at the slightest eyebrow raised, running
from every badge that passed by, every jingle from the draft
board. We milled around, many of us, grasping not just at
heroin or methedrine or LSD, but at who we had been when we
arrived here. We were new, like sunrises, but no one had
told us that the sun always sets, or maybe they did and we
just didn't believe it because our suns were so bright, so
pure, so devoted to changing the world, that we knew we
would be the hallelujah exception to the laws of nature.

This reporter talked too much to no one, babbling and
blathering and moving from stoop to stoop, occasionally
climbing inside someone's place to sleep on a mattress or a
cigarette-burned rug. He stole people's cash and stash and
drank their teas and organic juice mixes. He woke up one day,
stripped of everything but his blanket, ribs aching, shoes
gone, and decided to check himself into the Langley Porter
Neurological Institute. He simply didn't know what else to
do. He couldn't even sign his name when he checked in, his
hand shivering over the paper, so he just made an "X" and

later, when he remembered what came before it, claimed it as his last name.

Paranoia never really leaves a person. You learn tools that help. You learn how to talk yourself out of sliding into that place. But you forever walk with it, knowing it's looming just behind that street light, just underneath that bus seat, and all it will take is one slip, one bad choice, and it will be back, and this time you'll be devoured by it. No one escapes twice.

When he left the hospital, he didn't know what to do. He looked out at his Street and didn't know how to talk to it anymore. So he thought he'd try writing to it instead. He wrote about his questions, and soon those questions turned into answers, or at least paragraphs, and then those paragraphs turned into stories and he realized he might have found a way to make his life work.

The Hashbury Daily Times had its inaugural issue on February 14, 1973, and has been distributed daily since then. This reporter printed a story he'd written in '67 and dedicated it to the Collabria at the *Oracle*, even though they were no longer a Collabria. There used to be ads, even some personals and some searches for lost kids or lovers, but after a few years, those stopped. There used to be twelve pages per issue, but now there's only one. It still sells for a quarter, and that quarter gets dropped in the fingerless-gloved hands of the Street's residents. It's blood money for this reporter's life. It's a bribe to keep the shadows in the corners. But on August 30, 2007, no one bought a single paper for the first time in all these years. So there was no quarter for the Street and everything that's been held back is leaking through that coin-sized hole.

This reporter apologizes for the misleading title. This may not be a birth story after all.

Remmy X: Hashbury Daily Times

2007

Brian's tongue was thick in his mouth. His mother had once told him that he should keep his mouth shut on buses because he might find himself telling a complete stranger all his personal business. He wondered why he would do that. "Strangers are safe," she said. "They're just going to hold your stories, not hold them against you." He couldn't imagine himself speaking to someone on a bus who hadn't spoken to him first, but that was long, long ago, and he'd noticed lately that his lips were loosening up. He was becoming the old guy to move away from on the Van Ness bus. He had begun smiling at children, trying to talk to young men wearing ear buds and pants that belted at their knees. He helped a Vietnamese woman with her brown paper bags board the bus and then he helped her get off at her stop. "I hope you have a nice day, ma'am," he'd said, but she just walked quickly into the fog. The driver was impatient with him as he held the railing and slowly re-entered the bus. "Move back! Move back!" the driver shouted, looking in the rear view mirror. "All the way to the back! There ain't no assigned seats." Brian smiled, grateful for the conversation, but the driver just pulled the doors closed and jerked into traffic.

"Do you want to go have a drink?" Brian asked.

"Actually, I do," said Frank.

"Somewhere quiet?" Brian couldn't hear well in crowded, enclosed places. He hoped he didn't sound like an ax murderer.

Frank nodded.

"I know just the place."

HER

Her body was put in ice and placed underneath the passengers on a flight from San Francisco to Atlanta. She had remained in the cold, green coroner's office as long as she could waiting for direction, but none came, so she left the boy for whom no one had yet arrived in his freezer and flew alongside her body at 30,000 feet. Occasionally, she would get a glimpse of the inside of the aircraft through a window. A small girl saw her, and she was so surprised she almost tumbled back to the earth.

"Mama," said the girl. "Look."

The bouffanted mother, in rhinestone glasses that pointed up at the ends like index fingers, craned her neck to see out the tiny airplane window. "What, honey? There's nothing out there but clouds."

The girl stared at out the window, mouth open. "No, Mama. Right there. A girl."

She tried to smile back at the child, but was not sure how to make her lips work, or even if she had any.

"You've got an overactive imagination," said the mother, pulling the window shade closed.

She slipped down to the wing and held on, wishing she could melt into the clouds that jetted past her, wishing the icicles caused her to feel cold, that the lack of oxygen caused her to stop breathing. The pieces of her lay among pieces of black and navy luggage, golf clubs, baby carriages and cargo. The pieces of her with the note in her jeans' pocket, her bloodied hair and her coagulated eyes bounced along against the clothes of those living, eating in the cabin of the plane, smoking their cigarettes and drinking their shots of vodka, believing, even at 30,000 feet, that they would live forever.

When the plane landed, she was the last to come out of the cargo hold. No one was waiting for her. No one was there with hugs or flowers or presents. No one missed her. She wanted to touch her box, but thought if she made contact, she might get pulled into it and she didn't want to be trapped like the smallest doll in the nesting dolls she'd gotten from her mother before she ran off with the revivalist. At least she could move around where she was, wherever that was. She did want to touch her face, though, and see if she could remember it before it bruised and colored. She wanted to touch her chin, trace the outline of her nose, smooth her eyebrows, trace the butterflies on her cheeks.

1967

There were just so many boys. How else could she describe it? Elle had never been the popular one, never been the one who knew how to behave with boys. She was the wallflower, wearing the dress with too much poof in the sleeves and the shoes with not enough lift in the heels. She had that one experience with Timothy and then Brian, but now—suddenly she was an adult. All it took was crossing the Mississippi River and coming to the City.

The black men looked at her and smiled. The Indian men looked at her and smiled. Everywhere she went, men smiled. She didn't know what she was doing differently, or why they smiled here but not in Georgia, but she loved it and she smiled back at every single one of them, even the stinky ones. She drew pictures of butterflies and flowers on her cheeks and around her eyes, feeling like a princess. She piled on layers of beads and put purple feathers in her hair because Janis did. She learned how to smoke and drink and stand with her hips just so, and she took everything the boys gave her because that was the polite thing to do, and she had not been the kind of girl to whom gifts were given. She took their drugs and their flowers and their guitar songs and their stoned promises. She took their beads, their fluids, and their dreams.

She had no idea what she was doing. There were just so many boys and the beat was so fierce and constant and she had never been in a situation in any way like this one before. They called her their flower child, their baby, their mama, their muse. She took it all. All their words and touches and kisses and reconstructed herself with them. She was playing every minute of every day and she thought everyone else was too.

"Why Miss Elena Mae," she would say to herself in an exaggerated Southern accent on those few occasions she was alone. She would trace the hearts on her cheeks, cock her hat on her head. "Why Miss Elena Mae, I daresay I would not have recognized you."

She'd giggle, even blush a little, then reply to herself. "Why thank you. I have indeed tried my hardest to vanish."

HER

Only Aunt Sadie had come to see her box. Aunt Sadie and a gravedigger and the minister from the only church in town.

"She left me a note," said Sadie, holding the piece of paper in her hands like a gift.

The minister took it and read it. "It's the times we're in ma'am. The end-times for sure. The kids are just being taken from us left and right. We have to pray, ma'am. We have to keep praying."

Sadie nodded, lowered her chin to her chest and watched her box. The gravedigger kept a respectful distance, sitting on top of his giant earthmover shovel.

"Shall I lead us, ma'am?" asked the minister.

"Yes, please, Reverend."

"Heavenly Father, we ask that you look out for this lost soul who has surely tasted the temptations of Satan. We know her to have been a good child, a good niece for Miss Sadie, and a good friend to all who knew her. We know that even your Son faced forty days of temptations in the desert, so we ask humbly for thy forgiveness for this innocent. She flew too far away, Lord, yes she did, but she was human and unable to resist her nature. Forgive her, Lord, and allow her thy most precious gift of eternal respite in thy heavenly kingdom."

Sadie sobbed.

"In the name of the Father, Son, and Holy Spirit, Amen."

"Amen," said Sadie.

The gravedigger leapt off his shovel. The time was getting closer. The minister opened his eyes and took Sadie's hands. "It's time to say good-bye. You will see her again."

"Yes," said Sadie, and then, "good-bye."

"God bless you, Miss Sadie."

"Thank you, Reverend."

The two walked away from the open grave. Neither looked back. The gravedigger moved closer and then began cranking the box into the earth. Elle watched from the edge of the six-foot hole. Such a very long way down there. Such a lot of dirt. She thought about how silly it was to feed the earth dead bodies. What if the earth didn't want them? The gravedigger smelled of alcohol and his fingers were dark with soil. He whistled while he lowered her box.

The note! What had Brian written? But it was too late. The gravedigger was beginning to fill back up the hole, the shovelfuls of earth splattering on her box like rain. She could not see it now. It would be part of the ground. She watched until she couldn't watch anymore. With each shovelful of earth that fell into the hole, she could see brighter colors. As her pieces became cloaked in darkness, her vision expanded and she found she could see not only what was right here with her, but what was happening in Sadie's car as she drove home (crying, shouting, and a nip or two from a dark bottle in the glove box). She whispered without sound to the gravedigger. *Thank you.* And then she flew.

For a few days, or what she perceived as days, she played. She experimented with what she could do. She could not, much to her dismay, pass through walls. She could, though, move small objects like salt and pepper shakers from one side of the table to another. She didn't seem to need sleep, but there were periods where she had no memory of what she might have done. She could still smell the world, almost too much to bear—the cacophony of fragrances from fresh-mown grass to lilies to sewage to the musk scent of the underside of a bird's wing. She could curl on the thin uppermost branches of a pine tree and see a span of four states. But except for the girl on the plane, no one had been able to see her.

For a time, she visited her box and her mound of dirt, hoping Sadie might come back again, but she didn't. Two other people had been put in the ground since her funeral and she had been able to get closer to their boxes than she'd gotten to her own. One was an old man, stiff like an upended spider, in his box. He'd just run out of breath. The other was a young boy, who was wearing a Sunday suit he'd hated while he was alive, his tiny hands folded over his chest on top of a gilt-edged Bible. He hadn't run out of breath at all, but had run out of heartbeats. It seemed like a person got only so many and once they were used up, whether you were ten or a hundred, you left. She wondered what kind of lottery determined those numbers.

She whispered to both of the boxes. *Hello? I am here.* The old man was already dried and transitioning into something else. If he were a leaf, he would have blown away. She thought the boy might have heard her. His pinky finger moved just a bit in the dark of his box, but it had just been a box-creature settling in for its final feast. *I'm sorry you're gone,* she whispered to the boy, even though she knew he couldn't hear her. She'd seen the boy's mama come day after day, spread out a red and white tablecloth and slowly butter one piece of bread after another and eat, chewing each bite a hundred times or more until the sun disappeared and she folded the tablecloth back up and returned to her car and drove home. She felt certain that wherever the boy was he was in the right place. One day, watching the boy's mama eat slice after slice of buttered bread, she slipped down from the tree and curled herself around the mama's neck. The boy's mama was warm and she felt she was beginning to understand that whatever she was was neither warm nor cold. She was in the place in between.

She kissed the boy's mama's cheek and told her as best she could, *He's gone where he's supposed to.* And then, mostly to herself, *Can you help me get there?* The boy's mama leaned against her tree sometimes when she needed some shade, and sometime's she'd sing a lullaby. Most of the time she stared at the earth. If she cried, it wasn't visible. No one ever came to sit with the boy's mama, and the boy's mama never uttered a prayer. When the boy's mama stopped coming, the leaves had fallen into the earth and become part of the boy and his box.

She missed the boy's mama. She missed the bread and the butter and the music. When the frost came, she didn't notice its sting.

She toyed with several different scenarios. Her favorite one was that she was somewhere in a coma, her body still alive, fed automatically, lungs pumped up and released with electricity, and that this entire experience was one of those coma-dreams she'd heard about. Maybe, like with Scrooge in *A Christmas Carol*, she was being given some kind of chance to review her life and make some different choices. When she's finished in this grand adventure, she'll return to her body and the nurses and doctors who had long given up on her would be amazed and fall to their knees at her power to transcend certain death. Another favorite was that she had been kidnapped by a secret agency of a foreign government—somewhere southern, like Chile or Cuba—and she was in a holding cell dripping with mold being administered hallucinogenics until she revealed the secrets of her government. She liked that one, not because it was pleasant, but because it was the most dramatic option. The explanation she liked least was the one that was increasingly becoming evident was the truth. She was simply stuck. There had been a misfire of a synapse or a hinge on a door had rusted shut. There was someone who was supposed to have met her, supposed to have given her direction, but that someone got lost, or didn't get the message, or, unthinkably, didn't want to help her. Maybe there really was nothing afterwards and a person just wandered and wandered until, well, until when?

She could find a way to seduce the secret government agent, who hated his job and didn't want to be torturing her like this. Instead, he wanted to free her from the dungeon and take her home to be his wife. He would sing ballads and play guitar and cook splendid foods with exotic spices and she would forgive him, though of course not right away, and they would live forever happily at the base of a lush mountain with deer and large cats. That fantasy was starting to lose its grip as she journeyed from one side of the cemetery to the other, one side of the town she grew up in to the other touching nothing, feeling no three-dimensional object or person against her. She was wind. She was stillness. She was the beginning of a shout that could not complete its breath.

A tether was attached from whatever she had become to her box in the ground, and the attachment was both a comfort and a prison. She knew this area, knew the peach trees and the animals, the single street light and the tin roof smells, but being with them now was like watching a movie of a place she once walked through. The movie gave her enough to stir up the longing to reach and touch the cheek of the man who worked the night shift at the Piggly Wiggly who had let her sneak candy out in her ratty jeans' pockets, to touch the dry and graying hair of the woman who was the closest thing to mama she'd had and smell her flaking scalp and brush her forehead with her lips. The kittens born under her porch had become cats several times over, and the school that had been full of all white children when she attended had begun to be integrated with black children, though not without guns, not without murder, not without explosions that she watched from wherever she was and wondered whether the victims would join her, but they never did.

The tether attached to her began to fester at its connection. The fascia contracted, the tendrils of muscle began to flay, and the itching became unbearable. One night the owls were out in force. The usually solitary birds circled her, this time in pairs, groups, a parliament of owls of all sizes, all kinds—barn owls, elf owls, screech owls, dwarf owls. She watched the way they spun their heads, the breadth of their wingspans, the precision of their hunt. Was it the owls she'd been waiting for? A great horned owl passed so close above her the ripples of air blew her off her branch. The owl didn't seem to notice her, but it circled back again, this time passing even closer. She thought the next time it passed by, she would try to catch its wing and see where it would take her. One more circle around and the bird perched next to her, eyes gazing straight ahead. She heard its quick heartbeat through the branch. She waited. The bird waited. The flurry of owls that had heralded the horned one had vanished.

What am I supposed to do? She asked, but the bird didn't hear. *I don't want to be here.* The bird lifted off the branch, talons expanded, and swooped to the earth, returning with a field mouse that it ripped in two. The mouse's blood dripped down the talons, down the tree. The other owls had returned and hovered. The horned owl made fast work of the mouse, even ingesting its bones. When it finished, it looked at her. She smelled its feathers, imagined the fierceness of the tip of its beak. Her tether burned. It had become infected. The bird could probably smell that. She could only see pieces of the tether. At parts it was a thick rope, the kind she climbed up in the all-white kids' school's gym. At other parts it was the finest hair, braided together like a doll's, and other parts were worm-like, living, squiggling, blind and knotted. The place it connected with her was bubbling and pink and reminded her of a volcanic eruption. The owl swiped at it with its talons.

What am I supposed to do? She tried again, but the owl returned to its stillness. Blood that only she could see was spilling from the tether and from her spine where it was still clinging, an umbilical cord to her rotting pieces in the ground. The pain contracted her, though she was grateful for such a strong sensation. The owl flew off, taking its wisdom of companions with it.

She couldn't move the tether on its own. She tried to fly higher, but the cord kept her bound to her box. The wound tore. Finally, she reached for it and twisted herself so she could gnaw at the connection with her teeth. The blood fed her. She chewed frantically, hungrier than she'd ever remembered being. At last, the tether released itself and tumbled back to the earth, curling around her gravestone, twitching twice before settling into the grooves where stone met earth. She felt her nostrils flaring, a wild horse's breathing, and she coughed and coughed, disturbing the leaves on the branch. The itching was gone. The burning was gone. She panted, exhausted and invigorated.

The first note she heard was D-sharp. Then an A. Then B-flat. Her fiddle! The sparks of blue and green from the notes drizzled down in front of her, a welcome shower. Two bars, then three, then four. Oh! She would find it, hold it, make its strings electric. You found me, she whispered, and if she could have cried, she would have, but instead, she gathered up her wits and pointed herself northwest toward the music.

1970

Brian found out about Janis Joplin's death on October 6, 1970, two days after her body was found. He'd been on his way home from work at Boudin when he happened to pick up an old paper someone had left on the bus. He was seeing this chick named Felicia at the time. Felicia made brownies (without anything special in them) and she crocheted place mats and lampshades and wanted more than anything in life to have a baby. Felicia was sweet, like Brian, and he was bored to tears.

When he got back to the apartment, a studio third floor walk-up in the Tenderloin, he hoped she wasn't there. He didn't want to talk about his day and he didn't want to have any brownies and he certainly didn't want to talk anymore about having a baby. Whenever the thought of a child darkened his mind, he thought of Elle, and he knew that the only person he would have wanted a baby with was gone. Felicia was all about dresses and matching flatware and construction paper mobiles that he hit his head on every time he stepped into the tiny bathroom. He'd tried to remember they were there, but in the darkness he was always startled by their dangling ovals and paper spirals. Felicia said it helped the feng shui in the room to have something hanging, something that continually moved the air around, but Brian thought she spent too much time trying to understand nonsense. Rooms that don't have a source of fresh air don't have good air quality. It was really as simple as that. He drew the line when she wanted to keep the kitchen faucet running all night to so there would be moving water in their prosperity corner. "We can't afford a fountain," she'd said.

"You're right," he'd said. "Turn off the sink."

But he knew as soon as he walked out of the door, she turned it back on. There were rocks she'd picked up, pieces of basalt and granite, and a tiny pink crystal she found on the street that she'd arranged in the rusted bowl of the sink so the water could cascade over them. No matter how much he pushed her away, she stayed. Once he even called her "Elle" on purpose in the middle of the night, but she only held him closer. "I know you miss her," she said. "It's OK. Love is forever." And she'd try to pull him into her, but he couldn't, once again.

"I'm sorry," he'd said.

"I love you," she'd said, but Brian had pulled the sheet over his face and pretended to be asleep.

He had taken the newspaper, a day-old *New York Times*, from the bus seat next to him. Page 1. Reuters. **Janis Joplin Dies; Rock Star Was 27**. He had been surprised, not by her death, but by his visceral response to the headline. He couldn't bear to read the article on the bus. He was too fearful of an unpredictable reaction.

"I made real chai tea," said Felicia when he walked in the apartment. She stood in front of the hot plate, a black pot bubbling with cinnamon. "I've been practicing." She used a ladle to scoop out a cup. "Here. Tell me what you think."

He had to drop the paper to the floor to take the cup. "Thank you. But I really don't—"

Felicia had seen the headline and picked the paper up. "I saw this earlier," she said. "It looks like she was a really nice person before she got all wild and strung out all the time. No surprise that it ended up like this, don't you agree? You can't do all these things and think you are going to be OK. Do you like the tea?"

"It's too hot."

Felicia's blue eyes filled. "I just wanted to make you something nice."

"Give me back the paper."

"Why do you want it?"

"I just do. Can't I do anything without you wanting to know everything about it?"

Felicia was a small girl, a bird-girl, really, and Brian had been drawn to that at first. She would need him. She would want his help, need his strength and demand nothing. Her fragility, her innate gentleness, was killing him.

"Can't you want something? Fight for something?" He wanted to throw the teacup across the room, but he couldn't quite do that. He set it on the thin gray carpet. "How can you judge someone you've never even met? Have you ever even seen Janis sing?"

"Of course I've never seen Janis sing."

"Then you have no idea what you're talking about."

"Brian, what are *you* talking about? You don't like all that kind of music. You don't like all that stuff that's going on over on the other side of town. Come on baby, sit down. Let me put on some Ravi Shankar."

"I don't want to sit down and I don't want to hear any fucking Ravi Shankar. You don't have any idea what I like."

Felicia froze mid-step. He'd never sworn at her. Brian's instinct was to take the words back, but he couldn't. He let them stand in the room, hovering between them. Felicia picked up her bag, one she'd crocheted herself, a large white daisy with a smiley-face in the center. "I'm just going to go for a walk until you calm down."

Brian remained unmoving. He was not going to stop her this time. He wasn't going to hurt her on purpose again, but he wasn't going to keep her here. Not when he so desperately wanted her to go.

"Brian?" The door was still open. "I might not come back." She waited, then brushed tears away. "I hope you enjoy the tea," she said softly and walked down the hall, door to their apartment still open.

Brian closed it, opened the paper again.

And there were those who said that neither her voice nor her health could stand the demands she made upon them, on stage and off. Her answer: "Maybe I won't last as long as other singers, but I think you can destroy your now worrying about tomorrow."

He let out a scream, his first in his life. He tried to mimic Janis. "Oh-oh-o-o-oh. Oh-oh-o-o-oh." Her banshee shriek had terrified him when he first heard it with Elle in the Park. And it terrified him again when they heard it at the Fillmore and the Avalon and on the occasions they heard her walking down the street, laughing, screaming, speaking in octaves the rest of her crowd could not touch. He couldn't look at her, she shook and shimmied and sweated. She screamed and slithered and sabotaged. But Elle could. Elle stared right at her, drank her in like Southern Comfort. Elle could watch.

Brian looked at the photo placed with the article. Janis was a girl then, not yet Janis, only a kid who didn't fit in in Port Arthur, Texas. Only a kid who wanted the other kids to like her.

The apartment had one tiny closet. Enough for two coats, two umbrellas, and Elle's fiddle. He'd never repaired the case, simply wrapped it with tape, and he'd never held the fiddle in his own hands. He lifted the case out of the back corner where he'd placed it. "Some girl would love to have that fiddle," Felicia had said when she noticed he still carried it. When Brian didn't answer, she stroked his hair. "When you're ready you'll let it go. I know you will." And when Brian didn't answer again, she kissed him and he let her, but he knew he would never give that instrument away. He peeled back the masking tape. The glue residue stuck to the case. Elle would have hated that.

"I'm sorry," he said. "I'll get it fixed."

He held the fiddle by the neck as lightly as he could. He didn't know how to tune it, how to hold it, how to make it sound like her. The bow hadn't been damaged in the fall from the fourth story window. How were you supposed to take care of a bow? Did you have to clean it with something? What if a string breaks on the fiddle? He rested his chin on the chin rest. He hadn't realized the weight of the instrument, how much strength it took to hold it. His hands shook as he raised the bow and dragged it, screeching, across the strings. It sounded like *Janis*. He tried again. D-sharp. A. Then B-flat.

He couldn't hold it anymore; the fiddle slipped to his lap, the bow slid to the floor. He looked down deep in himself to a place he'd never let himself see and pushed a scream out that Elle would have been proud of. Once one was set free, the rest soon followed, and when he woke a few hours later, curled on the floor around the fiddle, his nose was running and his throat hurt, but his chest had expanded, his breath wasn't rattling anymore, and he left the apartment to buy his first 45 of "Ball and Chain".

2007

Brian wove through the crowds milling outside Vesuvio, heading south on Columbus. He looked behind him to make sure Frank was keeping up.

"I'm here," said Frank.

"Just up the way is a place nobody knows about." Brian walked quicker than he was accustomed to. He wanted suddenly to be out of the streetlights, out of the thumping music and the honking traffic. He didn't want to hear a bus kneel or a foghorn blurt or a tranny shout at the world. He wanted to be at his friend Mel's place, more of a living room than a bar, more of a crash pad than a drinking establishment, in his favorite red vinyl booth with the broken lamp and a shot of Southern Comfort. Brian ducked down a cobblestoned alley and knocked four times on the black wooden door. Five knocks were returned. Frank looked puzzled. "It's OK," said Brian, and knocked four more times. The door opened and a squat man wearing a stained white apron stood in the doorway.

"Brian!" he shouted in a heavy Russian accent. The man eyed Frank with a squint.

"He's good," said Brian.

The man nodded and stepped aside.

"Frank, this is Mel. Mel, Frank."

Frank held out his hand but Mel refused it.

"It's been awhile, Brian," said Mel.

"Too long."

The room was lit only by candles and a flickering fluorescent strip over the bar. Four empty red barstools greeted them. The place was empty, the corners shadowed. A single black ceiling fan wobbled the air.

Mel clapped Brian on the back. "Come! Sit! Drink!"

"Exactly what I had in mind," said Brian. "Frank?"

Frank had already taken off his coat and rooted himself on a barstool. "Scotch," he said.

Mel laughed. "That's my man!" He extended his hand. "Welcome to my place, Frank."

Frank shook his hand. "Thank you. Do you have Justerini and Brooks?"

"Getting your Capote on tonight, my new friend?" said Mel.

Frank shook his head. "I just like it."

"He just likes it," said Mel, poking Brian in the shoulder. "Sorry, Charlie. Got us some Johnny Walker."

"Fine," said Frank.

"Ah," said Mel as he poured. "What a night it's going to be, don't you think? The hippies are coming back on Sunday, you know. The mayor said they could come this time. But only for one day." His laugh was stiff this time.

"Yeah," said Brian. "I heard. I'm thinking that might be what's got me all messed up today."

Mel didn't ask Brian what drink Brian wanted; he just poured a big tumbler of the amber liquid. "The New Orleans Original," he said.

Brian drank half the tumbler in one swallow. "God bless the South." He raised his glass. "To Dixie!"

Frank lifted his scotch glass, and Mel retrieved a glass of an unknown liquor from beneath the counter. "To Dixie!" they said.

Brian and Frank slid their empties across the bar. "Gentlemen," said Mel. "I do believe we've got us a goin' on."

Brian wanted to keep drinking, glass after beautiful warm glass, until he dripped off the bar stool and Mel put him on the cot in the back room, covered him with an Army blanket and turned out the light.

"I came here to get divorced," said Frank.

"I walked off my job today," said Brian.

"I let my brother drown," said Frank.

Brian paused. "I left mine in the ground." He downed his third. "And I stole my girl's instrument."

"Well," said Mel. "If this isn't the strangest drinking game. Um, I killed my step-daughter's pet frog!"

"Seriously?" said Frank.

"Of course not. We're all kidding, right?"

Silence.

Mel leaned against the back bar. His reflection a Pillsbury doughboy of a man. "I see. You two stay put. I'm going to get the good stuff."

Buena Vista Park
A Hidden Haight Gem

Buena Vista Park was established in 1867 and is the oldest official park in San Francisco. If you climb into it, you'll find yourself going up 575 feet. This sudden climb surprises many wanderers.

The hill is made up of mostly San Francisco chert, which formed during the Mesozoic era. Chert, for those of you who don't know, is a sedimentary rock that sometimes holds small fossils. At the very top of Buena Vista Park is a lawn where a body can see north, east, and west, even to the Golden Gate Bridge, assuming the fog is cooperating.

The west side of the park is where the gutters lined with headstones are. If fossils are to be found, look here first. WPA folks built the gutters from the Lone Mountain cemeteries that were broken up in the 1930s and replanted over in Colma.

A person can score in the park in just about any way he wants to, but it's safe if you have your feet underneath you. If you don't, there's no place you can go that won't sweep you away, so you might as well get lost looking out at the most beautiful place on earth.

Remmy's Reflective Moment: We used to come here all the time and wait. We never knew exactly what we were waiting for. We'd hold our candles, wrap our Mexican blankets around our shoulders, let the tabs dissolve on our tongues and watch the skies. When the moon was full on those nights, the whole park lit up. The scraps of tombstones that made up the rain ditches and some of the sidewalks glowed. We waited for their residents to come back, or we waited for a space ship to land, or we waited just for the trees to stretch their arms around us and whisper that we were the ones they'd been waiting for.

Remmy X: Hashbury Daily Times

2007

Frank decided to be brave and initiate the conversation. He wasn't sure about Mel and he wasn't sure about this place, but he also didn't want to lose sight of his new friend. He was more afraid that he'd find himself left alone in this dark part of the City. He was starting to get tangled up about the reasons for coming to San Francisco in the first place. It was supposed to be a birthday trip for Helen. It was supposed to be a civilized way to end a marriage—a lovely trip, a fortieth birthday, and a little bit of pre-packaged nostalgia from the Summer of Love. All of those reasons made sense separately, but they didn't work together anymore. He was beginning to feel Helen's absence next to him like a living thing. The vacant space breathed and beat its heart and he wanted to touch her but no one was there.

He swallowed his third shot. "I don't understand poetry," he declared.

"No one understands poetry," said Mel. "It's not meant for the head." He thumped his chest. "Meant for the heart." He poured another shot for Frank.

Frank downed it, hoping he masked the shock of the fire in his throat. "What's the deal with the bookstore?"

"I never considered myself one for poetry," said Brian, in a tone Frank felt far too measured for the amount of alcohol he'd drunk. "It didn't make any sense to me in school, and to be honest, it didn't make a lot of sense to me here, except that I could feel it."

Frank forced a laugh. "I'm more of a science man, myself."

Fortunately, Brian ignored him. "I had known someone once who could see things that I couldn't. Until I met her, I thought I had a pretty good understanding of the way the world worked. Whether I liked it or not, there were rules and an order to things that made sense. But she heard voices when no one was there. She heard things different too. Heard music like it was three-dimensional somehow. Like each note had its own soul. Even said sounds had colors."

Frank heard what Brian hadn't said and his intuition surprised him. "What happened to her?"

"Anybody want some music?" asked Mel, laughing a bit too hard. "Come on Brian, what's your song?"

Brian waved Mel quiet. "She died."

"When?" asked Frank. Mel glared at him. He'd done it again. Gotten so close and then said the wrong thing.

"Forty years now."

Frank hadn't been expecting that. Brian's sadness was recent, the raw sadness of someone who just had his foundation ripped from underneath him. He kept his mouth shut.

Mel raised his glass. "To Elle!"

Brian raised his gaze, but not his glass. He nodded, but remained quiet. Frank thought Mel had said Helen, so he raised his newly empty glass. "To Helen!"

"Helen?" asked Mel.

"My wife," said Frank, realizing his error once again.

"Elle," said Brian.

"Elle," said Mel.

"Elle," said Frank, but he thought *Helen*. My Helen.

Brian felt his world shrinking. He couldn't understand why the liquor hadn't softened him, loosened his tongue. Instead, he felt alert, precise, and tiny. Alcohol usually made him feel large. Made him, to his eyes anyway, young and wise. What could he tell this middle-aged kid about City Lights that would make any difference? Nothing. He read essays.

After Felicia had left him—taking her smiley-faced daisy bag and her teacups—he'd found himself wandering. He'd leave for work an hour before he had to so he could meander up and down alleys and hills. After work, if it wasn't too cold, he'd wander some more, finding the smallest corner of the smallest bars and nursing a single drink until closing time. He'd talk to whomever walked by—male or female—but not for very long, and no one wanted to stay too long with a sullen man whose beard had grown too wild. Even though the times were shifting, darkening; the war was not ending only escalating, the body count not dropping; most people still just wanted an escape chute. A person they could slip inside for a time and be someone else until all the madness spun to a stop and *real life* could begin. Brian couldn't be that person so they moved on, drifting from person to person until a the next almost-right revealed itself with arms in leather jackets, crocheted sweaters, or henna tattoos.

He didn't miss Felicia like he knew he should, and he was embarrassed to realize that he thought of her as Elle must have thought of him. Sweet. Reliable. Dependable. Utterly dull. Felicia had been a virgin, had believed that love was forever, not just in the abstract, and she had established herself as a fixture that for a few months provided Brian with a safe harbor that soon became cement shoes. He tried to miss her. He saw her once after she'd left, hanging tightly to a man with a guitar and a ferret. She was still smiling big, smiling sincerely, and he wanted her to notice him, but she didn't, her gaze fixed and all-encompassing on the man whose hand she held. He tried to miss her because he wanted to believe Elle missed him, wherever she was, that she'd read his note somehow and would watch over him.

He even started wandering around the Haight from time to time, but he couldn't stay long. The Haight had begun to grow arms of its own and when he walked the streets that once had been his home, he dodged them, avoiding the reaching fingers, the hungry eyes, the whimpering dogs. He wound himself around the limbs, stepping over legs and ankles and bare feet like he was playing hopscotch.

The Haight was holding its breath, and he didn't want to be in it when it exhaled. The rainbows and prayer beads and newspapers and posters of earlier years had grayed and broken and torn. The dancers in the park, the mothers and babies, the black and white couples who had once thought simply being together would be enough to change the world, had drifted to other places and what was left was fear. The edges and innards of what had brought them all out there, freshly scrubbed and polished from middle America, lined the sidewalks, strumming a ukulele, begging for food, shooting a new numbness into their veins by the thousands.

He wanted to stay longer, looking for Elle, walking where they'd walked, standing where they stood, but the grasping limbs scared him. He often heard Janis' voice when he walked the yearning neighborhoods. He heard her shriek, heard Elle's tinkling laugh, and tried to tell himself there was nothing he could have done differently. There was nothing he could have done that would have made her love him, made her stay with him, made her feel whole. She was always one of those hungry ghosts, and as much as it pained him to admit it, she would have fit in perfectly with the tangle of mouths and protruding bellies he turned his gaze from.

After a time, he moved from aimless walking in the Haight to full-time hanging out in City Lights. He saw Allen Ginsberg discussing incomprehensible things with thin young men, smoking cigarettes and swallowing booze and slamming palms in front of the store between the paperback carts. He heard Ferlinghetti read and read and read again and he thought he saw a little bit of Elle in these men, though they were rougher, more jagged in their conversation and their art, and as much as he could see the genius in them, he knew that the notes Elle could pull from her fiddle topped them all. He knew that if these men, these aging Beats, these loudmouths who did, in fact, change the world, could hear her play they would have stopped mid-word, mid-breath. Even Kerouac would have put his glass down and whispered, "Brava," before falling to the floor.

Brian hovered around these men. He attended all the readings. He took up serious smoking. He grew a dark beard and wore black. He occasionally wandered into their sphere, but they didn't see him. He picked up a napkin Ginsberg had dropped once, handed it back to him. "Thanks," Allen had said, and Brian had carried that word with him for days. He didn't understand what the men talked about, argued about, but he understood it mattered to them in the same way that music had mattered to Elle and he wanted to understand the root ball of that kind of passion. He didn't know how to plant something like that inside of himself. He hoped some pollination might occur by simply being in their garden.

He looked at Frank, who perched on the very edge of his barstool, truly wanting to understand. "City Lights," he said, "was where I hid."

Frank could understand hiding. He could understand disappearing in shadows and pretending to be invisible and hoping at the same time that he'd be noticed and ignored. He thought he could fairly be accused of hiding in his marriage with Helen. He hadn't planned that, but he could see how it could be interpreted that way. She was the one who always arranged social events. He'd preferred to stay home reading *American Archaeology* and drinking tea, but she kept insisting they needed to go out, needed to make friends, otherwise, there would just be the two of them and that was not healthy. Those were Helen's words. *Not healthy.*

After Benjamin's body was pulled from the lake, he hid under the raft they'd floated on which had remained untouched at the water's edge. A few days had passed, the storm that took him had subsided, and his parents had become people he'd never seen. His father, rather than drinking and shouting more, which Frank would have expected, turned inward and seemed to sink, one bone settling atop another until there was no buoyancy in his body; he moved as a single rigid unit, lurching from one place to another. His utterances became whispers. "Pass me the paper, son," and "thank you," and "shhhhhhhh" that he spoke to himself as he rocked on the porch or nursed cold coffee. This father was the most frightening father of all because he was not behaving according to pattern. Frank had charted his life based on the patterns of his father. He'd used them to help Benjamin escape trouble, and he'd used them to deflect his own imminent punishments.

His mother, normally quiet, mousing from one room to another, became chatty, her laughter piercing the edges of the walls causing the paper to peel into toothpick-sized strips. She busied herself feeding everyone, the whole neighborhood, and when the ladies from the church came with their casseroles and their prayers, she welcomed them in, smiling, and they played Old Maid and Uno, eating plates of orange jell-o with marshmallows, laughing and laughing until his father came in the dining room and stood in the doorway, shrinking inch by inch to the linoleum. He said nothing, even when his wife said, "Come! Join us! We'll deal you in!" so eventually the church ladies left, leaving their Tupperware and their Pyrex and the house shivered again.

Frank watched these strangers from the kitchen table. Neither one paid attention to him. When the Sheriff came to the door, big hat in hand, and said, "I sure am sorry, folks, but we've found your boy," Stranger-Father and Stranger-Mother moved close to each other and Stranger-Mother pressed her head on Stranger-Father's shoulders and Stranger-Father wrapped his twig arms around her and they stood there until dark fell and the crickets and the bullfrogs took up singing.

Frank crept past them and ran to the lake, the wind carrying his voice away, and he crawled under the damp raft and pulled it onto him, an awkward cave, and he scratched at it in the darkness for some piece of Benjamin, some scrap of shirt or worse, but he found nothing, and the raft didn't keep him warm and the raft didn't keep him hidden, but the raft did press its weight into him, light enough to float, heavy enough to burden.

"I understand," said Frank to Brian, because he actually did. He was envious, in fact, that Brian had an actual place to go to when he wanted to hide. Frank had had to learn to hide in plain sight. Many times Helen would trip over him or accidentally sit on him on the sofa. He'd become that good at being invisible. It was the only way he knew to have any sort of control.

"How is it possible that you're right here and I don't see you?" Helen would say, after a stubbing her toe on his outstretched feet.

"How is it possible you don't see me when I'm sitting right here?" he'd say back. He was starting to understand how that might have been the wrong response.

"You just try to go away, don't you?" she'd say. "No matter what I do or what I say, you can't wait to get away."

That's not true, he thought, but didn't say. He should have said that. It might have made a difference.

"My wife says I'm not here even when I'm here," said Frank.

Brian nodded. Mel leaned against the back bar, a flashing neon "Drink Me" sign above him. There was a knock at the door.

"We're closed!" shouted Mel, but the knock persisted. Brian spun aimlessly on his barstool. Frank curled into himself, hunched over his fourth—or fifth—shot. He couldn't remember the last time he had so much alcohol. The bar had a padded leather wrist rest, and the bar itself was a dull wood he couldn't identify. Penknife scratches dotted its surface.

"It's OK," said Brian. "Someone else can come in."

LARAINE HERRING

Mel's lips pressed together, widening his red nose. "Asshole doesn't know the knock." He walked to the door. "We're closed!"

The knocking grew fiercer.

"Is there some parade I don't know about?" asked Mel. "I hate those damn parades. Everybody trying to be somebody else, knocking on doors that aren't theirs, making all kinds of racket."

"You got old on me, my friend," said Brian.

"Me? Take a look in the mirror yourself, hot stuff."

"Yeah, yeah."

Mel unbolted the door but left it chained. He stuck his bulbous nose out into the cold. "Who the hell are you?"

Frank worried about being robbed or worse. Maybe this was one elaborate set-up. Brian spotted him and made him as easy prey, lured him here with poetry and alcohol, and now the game was beginning and he'd not only figuratively disappear, but literally disappear, parts of his body floating in the Bay by noon tomorrow. Maybe the door behind the bar led to an altar where they did ritual sacrificing. Didn't the Mansons live in San Francisco once? Helen would be quite surprised at his dramatic end.

Brian had stopped spinning and now twirled his empty glass on the bar. How old did he say he was? Sixty-something? Sixty was supposed to be the new forty, right? The longevity movement, Andrew Weil, something, he was remembering reading something—fish oils made it possible? A sixty-is-the-new-forty-year old man hopped up on fish oils and gingko biloba could certainly take him out.

Mel slid the chain off the door. "Sorry, hon," he said. "You didn't use the knock."

"What you got to go having such a crazy knock for? You ain't James Bond." She gave Mel a kiss on his cheek, leaving a pink lipstick mark.

Frank had never seen a woman like this. She was taller than Mel, and her make-up shimmered, even in the poorly lit room. Her hair was a bouffant of color, and her legs were athletic, though the ankles were a little large for the six-inch emerald green stilettos she was wearing. Helen never wore shoes like that.

She extended her hand first to Brian. It was bejeweled and brace-leted. "Nice to see you again, sugar."

Brian kissed the top of her hand. "My pleasure, I assure you."

She smiled wide, ran a manicured hand over the top of Brian's head.

She stepped past him to Frank and towered over him. "Penny Lane. Pleased to make your acquaintance. And you might be?"

"Frank."

She rolled her eyes. "Just Frank? Bo-o-o-ring." Frank noticed the incredible false eyelashes. They had sparkle tips!

"Connor! Connor!" he said quickly. "My name is Frank Connor."

Penny Lane rewarded him with a kiss on the top of his middle-aged head. He felt a warmth in his belly, or maybe a little lower. He'd been drinking quite a lot, he reminded himself. He was still married, he reminded himself further.

"You're very tall," he blurted out and both Brian and Mel burst out laughing.

Penny Lane put a hand on her hip, silver evening bag swinging. "He ain't from around here, is he?"

"No," said Brian and Mel at the same time.

"Cute," said Penny Lane and kissed him again. Frank wiggled on his stool. "Can I have a Zinfandel, please?" she asked Mel.

"Only for you, sugar," said Mel. He slid a remarkably clean glass of white zin across the bar to her. She drank it in two swallows.

"Lord, what a night," she said. "I knocked 'em dead, though."

Mel beamed. "I bet you did."

"You ought to come see me one of these nights. It's just down the street."

"I know, but I don't really fit in those places."

Penny Lane took the stage with her presence. "*Those* places." She clicked her tongue. "And what is this place if not one of *those* places.

Honey one of these days you got to walk yourself out into the sun and drink in the life you got. Hiding out here like you're a vampire with your secret knock and middle of the night visits isn't healthy. You need vitamin D."

Frank was confused. Mel seemed to have melted a bit, and Frank was embarrassed that he'd thought they were going to sacrifice him to Satan in the back room.

"Can I stay here tonight?" asked Penny Lane. She twirled her hair with her left hand. "I don't think tonight's a good night to go home."

"Sure, sure," said Mel. "Any night. I told you. Any night."

She smiled a real smile, less teeth, more cheeks. "I'm just going to go freshen up." She took her silver clutch evening bag and teetered to the tiny unisex.

"Who is she?" asked Frank when he thought she was safely in the bathroom. He still hadn't stopped tingling.

Mel and Brian exchanged glances. Had he said something wrong again?

"She," Mel said, taking a deep breath and exhaling. "Is my son. Isn't she the most beautiful girl?"

"She is," said Frank, because it was true, because he was still a little tingly, and because the world he thought he had figured out made no delightful sense at all.

Penny Lane came back, walking with more confidence this time. "I don't want to interrupt anything you men-types are doing," she said. "I'll just go on up and get my beauty rest."

Stay! Frank thought her hands were the most beautiful hands he'd ever seen. So feminine but strong. He had drunk way too much. He'd had wine before coming to Chinatown. Frank was not a man who could drink and maintain his dignity.

"We're just drinking, love," said Mel. "Stay. It'd be good to hear what you've been up to."

She slid into a bar stool and crossed her legs. Frank wondered if it would be too strange if he switched stools and sat beside her. Brian had stopped drinking and was staring off at something Frank couldn't see.

"Has my daddy been regaling you with his war stories?"

Brian shook his head. "We weren't really talking. Mostly thinking."

Penny Lane applied lipstick, even though, to Frank's best guess, it was two or three a.m. Who needs lipstick then? "Did the earth move?" She laughed to herself.

"I got lost in Chinatown," said Frank.

"Well, you're not the first," said Penny Lane.

Frank didn't know how to explain to her what he meant. Alcohol. Too much alcohol. He passed his glass to Mel. "Can I have one more?"

"You sure?" asked Mel.

"Yeah. I'm getting divorced."

"You sure?"

Penny Lane had gotten up and was suddenly beside him. Frank was staring at her gray-ocean colored sequined dress, her layers of gold and silver necklaces that shimmered even in the dark of the bar. He should raise his gaze. He was being rude.

Mel slid the drink back. "Last one, man. I can tell you're done."

Frank nodded. Penny Lane was behind him now, rubbing his temples.

"You just relax, old man," she said. "Let Penny Lane make it all better."

"Who are you really?" he said, but he thought he'd kept his lips closed.

"I'm Penny Lane. You have had too much to drink."

"Yeah."

"Tell me about your wife," she said.

"She's nothing like you," he said, and when Brian and Mel laughed, he knew he shouldn't have said that.

"There's no one like me, honey."

"Why do you want to know?"

"Just thought since we're all here in the middle of the night we might as well get to know each other. And you, you don't belong here. No disrespect." She began massaging his shoulders. Frank felt a moan beginning.

"I know I don't belong here. I just got lost."

"In Chinatown," she said.

"In Chinatown."

"So tell me about her."

"Her name's Helen," said Mel. "He told us that before."

"I didn't mean to," said Frank.

"It's fine, Frank. You don't have to apologize for being alive."

Penny Lane walked her knuckles up and down his spine. The vertebrae popped and sent a sizzle through him.

"Her name is Helen."

"Uh-huh. Got that."

"She's a good person. We like to fall asleep with the television on."

Penny Lane fanned herself with her right hand. "I can't bear the heat! What about the romance, Frank Connor? What do you love about her?"

"We fall asleep together. Is that enough?" Frank swirled the last of the amber liquid in his shot glass.

"I don't know. Ask Brian. He can't fall asleep next to anyone anymore since his girl gone. It's been a long long time since she was here and he still wanders around."

Brian didn't say anything. Mel, who had been wiping the same corner of the bar for the whole conversation, put his rag down and clapped Brian on the back. "Brian and me—we go way back. We were wanderers, weren't we? Just like the Merry Band of Pranksters."

"Who?" asked Frank.

"Doesn't matter," said Mel. "I think all I'm saying is that wandering is just a little better with somebody else."

"Don't let Daddy get all sentimental on you. He plays all tough and gruff like a billy goat, but he's nothing but squish and squeeze, isn't that right?"

Mel blushed and let out a little roar, but it was light and airy and everyone just laughed.

"Tell me about her hair," said Penny Lane.

"Shiny," said Frank. "And blonde. She wears it in a pony tail some-times." He finished the last swallow of his last drink. "I like to touch it."

"I am not at all sure that you're done, sugar," said Penny Lane. "Life isn't a line, honey-buns. Life is a spiral, and you keep revisiting, re-connecting, re-everything with each little loop you take. Did you ever think this morning that you'd be here tonight with me?"

Frank honestly could say he did not think that was a possibility.

"But here you are. And here I am, and here we all are. It's just too much sometimes I know, but from what I hear you not telling me, you and your Helen are still on a loop."

"She wants the divorce too," and then, "Today's Saturday! It's her birthday."

"Honey, no woman wants a divorce on her birthday, take that to the bank."

Frank was sleepy, hard, lead-sleepy. He thought he was going to slide right onto the floor in a puddle.

"Daddy, Frank's going to stay with us tonight. He needs to be in better shape for his wife's birthday."

"Why don't you all stay," said Mel. "I could sure use the company. I'll make omelets and lots of coffee in the morning. Brian?"

Brian hadn't stopped staring at the place Frank couldn't see. He hadn't finished his drink. "I'll stay." He turned to Frank who was all but asleep. "Your wife's birthday is today?"

"Uh-huh. Forty." If Penny Lane would just stop pressing on his spine he could stay awake for a few more minutes.

"My girl died forty years ago yesterday. Isn't that a wonder."

"I'm sorry."

LARAINE HERRING

"She had long blonde hair, too, but she never wore it in a pony tail. She always had it loose."

Frank blinked his eyes hard. Stay. Awake.

"It was a wild time, Brian," said Mel.

"Yeah."

"Let me go get a sleeping bag," said Mel.

"OK." Brian held onto the bar as he stood. Penny Lane extended her hand and he took it.

"Go on up to sleep, love," she said. "May your ghosts be friendly."

Brian kissed her. "Good to see you. See you in the morning. You going to make cheese grits?"

"You know it."

"Night, Frank." Brian held Frank's gaze too long and Frank was frightened by the water in them, by the wild pupils that were always looking for something past.

"Night, Brian. Thanks."

Brian nodded and he and Mel went through the tiny door that led upstairs. Mel flicked the lights out on his way, leaving only a few tea light candles still burning around the bar.

Penny Lane spun Frank around on the barstool. He was glad he was too tired to retch. "Why don't we go over in that booth over there and stretch out a bit?"

Frank watched himself say yes from some other place. "What does 'may your ghosts be friendly' mean?"

"Something Daddy always said when we went to sleep. Kind of like sweet dreams, I guess. But it's more real, don't you think?"

He did. Benjamin had never been a particularly unfriendly ghost, just a persistent one.

"Do you believe in ghosts, Mr. Frank Connor?"

They reached the round red booth. The seat was just wide enough for them to lie together on their sides. "Go ahead, take your shoes off," she said.

He was grateful for the Dockers slip ons and the cool vinyl of the booth. He slipped into it like it was a pillow top at the St. Francis. She began to rub his feet, and even through his socks, he felt loved. "I do believe in ghosts," he said. "I didn't think I did before tonight."

"I'll tell you a secret, only because you're not from around here and your wife is having her fortieth birthday right this minute and you're here on a dirty vinyl booth with me. The way to get yourself straight is to look at those ghosts, no matter what kind of ghost you got hanging around. Don't run away from them. They can out run you. Trust me."

Frank was using every ounce of will to stay awake. A collage of gum lined the underside of the table. He had a passing thought of the unsanitary conditions, but as fast as it emerged, it left. Penny Lane stopped rubbing his feet and began humming a song he couldn't place.

"Go to sleep," she said. "I'll be right here watching. I'll keep the ghosts from you tonight. But in the morning, you've got to go find them yourself."

In the morning. In the morning. It was already morning. Helen was going to wake up soon and discover he never came back. She would maybe even repack his toiletries and decide to go back to Phoenix. In the morning.

"I love you, Penny Lane," said Frank, slurring but solid.

She stopped humming and laughed. "Of course you do, honey-buns. Of course you do. Now scrunch your ass on over and let me have a little room."

He pressed his back into the curve of the booth and she lay in front of him and pressed her spine into his soft belly. He rested his hands over her and she grasped them tight.

"May your ghosts be friendly," she whispered.

HER

Nothing mattered but the music. Nothing mattered but the notes and she saw them stretched in front of her, a highway of sound. The briefest of thoughts passed through her. She would never see Sadie again. Then a strange thought that Sadie had died, but that couldn't be possible. She wasn't even sick, unless you counted sick of heart, which everyone knew a person could live with a very long time before keeling over. Perhaps she was now at last in the tunnel.

The notes wove with one another, dancing with each other, one stretching out long and low while another bounced staccato along the surface. The third note waited for a break before slipping in to alter the direction of the other two. Phantom limbs grew from her center and she held her ghost fiddle and answered the notes back. She was stiff, her arms translucent and shining.

Her voice. Her own voice was calling her.

She hurled herself headfirst toward the notes. The soft fur of the kittens that had become cats faded like the front porch's peeling paint. The lullaby from the boy's mama at the graveyard played its loop for someone else. The airplanes flew over her, under her, around her, followed by flocks of ducks that broke their 'v' so she could continue west unhindered. How long had it been? Minutes? Hours? Days? No more than a year or so, certainly, since she'd held her instrument. *I am coming,* she said. *Keep singing.*

A tripping in a crosswalk. A fragment of a windowsill. A woman on the bed. She was moving too fast to stop and when she slammed once again into a window, this time from the outside, she was as surprised as the middle-aged woman who tried to catch her.

She dropped to the sidewalk after impacting the window, only this time the fall didn't stop her. She didn't leak out of her skull. No one gathered around her broken body. No one stopped doing anything. They walked over her without realizing it. The doorman in his tasseled polyester uniform hailed cab after cab. Men, women and children stepped through her into the backseats. The honking and the skidding, the exhaust from the tailpipes, the cacophony of the street vendors plying tourists with jade beads, feathered earrings and woven bracelets assaulted her.

She tried to regroup. The town was San Francisco. She was certain of that. When she rose above the sidewalk and the street lamps, she saw the Ferry Building and Coit Tower and a glimpse of the Golden Gate Bridge. This was San Francisco but *not* San Francisco. She didn't know how to explain what she was feeling. It was like the memories of San Francisco that she carried merged with whatever this San Francisco was and together they made a different place—a place where she *had been* but *no longer was,* and she saw places that should be familiar but had shifted, retrofitted themselves, wore different clothes, sang different songs—and she was unsure that she belonged here, unsure that she could sing the sounds of these streets.

The revolving doors of the Hotel Gladmore spun. She liked the play of the light that splattered against the glass doors as they twirled, eating people and spitting them back out onto the sidewalk. She was afraid of the doors, afraid they'd eat her and digest her and she'd be stuck again wherever she had been. If no one could see her, why could she not pass through walls? Wasn't that supposed to be one of the bonuses of being a ghost?

But she wasn't a ghost. She knew that from the beginning. She was something more solid. She rooted herself to earth with something of substance; something that was too heavy to let her take flight, slide through walls and glass, enter people's thoughts or closets. That was it, wasn't it? She needed the rest of her. She needed the rest of her substance to find her fiddle. She needed help, and never having been one to ask for it, decided to take it from this middle-aged woman who had tried to catch her. The next time the revolving door opened its mouth to her, she dove in and tumbled out the other side into the lobby.

Now that she was in San Francisco, or this new San Francisco, she was forgetting what had happened before. Her memory banks consisted now of stilled images. Her box. The airplane. The boy in the freezer. The boy's mama at the cemetery. Sadie crying. Remmy pressing his fingers on her forehead after she fell. The great horned owl. Images that began to curl at the edges and cocoon themselves into stasis. She clicked through them like they were a slide show. The time between when she jumped and when she returned to the City was mostly empty, a deflated balloon.

She watched the traffic in the lobby of the Gladmore, people twisting and turning around the red velvet ropes. They moved, feet on the ground, spines in "S" curves, skulls bobbing and tilting, jaws opening. They were solid. She curled into a corner by an elephant plant and tucked herself in the space between the pot and the mirrored wall. She could come up with no adverb to explain the time between then and now. *Where?* wasn't exactly a fit. *When?* didn't address the spectrum of experiences. *How?* Well, there could be no answer to that one.

Sometimes she saw dangling seaweed when she tried to remember. Other times, she felt a roaring cold that had no source. Bells. Cowbells, church bells, alarm bells, those she remembered. A dripping sound, as if she were in a cave far under the earth, but there was some light, a blue-green light like the old fluorescents in basements. A guppy, oval and shimmery, moved past her once but it didn't see her. The tentacles from the seaweed danced slowly, tempting her. Once she heard voices, or what she thought were voices, underneath her. A shout in a language she didn't know. A softening. A whisper.

"Why do I have to pay a $250 deposit when I already paid for the room?" a man in a Brooks Brothers suit coat asked the girl, Amy, behind the registration desk.

"We won't charge your card, sir, until you check out, and only then if you've used any sundries."

"Sundries? What constitutes a sundry? Is this conversation, for example, a sundry? Is the oxygen in this lobby a sundry?" He turned to face the lobby; his reflection mirrored back on three sides, a bearded man with thick-framed glasses. "Ladies and gentlemen, the Hotel Gladmore charges you *to breathe*."

The people behind the man murmured in their places behind the red velvet ropes.

"Sir, Mister—" said Amy.

"Shh! Do not utter my name."

She watched the Nameless Man begin to work up his insult from the deepest parts of himself in all three mirrors when she caught a glimpse of her own face below his knee in the mirror across from her. Oh! Her flowered face paint was smeared and her skin hovered over her skull bones. No one noticed her in the mirror; they were focused on the man in the suit coat.

"Sir," said Amy. "Please. Let me get my manager to better explain the policy."

"Do you know who I am?"

Elle let herself smile and saw no teeth but a dark inviting space between her lips. Oh.

"Yes, sir. But you won't let me say," said Amy.

"I am going to my room. You can tell your manager to ring me." He took his key card, credit card, and moved swiftly through the lobby. Elle moved swiftly as well, and slid between the doors just as they closed. *Thank you, Mr. Nameless Man.* They both exited on the seventh floor. He turned left and she turned right, the middle-aged woman's room directly ahead.

2007

Helen had fallen briefly asleep. She woke to her own fingers tracing patterns on her face, as if someone else were holding her hands. She was still naked and Frank was still gone, but there was light gilding the edges of the drapes. She wrapped herself with the towel that had fallen to the floor and went to the bathroom to fill the coffee maker from the sink. She slipped into the complimentary robe, embroidered in royal blue with "HG" and a rendering of the Golden Gate Bridge. She used her teeth to open the coffee packet and then pulled the drapes, standing, robed and steady on the carpet, in front of the window she'd tried to walk through just yesterday.

She traced the windowsill—some dust, a stray spider's web, the metal lock secured with blue paint. But hadn't she opened it yesterday? Hadn't she almost jumped through? The window panes were swirled, a thick opaque glass that she remembered from the bathroom in her grandmother's house. Had she just walked into the window and fallen back from the impact? Seven floors down, the sidewalk was splotched with old gum, cracked from years of shifting earth. A Yellow Cab waited in front of the hotel and a woman wearing a pillbox hat clutching a toy poodle emerged from the hotel's revolving doors and entered the cab.

It was 6:30 in the morning. The thin fog filtered by above her window level, then dissipated as it rose higher. She pressed on the windowsill with her full weight. It did not break. She tried the lock, but it did not budge. She stepped back, but did not see her reflection in the mirror. She cut left, cut right, returned to center, but still saw nothing in the glass but the air in front of the window.

The coffee was ready. Frank had always filled her cup. No matter how apart they'd grown over the years, every morning he brought her coffee before he went for his early morning run. Where could he have gone? She filled a second cup for him anyway. He'd need to come back and shower. He'd need to shave. He couldn't bear not to do these things. She'd forgotten to comb through her hair after the bath and it had dried into a tangled wasp's nest at the base of her neck. She set the coffee on the nightstand and began to tug a thick-toothed comb through her hair. Against her better judgment, she lifted her gaze to the dresser's mirror and screamed, knocking the coffee to the floor.

No one came in the room. The phone didn't ring. The window didn't open. The drapes didn't rustle. Icy fingers didn't walk down her spine. The face in the mirror didn't move, even as Helen looked away. She would wipe up the coffee, call downstairs and report the spill so the carpet wouldn't stain, and when a hotel staffer arrived, everything would be fine.

"Front desk."

Helen pulled her robe tighter. "Yes, this is Helen Connor in room 719. I have spilled some coffee on the floor. I just didn't want your carpet to ruin."

"Thank you, ma'am. We'll let housekeeping know."

"Wait—"

"Ma'am?"

"Do you think you could send someone up now?"

"It's 6:30 in the morning, ma'am."

"Of course."

"We'll let housekeeping know."

"Of course."

"Have a good morning, ma'am."

Helen replaced the receiver. She would turn around in three-two-one and the only face in the mirror would be hers. Three. Two. One.

The face in the mirror had smeared tattoos of butterflies and hearts on its face. The lips smiled but the eyes remained gray. "I need you," the lips said.

Helen grabbed Frank's cell phone and her purse and ran out of the room. She checked three times to make sure the door was locked before she fled down the stairs to the lobby.

The front desk manager was not excited to see Helen.

"You've got to get me out of here!" Helen shouted.

"Ma'am," said the front desk manager, whose nametag read Amy. "Please keep your voice down." Amy glanced around the lobby. The only other co-worker with her, a goateed kid, moved farther away.

Helen held her robe tight around her. Frank's cell phone weighed down the pocket. "I'm sorry." She had a vision of herself as she must appear to this young Amy. An old woman—Amy would think so since she was, at best, twenty—half naked in the dawn, no make-up, tangled hair, sagging flesh. "I'm not crazy."

"Of course not, ma'am," said Amy.

"There's another person in my room," Helen said.

"Well, did you invite another person in your room? Sometimes, we can get a little carried away, you know, and forget, like what happened the night before." Amy chewed green gum, snapping it sharply between her teeth.

"I did not invite another person in my room, miss."

Helen knew Amy was trying to figure out what part of the training video handled crazy women.

"I'm not drunk," said Helen.

"Of course not, ma'am."

Helen gripped Frank's phone. The lobby was covered floor to ceiling with mirrors on three walls. The sight of so many of her selves was disconcerting. Every angle revealed a stranger.

Amy pointed to a royal blue velvet fainting couch. "Why don't you have a seat over there, Miss—"

"Connor. My name is Helen Connor. And I don't want to go have a seat over there."

"Do you want me to call security?"

"I don't care. I just want you to call someone. There's another person in my room."

Amy picked up the desk phone and whispered something, keeping her gaze averted from Helen.

Whatever. Helen was not going back into that room. Not by herself, anyway. She sat on the fainting couch, thought of reclining dramatically and placing the back of her hand on her forehead, but she was beginning to believe she might be crazy. Frank would have a logical reason for this happening. He would explain the pre-dawn dream state. He would tell her maybe she was experiencing a fugue. There was scientific data to support a fugue state, however tenuous that research might be.

Amy looked up from the desk. "Is there someone you can call, Miss Connor?"

"Mrs," she said. "I have his phone."

Amy whispered something else into the receiver and then returned it to the cradle. "Someone will be right with you." And then, back on firmer ground, "Can I get you something? Perhaps some coffee to help perk you back up?"

"I don't need any coffee."

"Of course."

Helen was grateful for her short frame. The robe fell below her knees, keeping her concealed from all the mirrors. Amy brought her a paper cup of coffee anyway. Helen was dismayed by how thin the girl was. Her legs were more like strings.

"Thank you." She took the cup. The wax was sticky from the heat of the liquid. "I spilled coffee on the floor in my room."

"I know, Mrs. Connor. I have put a note in to housekeeping."

"Thank you."

Amy smiled too wide. "Here's a complimentary copy of *USA Today*."

"Well, look at who is here!"

Helen looked up from the headline. At first she didn't recognize the man.

"Omar," said Amy. "Mrs. Connor is not well."

Omar waved Amy away. "Nonsense! Helen! Where'd you end up last night?"

The doorman!

"Well, I didn't go to Oakland," said Helen.

"Would have been quite a walk."

Helen slid to the left and Omar sat next to her. His thighs were larger than her hands. The cheapness of the polyester uniform was apparent by the way it clung to his body.

"What's going on, Helen?"

His eyes were soft, like those of a greyhound, and she wanted to believe he wanted to know, wasn't just killing a few minutes before his shift.

"My husband didn't come home last night."

Amy nodded knowingly from her perch behind the desk. "I can change the lock code for you," she said.

Helen ignored her. Omar kept quiet. "And there's another person in my room," said Helen.

"Would this be a friend?" asked Omar.

"I don't think so." Helen realized she hadn't released her grip on Frank's phone. She withdrew her hand from the pocket and pressed her fingers to her throat. "I don't know who she is."

"That is odd," said Omar. "Usually when someone ends up in our room, we know who they are."

If Amy had said those words, Helen would have snapped, but Omar spoke with such softness he brought tears instead. She clenched her jaw to try and stop them.

"Hey!" said Amy. "I know who you are! You're the woman from last night's shift who tried to kill herself!"

Her goateed co-worker glared at her. "Be quiet," he whispered. "You're going to get us both fired."

Helen took a deep breath. "I did not try to kill myself."

"That's not what I heard."

Helen almost responded, but did not want to find herself in an argument with an adolescent.

"That lady was you?" asked Omar.

"Well, yes, that lady was me. But I didn't try to kill myself. The same person who is in my room now was in my room then and I was just trying to touch her."

Omar didn't pull away from her. He understood. She wanted to kiss him for his faith. "I got someone you need to meet," he said, pulling out his phone. "Hey, it's Omar. Look, there's this lady at the hotel and she's got something I think you need to hear. I'm going on shift. Call me." He flipped the phone closed. "Voice mail."

"Uh-huh." Helen didn't want to meet anybody. She didn't know who this person was. She didn't know where her husband was. She didn't know what was going on in her room. "Maybe I just need to lie down for a bit."

"Not here," said Omar. "This place'll be busier than Mardi Gras in a couple of hours. Go on back to your room."

"But I've already called the night manager," said Amy.

"Oh, mind your own business," said Omar.

"This is *my* business. I am the front desk manager. This woman came down in distress on *my* shift."

"Want me to walk you back to your room?" asked Omar. Helen recoiled, remembering her nakedness. "It's OK, I promise. There are cameras all over the place. I won't hurt you."

"I'm sorry. I just—this is not like me. It really isn't."

"I believe you."

"Thank you."

"Let's go on back upstairs."

REMMY X

It's Saturday morning but there's no sun up yet, and Shep and me haven't slept hardly a lick. The new family upstairs makes one helluva racket. Never thought I'd be that guy—the 'get off my lawn' kind of guy—but when you don't get your required eight hours of shut eye, a man can turn into a beast right before your eyes even if that man is your own self. Shep didn't sleep so good either. I can tell because he kept shifting around on the bed, waking me up, whining a little like he was having a bad dream, only I know he was wide awake too.

I don't like when I have the dreams. They've been coming a lot lately and I half want to go down to the Free Clinic and get something to help, but I know it's a slippery slope once you go putting things into your body thinking they're going to send you away from the places you're already trapped in. Against my better judgment, I decide Shep and I should go for a pre-dawn walk, try and shake loose whatever was in our brain-houses.

I put his leash on and he's not the least bit reluctant to go. We both got some old bladders. We climb the four stairs up out of the basement and turn west, straight up Haight's enormous hill. It always smells especially salty before the sun comes up, like the winds from the ocean pushed its perfume out over the City just to add a little seasoning to us before we wake up. Tomorrow is the City's official celebration of the 40th anniversary of the Summer of Love. It's going to be a grand time to make a lot of money writing poems in front of Ben and Jerry's, but to tell the truth, I don't know as I've got the gumption for it. I've known it was coming all week and I'm thinking that's why I'm not sleeping so much, why I'm seeing things that aren't there walking up and down the street, why Don would rather get bludgeoned to death on Geary Street by an ax-wielding Jimmy Dean than talk to me. This is a time of secrets coming up like sewage from a busted pipe. I can feel it.

Sunday there are going to be a lot of tourists who will give me ten bucks for a poem and permission to snap my photo on their smart phones so they can tell their friends they stood where Jerry Garcia stood. There are going to be a lot of people who are coming looking for something that never was, and there might be a few folks who are coming back because they were here then and they just can't understand how so much time has passed right on by without any revolution, without any peace, without any brotherhood of man. Of all the outcomes we envisioned, we never saw that one, the only possible one, coming.

My heart's pounding and I'm panting more than I'd like to admit walking up this hill. Shep's bouncing next to me like he's a young dog again, but I'm feeling heavy, feeling like I can't bear to see what's at the top of this hill before the sun comes up. We cross Divisadero against the light and are almost at Buena Vista Park. I know it's got to be the sun all starting to rise and get all jiggedy with the world that makes me see all the different layers of people, but the sun's not actually out yet, though I know she's a-coming. It has to be the sun, the way it creaks through the clouds and the fog and shows you things that a body can't see in regular light. But it was still gray-dawn and the sun comes up behind me when I'm walking toward the park, and I wish to heavens that I have a rational explanation for what I see at the edge of it.

I see the world all turned in on itself like some mad scientist's puzzle. We cross Broderick. We pass the Alcoholics Rehabilitation

Association. We are getting up into some nicer Victorians. Shep really likes the green one across the street from the park. As I get to the slope past Baker Street, it's like the whole place, all of its trees, all of its hills, had expelled everything and everyone who ever walked through it, slept on it, prayed on it or played on it. Only I could quarter-see everything. Like I see some people's feet. I see some people's eyes, some people holding candles, some crying. I see Tarot cards and teetotaling booklets. I see needles and wigs and high-heeled shoes and flowers, so many flowers, and I see the people everyone is carrying with them, like some kind of living Day of the Dead altar. I see it all like a Picasso painting. His cube phase. I see elbows where there ought to be noses and I see mouths where there ought to be legs. The earth herself has split apart into segments, like one of those crazy earthworms, and I see layers of soil—topsoil and then lower and then lower still where there are pottery shards, bones, and roots so deep and thick I wouldn't have dreamt so much hanging on happened underneath the surface. Some of the roots are cracked, long fingers dangling free. Others go straight through from the top layer to a place I can't see.

"Shep, you've been a good dog," I say to him because I am sure this is the gate of heaven or hell and I have just walked the last mile to my own death. Shep, who usually hides the fact that he's got any actual German shepherd in him, is not afraid of this. His brown ears perk up. He must hear one of those sounds that only dogs can hear. His big pink tongue hangs out of his mouth. I wrap his leash tighter around my wrist. Even at this early hour of a Saturday morning, there should have been some cars. There should have been some people stumbling back home or jogging themselves awake. The storefronts we passed, the smoke shops and the vinyl shops and the vintage shops, were dark. Even the 24-hour Walgreens on Fillmore, now that I think about it, had no one in front of it.

OK, Remmy, I say to myself and scrunch my eyes up tight. Enough is enough. You are having one of those bad experiences that folks have every so often. This is nothing to worry about. It is not real. It is not a problem. In fact, you are not even seeing it. You're back at home in your crazy bed with your crazy dog waiting for some decent hour to finally wake yourself up. You've just been thinking too much about the past lately. When you wake up, you're going to have you some of that fine Folger's coffee and you're going to stop at the Crepe Express and treat yourself to a gooey cheesy breakfast with even better coffee than that Folger's, and then you're going to set up your table and you're going to take money from tourists all day long, that's what you're going to do. You're going to just make a living like every other soul walking on this planet.

Shep barks and I open my eyes. The upside down earth in front of me is folding back together into an organic origami sculpture of a park. Whatever Shep is hearing must be getting louder because he's barking to beat the day. I wrap my orange scarf tighter around my throat as a strange fog moves in on us from the four directions. That may sound mystical to you, but that part is normal. We have microclimates in the City and all kinds of strange weather patterns just happen. (Excuse the diversion. I can't help it—providing information is in my bones.) The fog is so thick Shep and me feel wet, and my windbreaker has dots of water on it.

"Hey, boy, let's go on back home," I say, but neither of us moves. The fog turns warm, like a three-dimensional electric blanket, which frankly I am grateful for since I am getting pretty cold. The upside-down and backwards earth is now the same deep green of Buena Vista Park I've been walking by every day for forty years. I see the branches of trees through the fog and I see the base of the grassy slope that leads up to her vistas. Shep pulls free of his leash and bounds toward the green hill. I can't hear what he hears, but I can see what he sees. There's that ankle. That foot with the multi-colored toenails. The long leather fringe of skirt kissing calf. I hear a strand of Buffalo Springfield and I am in awe of her, once again, as I have always been, always, as I am admitting it now at the top of the hill in a screen of warm fog. Always and forever and I'm sorry to whoever is here listening.

The ankle and the foot move deeper into the park. I can't see them anymore, but I can't see Shep anymore either so I got to move and go find him. Maybe I'll finally find her.

Oh. Old Remmy didn't know all this was inside. The heat of the water in my body is scalding compared to the gentle warmth of the fog. I would cry right here in front of the green Victorian, but I got to find my dog. I got to find my girl.

I gather up every bit of my stupid-self courage. I knew this day was coming. I knew there was going to be a reckoning. There always is. Guess I just thought mine would be after I was already in the ground.

"Shep! Come on boy!" He's barking loud enough to call the saints back home. The fog is twisting around me now and I have a goofy image of being inside a chocolate swirl ice cream cone. I'm cold and I'm spinning. I can't see but a few steps in front of me. I start walking because what else am I going to do? There should have been at least two hissing buses going past by this time, rattling along on the electric cables. There should have been at least two. I try to access my best inner journalist. I try to stand outside myself and bear true and holy witness to what I see and what I do so I can record it for all ever, but I feel my objectivity swirling away with the fog. I feel the weight of Haight falling away and there's just light, just air. The ache in my knee's gone somewhere else. The cricking of my bones smoothed out. "Shep!" I haven't heard him for a beat too long.

A red rubber ball rolls to a stop at my feet. I'm going to do it. I'm going to step into this park and this fog. I pick up the ball. Shep barks. "OK, boy. Fetch it!" I throw it as far as I can and I hear the jingle-jangle of his dog tags as he chases the ball down and then the happy-trot of the tags as he comes closer to me. Only he doesn't come all the way out of the park. He sits, ball in his mouth, and waits. I'd sure as heck rather go into this park holding on to his leash. "Come here, buddy. Bring me the ball." The leash is a coiled snake beside him. He's panting, the ball in his mouth, tongue lolling to one side. "Come on, Shep." Shep hears something behind him, drops the ball, pushes it to me with his slimy nose and it arrives again at my feet, all gooey-slobbery and Sheppy. I pick it up and start to wipe it off on my jacket when Shep bounds back into the park.

I hear the soundtrack I never quite forgot. And then there's the first notes from the ghost fiddle. And then a voice, clear, unflinching.

"Nobody's right if everybody's wrong."

No. I start heaving like Shep had done. If my tongue could have hung out the side of my mouth it would have. I toss the slobbery ball into the fog and hear the bark again.

She sings back. "Hey, what's that sound?"

And my feet start moving without any direct order from my brain-house.

"Hey, what's that sound?"

And the fiddle crescendos and softens and I can see the music, the greens and yellows and oranges of the notes and then her voice, her waterfall of a voice explodes above it all.

"Nobody's right if everybody's wrong."

The park heaves, shifts, and settles. There's a crack of sunlight above the fog. The skin on my body contracts and I feel like I could step right on out of it and not miss it one single little bit.

"Everybody's wrong."

I know.

Shep barks.

"Everybody's wrong."

I gather all I got and open my mouth and sing it real slow. "Stop, children." I let the note carry like I was standing up in front of all creation.

She answers. "What's that sound?"

I can't stop the tears. I want to, standing here in the middle of the gates of heaven or hell, my dog missing barking somewhere in the fog, god knows I want to, but there's just an ocean in there, just an ever-loving ocean that I've tried so hard to keep pushed down in me, but I guess sooner or later water erodes even the best constructed dams. I tried to hold it, Elle. I did, I did. I cough out the words. "Everybody look what's going down."

And there she is. My girl. My beautiful ghost. She is dripping, all salt and slick like salmon, but she holds her fiddle high and her hair is golden and her legs aren't broken and Shep is barking like he'd never barked in his life and they both see me at the same time and then here we are, one puddle of saliva and fur and music and water tumbling on the dirt and grass and bones.

"Look at you," I say. "Just look at you."

She's smiling and her teeth aren't chipped and her eyes aren't sad. "I am almost home," she says.

"You are home," I say, not quite believing what my own two eyes are showing me. I feel only slightly better that Shep sees her too, or at least he's right here rolling around on the damp grass with us. I keep touching her—her cheeks, her neck, her long long hair. I press into her belly with my hands. "Are you there?"

She giggles.

"Shhh," she says. "Look at this place. It looks the same. The gravestones are still here in the park." And then, "Why did you send me back to Georgia?"

"I didn't, baby, I didn't. The men did."

"You should have stopped me from going back there."

"What could I do?"

"You should have stopped me. I came back. You could have stopped them."

Shep tosses the red ball up in the air with his jaw. He flings it up, then catches it, does a little side-step dance, and tosses it up again. I am no longer sixty-five years old. I am no longer aching and tired and full of memories. I am just full of shame. Full of the feelings that never went away. Full of the reasons I never left this Street. She smiles softly. "But you brought me back, didn't you?"

"What do you mean?"

"You have my fiddle. I heard you play."

She's playing catch with Shep now, and her arms are glowing in the fog. They're thinner than I remember, and they're full of right angles, her fingers stretching out long and slender like a fan of cigarettes from her wrist. Shep is happy as the day, running back and forth, stopping for ear rubs with each return of the ball.

I don't want to stop the play.

"Where is it?" she asks.

"What?"

"My fiddle."

Shep drops the ball at my feet. "I don't have it, Elle."

The flesh on her face sags, her bones pressing from beneath. Her gray eyes dull. The smile that comes next is ugly, a jack-o-lantern's twisted grin. "Where's my fiddle?"

"I don't know. I never saw it after—after—"

Shep lays down and presses his body against mine. I'm still lying on the sweet morning grass. I'm still thinking my girl, my girl, she came all the way back from I don't even know where. She's come back for me. I'm thinking this moment is why I'm the one still here. Why I'm the one who couldn't go.

"Where. Is. My. Fiddle!" She's taller and when she speaks the wind appears. "Did Brian take it?"

"I don't know. I swear I don't. I don't know that Brian took it. I haven't seen him in a thousand years."

The earth shifts beneath us. I think it's just a tremor, one of San Francisco's constant companions, until I see that Elle's face is scrunched, her teeth bared, and she's stomping on the ground.

"Hey, hey, calm down."

"Don't you tell me to calm down! I want my fiddle! I want my body back! I'm not finished!"

Shep whimpers and I want to whimper right along with him, but Elle would just make fun of me.

"Why did you run?" she asks.

"What?"

"When I jumped. Why did you run?"

"I didn't run."

"You did. You ran all the way to the ocean. I saw you."

I did, she was right. I ran all the way to the sea. I didn't know I could run that far or that fast, but my feet knew something I didn't. They carried me all on their own and when I hit the surf I wanted to just keep on running in until the salty water filled me up, but the gulls kept me back. They crowded and carried on and dove in and around me so much I had to stop moving and cry.

"I saw you." She stops stomping. "You left me."

"I never left you. I've been here ever since."

"You're old. When is this?"

"I am old. It's 2007."

She's clearly surprised by that. She sinks down to the grass with me and the fog dances around us. Shep's whining, not afraid exactly, but not completely comfortable either. I touch his special place between his eyes and rub, which seems to make him happier.

"Wow."

"You're telling me," I say. "I never thought I'd get to be this old."

"Me either." She's collapsed, suddenly, and I don't know what to do. She smells of the ocean.

"I'm sorry."

"For what?"

I want to say the real truth. I'm sorry I gave you the drugs that made you want to walk out the window, but I must not want to say it bad enough. "That I don't have your fiddle."

"Someone does," she says. "Will you help me find it?"

- X out.

2007

"Today's my birthday," Helen said, mostly to herself.

"Well, happy birthday, Helen!" said Omar. He let her exit the elevator first. She stepped out, but waited, wanting to walk side by side with him.

"I'm forty."

"You don't look a day over forty."

She laughed. "That is by far the most honest thing anyone has ever said to me."

She pulled out the key card and slid it through. Green. The access light flicked back to red.

"You're supposed to go in when the light's green," said Omar.

She slid the card again. Green. This time, Omar turned the heavy handle and opened the door. The door slithered its welcome across the plush carpet. Helen was embarrassed of the unmade bed.

"If you want, I'll wait out here while you get yourself some clothes."

"Thank you," and then, "Do you mind if I leave the door open—just a crack?"

She noticed the breadth of Omar's shoulders. Not even the silly polyester uniform could shrink them. The gold tassels on the shoulders were a nice touch. A little Buckingham Palace for the Bay. "I'll turn my back."

She slid the door as closed as she could before it would catch and pull shut on its own. The steam had long since cleared from the bathroom mirror. The coffee pot had shut itself off. The towel was still on the floor where she'd tried to mop up her spill. She unzipped her suitcase and pulled out a pair of jeans, a black cami and a burgundy cardigan with a rose filigree embroidered on the right chest panel. That would have to do. "OK, you can come in."

Omar filled the open doorway.

"You must think I'm a fool," said Helen.

"I think no such thing. You're one of the most exciting things to come to the Gladmore as long as I've worked here. Most of the jumpers go to the Bridge."

"I'm not a jumper."

"Of course you aren't. I'm sorry. I was just making bad conversation." Omar pulled up the blanket and bed sheets before sitting on the bed. "So, Miss Helen, where did you see this person?"

"In the mirror today and in the window and the crosswalk yesterday."

Omar took her at her word, nodding seriously. "I do sometimes think I see a stranger in the mirror. But I don't think you mean that kind of stranger."

Helen shook her head.

"Where's your husband, ma'am?"

Helen handed Omar the phone. "I have his phone. He left it here."

"Then I'd suppose he's going to come back for it."

"I suppose."

Omar stood and walked toward the closet. "May I?" Helen nodded and Omar pulled open the closet doors. Nothing but four wooden hangers permanently affixed to the closet bar. He turned on the light in the bathroom, looked in the shower, even looked under the bed. Helen pressed herself against the corner by the window, wanting to feel the solidity of the walls behind her. "I think who ever was here is gone for now," said Omar.

"What if she only wants me?"

"Well then, that's a different problem all together, isn't it? Hopefully my friend will call me back soon. I really think he's the one to help you."

"Who is he?"

"Fancies himself a reporter, but he's not really. He's more like a guy who publishes a diary or something like that. But he wrote about you yesterday. He'd be interested in talking to you."

"I don't want to talk to a reporter." She paused. "What do you mean he wrote about me yesterday?"

Omar laughed. "I'm not talking CNN or anything. Just an old hippie dude who never could move on. You'll like him. I met him when I started work here. He's a chatty guy. Him and his dog wandered by one night. We got to talking. He got me to subscribe to his paper, even though it's free. Well, he asks for a quarter, but he never does more than ask. That's where I read about you. It was nothing bad. Just his observations."

"Sounds like he's just a nosy old guy." She was surprised at her snappishness.

"Maybe that's the truth. But what does it matter what he is if he can help you? He's spent a lot of time talking about strange things in the City."

Frank's phone rang.

"Frank?" Helen answered. "Where are you? Oh, sorry, who is this? Hey. We're having a good time, thanks for asking. Um, no, he can't talk right this minute. Can I have him call you back? Thanks." She closed the phone.

"City's not that big," said Omar. "Seems big, but when you get right down to it, everybody's kinda always just a few feet from everybody else. You'd be surprised how small the neighborhoods are when you start to hang around in them. Your husband can't have gone far."

Helen began to imagine that he'd bought himself a one-way bus ticket somewhere—maybe Wyoming or Colorado. Somewhere the sky was big and the people quiet. It hurt he didn't even say good-bye.

"I probably just need to lie down some more," said Helen.

"You feeling safe enough for now?"

"Thanks, yes."

"I'm on shift until three. If I get a call back, I'll come find you."

"OK."

Omar let himself out, snapping closed the door. Helen opened it again, hung the Do Not Disturb sign, put the chain up and returned to the bed and tried to keep her eyes closed. She couldn't get comfortable, stretching out diagonally, then on her stomach, then on her side. Finally, she got up again and went to face the mirror. "Come out," she said. But the only reflection in the mirror was her own and the inverse arrangement of the hotel room furniture. "I'm waiting."

1967

The poet-man Remmy was the one who had gotten to Elle, but they kept it a secret as best they could. He'd been running from something too, and she knew part of what he liked about her was that she never asked. Brian was getting too heavy to carry around, though she was still interested in his haunted truck. He would be the kind of man she would marry one day many many years on down the road. He was the husband type, not the boyfriend type. And she didn't even want a boyfriend, but she did want the poet-man. He wrote her verses and slipped them in her Guatemalan bag for her to find later. Sometimes they wrote poems together, one line his, one line hers. He smelled good, like cinnamon and earth and he understood what she was about in a way she knew Brian desperately wanted to but couldn't. He understood her art and he pushed her to make it better.

"You should write a song for me," she said. "I'll play it and you could sing. We can make a ton of bread together."

"Poems ain't songs, Elle."

"Sure they are. What's a song if not a poem on wings?"

He didn't have an answer for her. "I just like to hear you play. I don't want my voice messing that up."

She kissed him hard. "You couldn't mess me up."

"Really?" he said. "I mess up just about most things."

"You'll never mess me up," she said, tracing his Adam's apple with her fingertips. "You're not responsible for me, sweet man."

He wrote a poem on her belly with his tongue and she giggled and pushed him lower. They lay together, leg over leg, in the small patch of sunlight that filtered through the window. "Did you ever think it could be like this?" he asked.

"I didn't know what anything could be," she said. "I just wanted to feel."

They heard footsteps on the stairs. "Get dressed," he said, and they threw their clothes on and sat together on the futon staring at the dust.

"Hey man," said Brian.

"Hey."

Brian kissed the top of Elle's head. "Got us soup."

"Thanks," she said, sneaking a bare toe toward her lover's leg.

"Summer's almost over," said Brian. "Do you think we should keep on going north?"

"North?" Elle stood up. "I'm not going anywhere. This is where I was coming and this is where I am staying. Forever and always."

"Nothing is forever," said Brian.

"You ruin things!" she shouted. "Why do you always ruin things? Why can't you just be happy?"

Brian handed her a bowl of soup. "Sit down. You don't always have to shout."

"I do! How else is anyone going to hear me? Look outside! See all those people? So many people! How do you get noticed if you don't make noise? How do you get noticed just bringing soup home every night?"

She knew she hurt him. Even though she'd been trying to, she still looked away when he flinched. "I don't know, Elle. But I guess you'd notice if suddenly there was no soup." He pulled a scarf from the pile of dirty clothes and opened the door. "See ya later."

"Just go," she said. "Eat all the soup you want!"

When Brian slammed the door, they burst into giggles. "Downer," Remmy said.

"You're telling me," said Elle. "I don't see why we can't just tell him about us."

"It's just not right," he said. "Not with a guy like him. He wouldn't understand all this. It would be too much for him."

"You're too poet-y and sensitive."

"Maybe."

"Good thing I think I love poets."

"Today."

She kissed him. "What other time is there?"

REMMY X

Shep asks first with his barking, then me with my words. "Can you come with me?" I ask, though I'm not completely sure that's what I want her to do. I feel like I'm standing outside myself watching all this. I feel all the different lifetimes all pressing together at once on my shoulder blades and I think I am just too old to carry it all. She is not who she was and I feel her watching me in a way that makes it like she sees my innards—not just my emotional innards but all the muscles and bones and organs. She stares through me and can see me work. Maybe she sees that blood clot that I'm pretty sure is about to hit my brain stem.

I start to hear other people. The fog has opened its doors and the City it had held frozen has been released. I feel my vibrating phone in my pocket. Maybe it's the American Academy of Journalism finally calling to recognize my lifetime of work in the field.

"What's that?" asks Elle.

"My phone," I say, pulling it out, a shivering thing in my palm.

Elle's not phased. "So people aren't trapped by a cord anymore."

"Nah. Trapped by other things."

"Like what?"

Is not that the ten-gazillion dollar question? Like all the little choices that turn into big choices that follow you around up and down hills for your whole life. Like the kisses you never finish. Like the sentences that don't complete. Like just about everything a person does in this world leads to one big spider's web of a tangle. "Like you," I say.

She likes that. Her bones recede a bit as her smile softens. "You've been trapped by me?"

"Forty years."

She doesn't just like that. She loves that. "What's the actual date?"

"Today is the first of September."

"I died yesterday. I died on August 31."

"You died yesterday forty years ago."

The phone stops shivering and chirps.

"Someone left a message," I say.

Shep barks a greeting at another dog, a Golden Lab, who is out for a walk with his human. The human nods at Shep and me. I gather he doesn't see Elle. "Where are you?"

"In between somewhere," she says. "Here. Somewhere."

The red double-decker tour bus is creeping up the Haight hill. The megaphoned tour guide drones: "This is the beginning of the site where hundreds of thousands of people came in the late sixties searching for peace, love, and understanding." Cameras flash from the top level. Condescending smiles. "Tomorrow will see the fortieth anniversary of the famous Summer of Love. Come on back if you've got the time. Should be a crazy show." The tourists pull their North Face wind blockers tighter, wrap their Old Navy fleece scarves around their necks and ears. They're not accustomed to the microclimates, and I think the Haight's trying to freeze them out. But I always think kind of like that.

"Brian might be dead," she says.

"Sure 'nough. Never know what might happen to a person."

"You never saw him at all?"

I did. I saw him quite a few times actually, though not in a really long time. I saw him wandering around the neighborhood a lot when I was in my really messed up time and I hadn't yet learned about my brain-house and all the things I could do to make sure I don't get stuck in there. He stepped over me a few times, looked at the needle by my leg. I don't think he recognized me. He was so clearly looking for her. One night I saw him, wrapped up in an Army blanket, leaning against the street sign where they used to live. He stood there all night, smoking, shifting his weight from one foot to another. People pushed past him. They asked him for things but he didn't say a word. They offered him things but he didn't take them. When the dawn broke, he crushed out his cigarette and tossed the butt to the pile he'd built up during the night. He raised the blanket up over his head like a hood and walked away. Think that was the last time I saw him. I went to the pile of butts and found a couple with a few puffs left in them. I wished he'd left the blanket.

"Nah," I say, lying once again. "I never saw him at all."

"It's a small town," she says.

"Sure it is. But if you don't want to see someone, you sure as hell can figure out a way not to."

"I'm tired. I am going to lie down right here. You go find my fiddle."

I don't believe her. She never in her life would have chosen to wait while someone else did something. That's when I find out that if she couldn't directly read thoughts, she could get pretty darn close to figuring out what was going on in my brain-house. She grins that bad pumpkin grin again.

"You're right," she says. "I'm not lying down anywhere. Find out who called you."

"I'm sure it's nothing important."

She points at the phone and it begins to ring again, dancing its jig on the grass. "Answer that phone."

She starts to loll around on the grass like an articulated snake. She presses her face into the earth and emerges with dirt and grass in her mouth. She rolls back and forth on her spine until she rocks an arc into the earth. The worms have been disturbed by her movements. She spreads out her arms and legs and makes snow angels even though there's no snow. She picks up a wriggling worm and eats it.

"Answer that phone."

And since I never had the courage of other, greater men, I do.

- X out.

2007

Frank woke up alone, a filtered stream of sunlight casting the bar in an Audrey Hepburn light. His shoes were off and his mouth felt like he'd been chewing on his tongue all night. He smelled coffee and bacon from another room. He needed to shower. He needed his toiletries. What time was it? Was Helen already awake alone on her birthday?

The bar that had appeared frightening and cave-like last night in the morning looked like what it was: a few tables, a very dirty floor, a bar with five bar stools, deep green walls and a tiny stage for what Frank could not possibly imagine. Maybe Penny Lane performed on it sometimes.

He smelled of her and some of the oils from her skin had rubbed off on him while they slept. He had never slept with a woman like that before—and certainly not on a vinyl booth in a bar that wasn't really a bar at all. She had felt familiar to him, and much to his surprise, he didn't feel like he had cheated. They really had only slept. She'd rubbed his feet and his shoulders and pushed something that had been lodged inside him loose.

Mel emerged through the back bar door with some coffee. "Thought I heard you moving around. Want some?"

He absolutely did. "Thank you."

"Penny Lane's making the grub. I make great coffee, though."

It was true. He did.

"It's Turkish."

"Ah," Frank didn't know what that meant, but it was clearly something Mel was proud of. Brian came through the same door, dressed and carrying a bath towel.

"If you want to shower, Frank, it's right back here."

Frank took the towel, which he knew had been used by someone else, but he let the thought of germs pass through. He wanted a shower. "Let me finish my coffee, but yeah."

"Who's ready for fabulous?" Penny Lane sang. Her wig was off, revealing short brown hair that stood on end. She was wearing a flowered housecoat and the fuzziest slippers he'd ever seen. Frank took another sip of coffee. It was beginning to untangle his tongue. "And how are you, stranger-man?" she asked.

"OK." He was afraid he looked like who he was—a mildly attractive, hung-over man.

"You're the first stranger Brian ever brought here," said Mel. "It's nice to have someone new. We get tired of our same old schtick."

"Speak for yourself, father-dear," said Penny Lane. "I do not get tiresome." She spun on her slippered heels back into the kitchen.

Frank stood and creaked out his joints. He finished the coffee.

"Got plenty," said Mel.

Brian had stepped outside and brought back in the paper. He settled in a tiny table under the swath of light with an ashtray. "Tomorrow's the thing," he said.

"You going?" asked Mel.

"It didn't even happen in September. It happened in June. What the hell was the City thinking? Now it's not the Summer of Love, it's the Fall of Love." He lit a cigarette. "Which is actually more accurate, I suppose."

"We should go," said Mel. "Get our tie-dye on."

"Bah. We are old, my friend. We saw it the first time. This is going to be like seeing an IMAX film of Niagara Falls after already tumbling down them in a barrel."

Penny Lane brought out steaming plates of eggs and, as she'd promised, cheesy grits. "You old folks talking about going to a party?"

"More like *not* going to a party," said Brian.

"I see you're still a mess," she said. "Eat some breakfast and put that cancer-stick out. You're destroying my pores."

"Then get out of the smoke," Brian said, but he was smiling and stubbed out the cigarette.

"Ain't those words of wisdom," she said. "Come on Frank. Eat. We'll go to a table where the atmosphere is better."

"I really want to get cleaned up first."

"Fine, but all the cheesy things will be gone by the time you get back."

"I'll take my chances."

The tiny bathroom was only a shower stall, cot-sized, with a toilet and a wall-mounted sink. Frank emptied his pockets and tried to line up his keys and wallet on the rim of the sink. He pulled out his loose change and wasn't sure where to put it when he found the fortune cookie fortune. *You will have a new addition to your life.* He had to admit, that had occurred. He didn't know what the numbers meant, but he figured that the odds of anything he gleaned from a paper fortune with a smiley-face on it was more than he could reasonably ask for. He flattened the paper out and slid it underneath the mirror bracket. He would pass it on, a gift, for the new additions to his life.

The shower was steaming hot. His muscles loosened with the pounding water. He lathered his hair, his arms, his legs and then rinsed and rinsed and rinsed. When he finished, he shook the water from him like he was a dog and laughed. He rubbed his teeth with his finger and redressed except for his socks and shoes. He was famished.

"About time, beauty-boy," said Penny Lane. "All the eggs are cold and there's no more cheesy grits."

Frank sat next to her. "I don't care. I just need to eat."

"That you do," she said. "That you do."

Frank pointed to a section of the paper. "Mind?"

Brian shook his head.

"Helen and I were going to go to that tomorrow. See what the sixties were all about."

"You should definitely go," said Penny Lane. "Even San Francisco's yuppie parties are better than most."

Brian took his empty plate and a few sections of the paper to the back. "When you kids figure out what the sixties were about, let us old farts know, OK? I'm going to the john."

"Too much *information*," said Penny Lane. Brian slammed the door. "Don't mind him. He gets this way from time to time. I've known him my whole life. If Mel here weren't my dad, I'd pick Brian."

Frank scooped out a heaping pile of eggs. He rarely ate breakfast—a grapefruit or a cup of non-fat yogurt if anything. These eggs had bell peppers and basil and tomatoes and enough cheese to certainly clog his heart. He couldn't remember anything tasting so good.

"So, stranger-man, you going back to your wife today?" asked Penny Lane.

"Um—well, I better go back to the hotel. She'll be worried."

"Uh-huh," Penny Lane smiled large. "Come on."

"I don't know. I have absolutely no idea what I'm doing. I thought I did. We planned this trip on purpose for God's sake. We made a plan."

"Honey, didn't we establish last night that plans never, ever work? Take these eggs. Was it in your plan to eat them for breakfast when you woke up yesterday?"

Frank shook his head.

"But they sure are good, aren't they?"

"They are."

Brian came out of the bathroom, towel wrapped around his waist.

"You OK?" asked Mel. "What happened to your clothes?"

Frank saw Brian was shaking, well, more like shivering. His legs looked so tiny, bare and wet and old. He held out the fortune. "Where did this come from?"

Mel took it. "You will have a new addition to your life. Sweet. These things are never wrong."

"Is it yours?"

"No," said Mel. "Penny Lane?"

"Penny Lane does not eat Chinese food."

Frank was puzzled. "It's mine. I got it yesterday at a restaurant in Chinatown. I had a weird conversation with the owner and, anyway, she told me to keep it. I forgot I had it until I was taking a shower this morning and I pulled it from my pockets. I thought I'd leave it there because—" He was suddenly embarrassed. What could have been the wrong thing about this? "Because it had already come true for me, so I thought maybe it would be true for someone else. It was stupid. I wasn't feeling quite myself this morning."

"It's not the saying. It's the numbers," said Brian.

"I don't remember what they were," said Frank. "I tried to make them mean something, but they don't."

Brian sat on the barstool. His towel fell away.

"Brian, what is it?" said Mel. He grabbed the towel from the floor. "Penny Lane, go get my robe."

"Give it back to me," said Brian. Mel handed him back the thin paper. It was wet from shower water. "27, 10, 6, 19, 70."

Penny Lane brought a thin black robe and wrapped it around Brian's shoulders. No one said anything.

"27, 10, 6, 19, 70." Brian's voice cracked.

"Hey, hey, what is it?" asked Penny Lane.

"That's the day I found out Janis died."

"I thought Elle was her name," said Frank. His eggs were growing colder. He tried to sneak a bite in without appearing rude. His stomach kept growling.

"Joplin. Janis Joplin."

"You knew Janis Joplin?"

All three turned to glare at Frank. He wiped his mouth with a paper napkin. "I mean—"

"It's OK," said Brian. "I didn't know her. I saw her a few times around. At some shows. Elle loved her though. Wanted to be her. I didn't find out right away. I saw the paper a few days after she died, but something about her being gone made Elle that much more gone."

Frank had to ask. "I don't understand the 27."

"Janis was twenty-seven when she died. Don't you see? Don't you all see?"

Penny Lane kissed the top of his head. "I see the ghosts are ready to talk to you now, Mr. Brian, so you're reading signs into a bunch of numbers. The bigger mystery is, are you ready to talk back?"

"They make these things by the gazillion," said Mel. "The numbers are random. You're trying too hard, man. I know you loved her, but—"

"I have to go back," said Brian.

"You have to have some breakfast. Some more coffee. You can even smoke your cancer-stick," said Penny Lane.

Frank felt like he was in a bad Woody Allen movie. He had stumbled in to a movie set and filming was in progress and he was supposed to understand the story line and follow along with whatever the actors said. Brian looked small underneath Mel's big robe. The tie dragged the floor.

"I miss her," Brian said and the sentence hung in the air among them, a fat bumblebee.

"It's just the weekend. The stuff at the park. The anniversary and all that. It makes everything spooky," said Mel.

"I don't just miss her this weekend."

Frank wondered if Helen were drying her hair in the hotel bathroom, using the round vent brush she always used. Had she gotten her own coffee that morning? Did it make her sad to pour only one cup?

"Frank," said Brian. "Want to go for a walk with me? I want to show you where I lived once."

"Brian, don't go wandering over there," said Mel. "It just messes you up, you know, to see it."

"I know," said Brian. "But I want to show Frank where I lived."

Mel nodded quickly at Frank. Frank was supposed to agree to this, but how long would it take? What if Helen actually did leave town before he got back to the Gladmore? Would she leave a note?

"Whaddya say, Frank? Work off some of these eggs. Clear your head before you go find your wife." Brian's voice was too chipper for the shivering bony man on the barstool.

"OK," said Frank, because that was what he'd been saying this whole trip and so far, that had worked out fine.

REMMY X

Excuse me for a second, everybody, I've got to stop the story for a minute because I just can't quite absorb everything that's happened. I need a breather before I answer that phone, before I follow this Elle-not-Elle creature wherever she wants to go because that's just what I'll do for her. It's what I'd have always done for her. She's eating worms and she's giggling and she's tossing a red ball with my dog. She's tall and then she's small and she's nice and then she's shouting and it's all just a little bit much for my brain-house.

I haven't had a drop or a tab or a smoke or any liquid gold since 1972. I have to keep telling myself that so I know the difference between where I was and where I am. I am in a good place now. I have a dog. I have a typewriter. I have a place in front of Ben and Jerry's where I advance the cause of literature. No one would have ever thought Remmy could have had those things, least of all me. I was supposed to die on this Street. I was supposed to just let it swallow me whole. I was trying everything I could think of to make that so. But one day I got tired of trying to be eaten and I decided I maybe could have a life, even if it were a little less bright of a life without Elle, without the scene, the bumper-to-bumper traffic, the gawking and the drumming and the soup.

They say no one escapes his life. That's sure coming true right now. I thought I was doing service for her. I thought I was paying homage to the Street and to our lives but maybe that was all some concocted crock of certified Remmy-fied bullshit. Maybe I thought I was speaking for the Haight, for Elle, for all we thought we were going to be, when I was really only speaking for me, or speaking to me, trying to find a way to move on. To pack up my typewriter and my plastic chair, take my dog, and leave. I am kerfuffled. Everything I ran away from is back, knocking down the door, and now I am much too old to fight it back.

I'm going to pick up the phone now. Thanks for waiting. I just had to stop.

"It's Remmy," I say into the phone.

"It's Omar, man, didn't you get my messages?"

"I've been busy this morning."

"Yeah, well, I've got a story for you. That woman you wrote about who tried to jump out of the Gladmore? I've been talking to her this morning. She's still seeing that blonde girl. She's freaked, man. I told her you could talk to her. Help her out. You know lots about hauntings. She's a nice lady. She's sad. Getting divorced and today's her birthday."

"Omar, I got more important things this morning. I'm sorry. You know normally I'd love to talk to anyone, but—"

"Come on, man. What's so important? You could get a follow-up story. I know how you like follow-up stories."

He is right. I do like follow-up stories. They provide more of a certainty about the first story, I think.

Elle's watching me.

"I'm sorry. Any other day, Omar."

I forget that Elle has strange senses. "I want to go meet this woman," she says. "I was there this morning."

I have not had a drop or a smoke or a toke or a shot since 1972. I have not. I have not. I have not.

"She has my fiddle."

What? "Omar, does this woman have a fiddle?"

"How should I know?"

"I don't know. You've just got to trust me. Today has not been normal."

"No day with you is normal, Rem."

Elle takes the phone. "Hello?" she says. "My name is Elle and I have come for my fiddle."

I grab the phone back. Omar's laughing. "Why didn't you tell me you were getting some. I'll call back."

"It's not that. It's—"

Elle is standing tall. People are walking past her without seeing her. Men are palming drugs in the shadows without seeing her. Joggers are moving through her. She doesn't budge.

"We—I will be there."

"Thanks, Rem. I owe you. I just felt bad for her."

"It's fine. I'll see you soon."

I close the phone. Elle is leading Shep out of the park without a leash. We step over the broken tombstones from the dug up cemeteries. I don't like to step directly on them. It's disrespectful, like stepping on someone's pants. Elle always liked to trace the letters and try and figure out what they'd said before they were chopped up into shards and used to make drains and stepping stones in a city park. We used to bring candles up here, and if it wasn't too windy, which wasn't much of the time, we'd tell ghost stories to each other in the flickering light. We'd let the purple Owsley tabs dissolve on our tongues and wait until the stone fragments started dancing. "They're so lonely," she'd say. "All those dead people. They want their houses back." And we'd feel the sea breeze and hear the drumming from Hippy Hill if the wind were just right, and we'd touch the fog's fingers and pull them toward us, wrapping ourselves in its cloak of icy fringe.

- X out.

HER

She was exhausted. She had failed at the hotel. She didn't know who the woman was or why it was so important to reach her, but if Remmy had gotten a phone call about her she must matter. She hadn't noticed a fiddle in her room, but she still wasn't good at this part yet and could have easily missed it. She liked the dog. He could see her and he didn't turn away. The people passing by on their super-thin roller skates and flashing running shoes turned away.

She used to wear a sheer blouse without a bra and walk down Haight, or even stand on the back of someone's old Chevy, and watch them watching her. Some of the girls couldn't take all that watching, but she could. She drank it in. The Hell's Angels, the freaks, the straights—they saw her and she would shiver under their gazes and feel exquisitely alive. It had never been so easy to make friends as it was then. Where were they when she was put into her box? Where did the honking and the "nice rack baby"s and the party invitations go when she became pieces? Brian never liked it when she did that, but that was just Brian. He never got with the scene.

She didn't know how long she could stay here. She didn't want to go back to the seaweed arms of the in-between. She wanted a foot that touched the ground. Toes that wiggled both in earth and sun.

2007

"It's a bit of a walk," said Brian. "Are you up for it?"

"Oh, put the man on the bus," said Penny Lane. "He's not from around here. He's not used to the hills, and besides, look at those shoes."

Frank's empty Dockers sat sadly under the vinyl booth where he'd slept. It was true, he was not used to the hills. His calves were killing him. His messed up toe hurt. He'd thought he was in decent shape. He walked four miles every morning in Phoenix before going to work, before the sun got too hot. Phoenix was flat.

"We'll go the flattest way," said Brian.

"And what way is that?" asked Penny Lane. "There is no flat between here and there."

Brian was pulling on his clothes. He folded Mel's robe and placed it beside his breakfast. "I said *est*. Flattest. Not flat. Are you up for it or not?"

Frank considered his no-plan plan of saying yes to things. He considered his shoes, which didn't have the best arch supports, but they had been on sale at Sears. When he left the hotel he hadn't thought he'd be gone this long. He hadn't thought he'd need walking shoes. Maybe that was the lesson—a person should always have walking shoes.

"Where is it we're going?" Frank asked.

"Home," said Brian.

That sounded like a fine place to go. "I can walk."

Brian smiled and Frank saw the young man he had been: his cheeks had more lift in them, his teeth less yellow, and his eyes, well, maybe they had never aged at all, or maybe it was just that everyone looked better in sunlight after Turkish coffee and eggs.

REMMY X

"She's in Union Square," I say, shout, really, because she's somewhere far in front of me with my dog. What a sight it must be, good old Shep tossing his ball to no one, catching it from nobody. The whole street's going to think it's tripping. There'll be a hundred YouTube videos up by the afternoon. I am itching to write about this for the *Hashbury Daily Times*, but I'm going to have to hold it until I can sit and catch my breath. I feel like I want to add some color to the next issue, maybe use something besides a Courier font.

My brain-house gets out of organization when I get afraid, and I'd be lying to you and Shep and all things holy if I didn't tell you that I am scared to death. I am scared of this thing, this Elle, not-Elle, and I am scared of what is coming. It's that wave far far out on the ocean that looks like only a bubble to the gulls that fly over it, but when it hits the land it wipes out villages and the scavengers are all that are left to circle back and pick out what the wave let go. Maybe it's a lucky-man thing to get washed in the wave while you're still living. I don't think my Elle got a chance to get washed in her wave before it was over and that seems to have left her mighty unrested.

I hear Shep behind me, heading west.

"Hey, wrong way! Did you forget? Union Square is east."

"I didn't forget," she says, but I can't see her. Her voice rolls around me like thunder. "I want to see my home."

I can't help but think this is a very bad idea. The kind of very bad idea that results in explosions or fires or floods or even locusts.

"There's nothing there anymore," I say. "Things aren't like they used to be." Shep barks. The red ball flies high. "Shep! Boy! Come on!"

The ball heads west, so my dog heads west, so what other choice is left for poor old Remmy? This wave, this wave, when it gets here it is going to unmoor us all.

"Elle! I don't think this is a good idea. Not at all. Let's go meet this woman and then we'll try and find your fiddle."

"Stay or come, Remmy," she says. "Those are the only two choices for you. First, I am going home."

The things I have done for this girl. I have watched her with other men. I have watched her dance in the candlelight. I have touched the backs of her knees with my tongue and I have given my life to re- membering her. I have given my life to this Street that took her. I have written about her. Every love poem I give to some wanna-be hippie kid is about her. Every sad whistle that leaves my lips is for her.

I don't know what went wrong that day. Maybe we mixed what we shouldn't have mixed. I didn't have a bad trip, but she did. And then she jumped and that was that. And now she wants to go back to that place. The last place we made love. The last place she danced.

Oh. Those two sentences are truth, but there's more, oh, there's more and it's pushing against the bars of my brain-house so hard I can't hold it back in anymore. How is it that I can know something that I didn't know? How can something I didn't understand be living in my brain-house be alive right this minute banging its gavel for me?

It was the last place *I* made love. It was the last place *I* danced.

Oh, Remmy, Remmy, what you have given her. What you have giv- en that girl.

- X out.

2007

"Can we stop by the hotel so I can at least tell Helen where I am?" asked Frank.

"It's most definitely not the flattest way back through Union Square," said Penny Lane. "You like to kill this stranger-man. But," she smacked her lipsticked lips. "He's going to find his ghost. Isn't that right, Frank?"

Frank had not thought he was doing any such thing. He thought he was going to do the polite thing and let her know he was alive. And maybe make sure she'd had her coffee.

"That's fine," said Brian. "We can go through the Stockton Tunnel."

"That's how I got to Chinatown!" Frank felt like a child at show and tell. "It was dark and loud."

"It is that," said Brian. "But didn't you feel like you were going on an adventure? And when you popped out in Chinatown didn't you think you'd crawled through the center of the earth?"

"Now that you put it like that, it did seem like a different world."

"Every street's a different world," said Penny Lane. "Ask daddy-Mel here. He won't go three feet down the street to watch me sing because it's a different world."

"Maybe this next weekend," said Mel. He had resumed wiping the bar furiously. A piece of bacon hung out of his mouth like a flattened cigar. Penny Lane curled her tongue and stuck it out. "Really, love.

Maybe this next weekend."

"I'll put that in my datebook," she said, and Frank could not tell if she were serious or sarcastic. He could always tell with Helen. Even when she wasn't talking, he could tell what she was feeling. That was something else. He should tell Penny Lane. They fall asleep together and he could tell what she was feeling. Two things. The number 2 was a good number, round and open.

Brian grabbed two bottled waters from under the bar and handed one to Frank. "Let's get going. It's almost noon."

Frank had a moment of awareness not familiar to him. He surveyed the bar—Mel scrubbing at a clean corner of the counter, Penny Lane sipping on a cup of coffee, the 'Drink Me' sign lit and blinking—and he knew he would never be back. Not because he didn't want to be, but because this place and these people were not his to carry and keep. They were just his to visit. He hadn't thought about things like that before. In Phoenix, well, this would have never happened in Phoenix, but if it had, he would have given them his business card, his cell phone number, and they would make plans for a drink or a Diamondbacks game, but for once in his life, he knew not to stretch the moment until it broke. Besides, he couldn't imagine Penny Lane at a Diamondbacks game.

Penny Lane wiped her mouth and stood. He smiled, hoping he didn't have bacon shreds in his teeth.

"Go find her," she said.

He gave her a hug, and he felt like he'd known her his whole life, this man in a housecoat and fuzzy slippers. This lipsticked, foot-rubbing, egg-making woman with an Adam's apple.

"Go, you old man. Some people are just for a moment. Some are for keeps." But her smile was warm and her kiss on his cheek was long. "I'll sing a song for you at the club."

Whatever she had lodged loose inside Frank was swimming around. His eyes heated and he broke her gaze before it was too late.

"I am different."

"You are that," she said.

Brian was at the door. "Come on. See ya, Mel. Penny Lane, always." He kissed her hand again.

"See you," said Mel.

"Bye, sugar. You go find her too. Be careful." Penny Lane closed the door softly behind them, and Frank once again found himself in the glare and noise of the City, but this time, he didn't feel uncertain. His feet filled his Dockers and they knew where they were going.

"What's the hotel?" asked Brian.

"Gladmore."

"Let's go, then. Won't she be surprised."

You have no idea, thought Frank. But he just said, "Yep," and the two men headed west.

Helen had been dozing on the fluffy chair when the hotel phone rang. "Hello? Frank?"

"Sorry, it's me, Omar."

She sat up, rubbing the back of her neck. "Hi."

"Just wanted to tell you my friend called me back. He's on his way over to talk to you, so don't go anywhere."

She'd trapped herself in her own hotel room for too long. "I told you I didn't want to talk to anyone, Omar. I think I'm just going to go out for a walk."

"You've got to stay, Helen. He's on his way right now. Just give him an hour, OK?"

Frank's cell phone lay unmoving on the dresser. She hadn't disturbed his toiletries when she got dressed. Would he really just go?

"Fine. I'll give him an hour. What's his name?"

"Remmy."

She was certainly certifiably insane. A reporter named Remmy was coming over to talk to her about her hallucinations and upcoming for-ay into a lifetime of pharmaceuticals. She was upholding her husband's obsessive-compulsive toiletry arrangements and she still had a rat's nest in the back of her hair.

"Remmy. Sounds marvelous."

"You'll like him. He's a hoot."

Helen put the phone back on the cradle. She'd better do something about her hair.

HER

She was surprised to find Downey Street right where she'd left it. She supposed after everything that had happened that the house would have moved, the corner would have been ripped up and turned into a Walgreens or another park or a parking lot. But there it was.

The house wasn't orange when she'd lived here. It was a dark blue and the paint had been peeling. The street had been lined with cars and people and tie-dyed window coverings. This house was quiet, the windows blinded and dark. This street corner was empty. A few parked cars, a few motorcycles, but not the Hell's Angels motorcycles she remembered.

She had fallen beside the One Way sign, head pointed toward Downey Street, body twisted toward Waller. There had been a woman who lived beneath the building who cooked burgers on an open grill on the street. She called them Love Burgers, and had handed them out to anyone who asked.

She touched the street. Remmy was still a ways behind her, undoubtedly trying to decide whether to run again. Shep had stopped playing and panted near the stoop of the next building.

This. She traced a circle on the sidewalk. This was where her head had broken. This was where she bled. Dried gum stuck to the concrete. A cigarette butt was pressed between the cracks. This corner. Buffalo

Springfield had sung out of the window. She had felt so warm. She had felt so alive, had felt every pulsing heartbeat through her entire body. She had heard her blood dancing in the vessels and veins. She had been so full. Each toe pressed to the floor. Each finger stretched and stretched wide—a web to catch everything, to hold everything she wanted. The curtains had fluttered and she heard the whispers, but she couldn't understand the words. She had felt unified. She felt connected to everything, the growing weeds between the buildings, the squirrels in the park, the sounds of the drumming, and her fiddle, her fiddle spoke so much she could hardly keep it all inside her. She'd just wanted to hear what the curtains were saying. It seemed so important.

And then the ground had come up so fast. She didn't know she'd stepped through the glass. Hadn't even realized she wanted to. She'd never been rooted enough. She'd always let herself be pulled from one thing to another, one whisper, one touch, one sound to another. She was singing when she stepped through the glass, and when she hit the sidewalk—this place where she now pressed her palm—she had just taken a full breath to sing the next verse.

REMMY X

Stop! Stop! Oh, everything just stop. I can't keep all this going any-more. I'm running down the street I've run down a thousand times before—running to her, running from her—running, always running. My lungs are about to give out.

I see her. The street is quiet, not at all like it was then. She's crouch-ing over the place on the sidewalk where she fell and I want to tell her I'd marked it with tape for awhile, but it got pulled up by shoes and feet and time. I want to tell her the world stopped when she fell, but that isn't the truth. I stopped. She stopped. But the world, well it kept right on going, faster and faster and faster, and it has most surely been exhausting to try and keep that world from spinning. I tried though. I tried.

I reach her, heaving, but she doesn't budge. She's touching that sidewalk and she's breathing, she's actually breathing, and I can see her spine, curved but not broken. Shep is pressing his nose into her legs and she's touching his ears and she's shaking and shaking and I hear her crying in my feet first. She's moving the earth with that sound.

She stands and floats to the top of the building. Shep's watching her, tongue hanging out his mouth. He's soaking wet from her tears. She reaches the window and presses her spine against it and kicks off it like a diver from a pier and this time she floats to the ground and hovers a moment before resting on the sidewalk, the very place she'd crashed. She's curled into herself and Shep is sniffing around her like he's found a dead pigeon or a rabbit. He starts howling and shaking himself dry. I'm here, Shep, I'm here, I say, but I can't speak. She took my voice. Elle, stop it. Stop it. I snap my fingers and Shep comes to me, tail between his legs. He's shivering now, and I wrap my arms around him. Good dog. Good dog Shep.

She has hardened on the sidewalk. I touch her shoulders, her hips, her legs, but they don't move. Her arms hide her eyes and I only hear her exhaling. She's exhaling over and over and over until she starts coughing. Elle. I'm here. She curls tighter into herself. I try to speak and my voice is far away, down a tunnel. "Tell me," I say. "I can hear you now."

She uncurls and the shell she'd been in becomes liquid, dripping down the sidewalk like her blood had done. Her lips are cracked and her hair, her golden hair that I have imagined in my hands for forty years, is full of dirt and worms and barnacles. Her eyes have deadened. She coughs again. "I was singing when I fell," she says. "I just want to finish my song."

The sun is straight overhead and Downey Street is clean and clear. Shep is howling. "Shhh, boy. Shhhh." But he won't stop braying. "I didn't know the stuff was bad," I say.

"I was singing."

"I didn't know what to do. Don—um, Starburst—thinks he gave it to you. But that afternoon—"

The wave is coming now. I always thought it would sneak up on me from behind and pull me under, but it's not outside of me at all. It's inside me and my bones are going to have to break to let it loose.

She lifts her arm. The skin that had shimmered in Buena Vista Park is gray. It's going to slip away soon. Elle. The back of her hand presses to my cheek. It's a block of ice. I don't pull away. The cold burns. Elle. Take me with you.

"I just wanted to have fun," she said, and her breath was rank. I saw her young and laughing, flashing her breasts at passing cars, drawing butterflies and peace symbols on anyone's flesh she could touch. I heard her fierce and fiery in the park playing her fiddle. So much alive.

"I'm sorry," I say.

"I know." She's coughing again, black phlegm, roots, pits and seeds. "Leave me here. Go find that woman. Go find my fiddle."

"I won't leave you again," I say, and her arm falls back to the sidewalk. I'm crying now too, and I'm grateful that I lived long enough to know this is one of those moments where everything I do will affect everything else I do. I didn't know those moments existed forty years ago. I thought there was a river and we all swam in it and it didn't much matter whether we did the breaststroke or the dog paddle or if we jumped too hard in the water and pulled some of the others into the rip tide. It was all going to wash out in the end. But now I know that's not how it is. I know it's most important to wash it all out while we're all still here. "Nobody's right," I whisper.

"If everybody's wrong," she whispers back, and I hold her, sticky and smelly, dead and alive, and watch the sun cross to the Pacific.

- X out.

2007

Helen was surprised to hear the key card in the door. She was glad she'd put up the chain. "Omar? I thought you'd call me to come down."

"It's me, Helen," Frank said through the small opening. "Can I come in?"

She stood beside the door, not removing the chain. His voice was lighter than she remembered. "You forgot your phone."

"I know."

"I can hand it to you through the door."

"Please."

"Fine." She unlocked the chain and stepped away. Frank didn't look like he'd been hurt. He looked healthy; a ruddy color in his cheeks, and his hair was curlier from being outside. "I guess you didn't get murdered last night."

"I'm sorry."

She opened the drapes, bathing the room in early afternoon light. "I'm going crazy."

"No you aren't." He hadn't stepped fully into the room yet. "I met someone."

Helen wanted to kick the door closed on him, but instead she resigned herself to the interpretation of events she'd thought the least likely—her accountant husband hooking up with a stranger.

"No, no, not like that. You know I always say the wrong thing."

She stayed on the other side of the room.

"Can I come in?"

She shrugged.

"He's waiting downstairs."

"He?"

"Not like that."

"Then like what, Frank? You've been gone for almost twenty-four hours. You never go anywhere for longer than four hours. You didn't even try and call the hotel, and I saw the girl in the mirror this morning and you didn't even try and call the hotel, Frank." She was breaking. She would not let him see her break.

"I know."

"You could have found a pay phone. They must exist still somewhere."

"I know."

Frank sat on the bed, smoothed the indention on Helen's pillow. "You only slept on one side." She didn't say anything. "His name is Brian. I met him in Chinatown. We're on our way to the Haight. He wants to show me something, and I—I wondered if you'd walk with us."

"Oh, you wondered if I'd walk with you? Today?"

"Happy birthday."

She couldn't hold it back anymore. She sank slowly to the carpet. Frank crossed to her and touched her ponytail. His fingers felt warm. They traveled to her neck and then her shoulders.

"Come go for a walk."

She turned and pulled him to the carpet. "Someone's supposed to come see me."

"We won't be gone long."

"It's about the girl in the window."

"I believe you," he said, sliding his hands to hers.

She didn't pull her hands away. "About what?"

"The girl."

"Why?"

"Come for a walk."

She nodded, too tired to argue.

"What does Brian want to show you in the Haight?"

"His ghost."

Brian paced the lobby, watching his posture in the three mirrored walls. There was no angle he could catch himself that didn't show him old. The elevator pinged open.

"You must be Helen," he said, holding out his hand.

She took it. "Brian?"

"Yes." He looked at Frank and raised his eyebrows.

"We're going for a walk," Frank said.

"We should go before it gets dark," said Brian.

"It's only two o'clock," said Frank.

"Sometimes it's dark when you don't think it should be," said Brian.

Helen looped her arm through Frank's. "I like you," she said to Brian.

Brian saw what Frank didn't see yet. Helen loved him still. They fit.

REMMY X

I don't know how long we stayed there on the sidewalk. Shep has curled up under a tree and is kicking his legs while he sleeps. I think quite a few times that she is just going to decay in my arms right back into the sidewalk, but she never does. She exhales loudly, coughing and coughing and I do my able best to hold her. She is in my lap, head cradled in my elbow, when they arrive. I knew I'd been waiting for something to crash up on this sidewalk, but I sure did not know it would be them.

"Remmy," Brian says to me as if we'd just had dinner last week. There are two other people I don't know with him. Elle stirs. "Have you had her all this time?" he asks.

I shake my head. "Not like this."

Brian's two companions stand across the street. The man is pointing up at our window. "Who are they?" I ask.

"Friends."

He sees her. We two old men see her. "It's getting dark," I say.

"Yeah."

"I saw you a few times."

"Yeah." He kneels beside us and picks up her hand. He rubs each finger. I don't let her go. He reaches her wrist and spreads out her fingers and starts to kiss each one. He's not troubled by the smell, the barnacles, the gray of her skin. She opens her eyes and turns her head.

I hear her neck creak.

"Brian," she says.

"Yeah," he says.

She opens her jaw and an eel slips out. Brian doesn't move. I jerk back, but I don't drop her. He just picks the eel up and tosses it in the grass.

"You have my fiddle."

"Yeah."

"I heard it."

"I didn't play it as good as you."

"You didn't." She tries to laugh, but her tongue is too thick.

"I need my fiddle."

"I kept it for you."

"Where is it?"

"Come with me."

No! I tighten my grip but she's too strong. She's slipping away again. She's unlocking herself from me limb by limb. When she's free of me, I stand, my wet shirt sticking to my chest and back. The air is cooling as the early evening fog is coming in. I don't know what to do. I'm getting washed away. I don't have any weight on me anymore. She presses close to Brian and he helps her stand. She's earth. She's water. He kisses her gray mouth and blows his air into her. He blows his anger at me in her and gives her fire. She puffs, a cloud, and rises above the sidewalk, holding his hand. She twists her head behind her like an owl and looks at me. I can only imagine what she's seeing. "I love you, Elle," I say. I want to tell you she said the same thing to me, but she didn't.

"Thank you for helping me find my fiddle, Remmy," she says.

Brian holds her hand tighter. His back is to me. He hasn't once made eye contact with me. The woman Brian brought with him is crying and pointing at us. The man is holding her, kissing the top of her head, stroking her ponytail. Who the hell are these people?

"You're welcome," I say because what else can I say? What else is there? Shep shakes himself awake and starts barking at Elle's back. She stops and scratches his ears and his tail wags and wags. She whispers something in his ear and he turns and bounds back to me, licking my face. "Take care of her, Brian." He stops and I both want him and don't want him to turn around. Doesn't matter what I want. He starts walking away again. His friends are waving at him.

"That's my friend, Remmy," he says to them, but he doesn't stop walking, doesn't let go of her hand, doesn't turn around. "Go take care of him." They're walking down Waller Street to Ashbury. He walks like a young man. His arm is around her waist and she is laughing and then the fog swallows them and I am alone on the place where she fell and I realize the wave has come and gone and left me tumbled, shiny and alive.

- X out.

2007

"It's Sunday already," said Frank to Helen. They were in their hotel room after an exhausting night with Remmy and his slobbering dog. "This is the second night in a row, the second night in my whole life, I've been out past midnight."

She flipped on the bathroom light and put toothpaste on her toothbrush, taking care not to disturb the placement of his. "Do you think he'll be OK?"

"Remmy or Brian?"

"Either one, I guess."

"I don't know." He took off his Dockers and lined them neatly, right foot on the right, left foot on the left, in front of the closet. He unbuckled his pants and slipped into his side of the bed. "All this time I thought Benjamin was my ghost."

"What? I didn't think you believed in ghosts."

"I don't. But ever since we got here, I've been thinking of Ben."

She spit her toothpaste into the sink. "You would have said that's a memory, not a ghost."

Frank let himself smile. "Yes, I would."

"Did you see him?" she asked.

"No. I just kept feeling him. Following him even." She turned off the bathroom light and came to bed. He lifted the sheet for her. "I think my ghost might be you."

She fluffed her pillow, sliding her hand underneath it. The peach pit was still there. She decided she'd offer it to the room, like a child leaves her tooth for the tooth fairy. "I didn't sleep well last night."

He thought of Penny Lane, decided to talk about her another day. "I slept in a booth."

"A booth?"

"I'll tell you about it."

"Today's the fortieth anniversary," she said. "Do you want to go to the Park when we wake up? See what happened the year we were born?" She crept her hand toward his. He opened his fingers. His wedding band was still on. "We can decide when we wake up," she said.

He touched her cheek, traced her lips and chin. "I've already decided," he said.

Her mouth opened. He pressed his finger to it. "You can decide tomorrow if you want to. Don't say anything. Not tonight."

She moved his finger from her lips. "I can take a few extra days off work if you'd like to stay a little longer."

"That'd be OK," he said. He could tell her then that he'd decided not to go back to work, and if she didn't want to go back either, maybe they could not go back together. He reached for the remote and turned the television on. It was *The Bob Newhart Show*. "I always thought he was old," said Frank. "We're older now than he was then."

"You have better hair." She moved closer to him and wrapped her arms around his thin waist, pressing into his back. "Turn the volume down just a little. I want to hear you breathe."

For the mile and a half walk to his apartment, Brian let himself stand tall. He let himself hold her hand, drink in her body as it was, not as it used to be, and he took each step like a man who knew where he was headed. There was only one possible end to this, he knew, but he was going to be present this time. She floated along beside him, leaving drops of water behind her. He pulled his windbreaker closed. He'd been away from home for a few days. Anastasia, his cat, would be hungry. They climbed the hills, stepped over the jagged sidewalk pieces, and stayed connected. He knew she was going, but she would wait until she got what she came for.

The big key got them in the lobby of his building. The floor had been lovely once, many many years before he moved in. Now, the white marble was chipped and scuffed, more yellow than white, the gold trim edges brown and peeling. A large vase of dead flowers graced the south corner of the lobby. The vase had been there the entire thirty-six years he'd lived there. The gift of rent control. She didn't seem to notice.

The elevator was on the ground floor. It had an iron pull-gate that always stuck a little before it gave way. They stepped through onto the threadbare gray carpet. He closed the gate, pressed the button to the fourth floor. One bare bulb lit the hallway, which had just been painted a glowing white after a spat of graffiti appeared over night. Brian had preferred the graffiti. He couldn't understand what it said, but seeing the bright colors, the oranges and reds and greens, made him feel that he lived someplace where there were others. The stark white paint reminded him of a death tunnel.

It always took a few tries to get the door key to click into place. She waited patiently, dripping. He had to let go of her hand to jimmy the doorknob. She didn't go. The apartment was dark and smelled of old coffee grounds and wilted lettuce. He'd forgotten to take the trash out before he went to work. Was that only two days ago? It was after midnight now. It was Sunday, wasn't it? Anastasia twisted around his legs, leaving bits of white fur on his pant legs. Elle remained outside.

"Come in," he said. "It's OK."

She was slithering now more than she was hovering. He wanted to wrap a cloth around his nose but he made himself breathe her in. Anastasia hissed when Elle entered and ran under the only chair in the room, tail swishing out the back of it. The door shut behind them with a snap. Elle found the center of the tiny room and spun twice and stopped.

"So this is where you have lived," she said.

"Yes."

"It's dark."

"Yes."

"You carried my fiddle for me." Her hair was a net over her eyes. Brian wanted to pick the creatures from it, but he wasn't sure they would separate. "I told you not to."

Brian sat in the worn La-Z-Boy he'd picked up from the Salvation Army for twenty bucks. Anastasia pulled her tail in closer. His hands were aging. The veins were moving toward the surface, liver spots dotting the lines. The knuckles ached in the morning and the evening now. His fingers hadn't loved anyone since Elle. They'd touched many whose names he could not recall or never knew, but they'd only loved Elle. "What do you want me to say?"

"Why?"

"Why what?"

"Why do you have my fiddle?"

"Because you loved it."

She cracked then, like a building in an earthquake. The crack began at her feet and moved up her spine and across her face, fracturing her into cubes. A warm amber liquid bubbled from the fissures.

"I never saw Stevie there, where ever I was," she said. "Your brother wasn't there."

Brian coughed into his aging hand.

"Nobody was there. Just me."

The liquid pooled around her until she was standing in a pond of shimmering light.

"I gave you a note."

"I couldn't read it."

"Remember the chanting we'd go to sometimes on the hill? The Hare Krishnas and every other group you could think of? You thought they needed some electric guitar."

"The Hare Krishnas were too slow," she said.

"There was the one night we went and there was Sufi dancing. You spun and spun and spun into a dervish. Your hair was a carpet. We laughed."

"Where is my fiddle?"

Brian stood and crossed to the tiny closet. The fiddle case was in the back behind a raincoat and a valise.

"I remember," she said.

"What?"

"That night."

"That's what was on the note. The chant we sang there."

The amber liquid swirled around her. A fin cut through the surface. Her cracked body splintered and hit the hardwood floor. All that was left was her skeleton standing, bending, twisting in the liquid. Her eyes remained, glittering, no longer gray but a crystal blue.

"Sing it to me."

"No," said Brian. "It was a long time ago."

"What other time is there?"

He lifted the fiddle case from the back of the closet and closed the door. She watched it as it lay on the floor, but she didn't move toward it.

"Sing it to me," she said.

"Sing it with me."

Her lower jaw opened. Her ribs heaved. "All I ask of you," she sang and her voice was pure, no longer hoarse and trapped.

"Is forever to remember me," sang Brian.

"As loving you," she said.

And together, "All I ask of you is forever to remember me as loving you."

They sang the chant over and over, growing louder and softer, faster and slower. The dawn was breaking through the fog. The City was waking up.

"I have to go," she said.

"I know." He opened the fiddle case and handed her the instrument. Her bones curved around its handle, her chin resting on its chin. He gave her the bow and it stretched out from her forearm, a limb of its own. Her elbow bent, her fingers gripped, and she drew the bow slowly across the strings. The fiddle cried. "I didn't carry it to keep it, Elle. I carried it to give it back."

She bent into the instrument, fierce and fiery, jaw slightly open, eyes sparking. The notes filled the room and Brian saw their colors. He smelled them, blueberries, chocolate, cinnamon and Tabasco. The light bulb in his table lamp sizzled and exploded. The floorboards shook and the amber liquid she stood in boiled. She played and played and played and played. His cell phone rang. The faucet turned on. The two chairs at the dining table slid away from her. Brian didn't know a fiddle could make the sounds she made with it, crescendoing and crescendoing. The window rattled. The chain on the door shook. Sparks flew from the frets and the bowstrings began to melt.

"You carried me home, Brian," she said, only it was the fiddle that told him. The fiddle with its electric dancing and shrieking synesthesia. She was almost gone. She was playing so fast, her bones blurred white.

Elle. Good-bye.

The liquid turned to steam and her spine became ash. The fiddle and bow clattered to the floor, smoking but not burning. A small puddle of liquid remained on the floor. His phone stopped ringing. The faucet shut off. He breathed in and out, holding his chest tight with his hands. In and out. In and out. A piece of paper fluttered in the strings. He picked it up carefully; the fiddle was too hot to touch. He read it, stutter-breathed a moment, and slipped the note in his pocket.

Anastasia crept out from under the chair. He pulled up the blinds and lifted the window the few inches it would budge. The cat leapt onto the sill, rubbing the glass. In the small kitchen, he put water on to boil, then took a dishtowel and wiped up the puddle on the floor. He wrung the towel out into the kettle and when it boiled, poured a cup of the hot water, tossed in a slice of lemon, and drank standing up.

He cleared a space on his bookshelf, and when the fiddle and bow cooled, he picked them up placed them there, alive and breathing. He slid the case under his single bed, turned down the blankets and in the new light of morning, lay back into the pillows and closed his eyes.

REMMY X

It's the next day dawn and Shep and me are wrapped up in each other in my apartment. It's cold this morning. We are a pile together. His feet twitch him awake.

"Hey boy."

His tail thumps the mattress. The red ball has rolled under the bed, but I know he wants it. It smells of her. I want it too, but she's gone. He pushes out of the bed. He needs to go out. Maybe today I can get me some of that good coffee.

"OK." I pull on sweatpants and a sweatshirt. My good walking shoes. I got to go visit Don today. I got to tell him it was me what gave her the bad stuff so he can stop carrying it—maybe stop not caring if he gets killed in his neighborhood. I hope he don't shoot me. Be a shame to get this far to end like that.

When I open the door, we both bound up the stairs to street level. Shep turns west, up the hill again. I walk a ways with my eyes closed, trying to feel the sidewalk through my shoes, wanting to know where I am by touch. I am behind on my *Hashbury Daily Times*. I haven't missed a day until this weekend. My brain-house, normally so full of ideas for what to write, is like a bank vault. I can tell there's stories still in there, but right now they're locked away and all I got is a sterile space that echoes.

We get to Buena Vista Park and I want to keep on going. I want to go to Golden Gate today, see the celebration, even if it's fake and full of the wrong people. I want to see it because maybe it'll make me dance a little. Shep wants to go into Buena Vista though. He thinks he'll see her there, but he won't. The park looks like it always does, but he leaps ahead of me into its fog and climbs the stone staircase. I think I may be getting too old for a dog. Too old for all this activity. But he's waiting for me at the top and I know I'm just being silly, my usual self-deprecating thoughts. They call that negative self-talk at the Free Clinic. I say it's just being a person and there's supposed to be some of that negative self-talk to balance out the positive self-talk so we don't go thinking we're invincible.

"They want their houses back," Elle said to me so many years ago when we traced the edges of the crumbling tombstones in the park. "The dead are so lonely."

We get to the very top of the hill in the park, a place I haven't been in too long. The City stretches out in front of us, and today it's clear enough to see all the way to the Golden Gate Bridge. The City stoops and rises, kneeling and praising. The Pacific is a stripe of dark blue and the fog is only wispy, just enough so that we know it's there, that we know at any minute we can be swallowed up. At any minute we can lose ourselves.

I have to sit, so Shep sits beside me. He drops the red ball in my lap. I rest my head on his shoulders for a minute. "Look at all that, Shep." I try to point out landmarks but he gets bored and nudges the ball.

One day Shep and me are going to be bones. We're going to be part of the underneath of this park, part of the underneath of this City. Maybe we'll see her again there. Maybe not. I smell Shep's oily doggy smell and rub his fur backwards at his neck like he likes it. That's what it's all about really; having your fur rubbed backwards by someone you love.

I toss the ball in the air and he barks. "Ready?" He wags his tail, crouches. I throw the ball ahead of me and Shep goes first into the trees, single-minded in his pursuit. "I'm right behind you," I say, and take one more look at the bridges and rooftops of my City before chasing after his ever-loving living bones.

- X out.

Acknowledgments

I am so grateful to my writing partners, Gayle Brandeis and Michaela Carter, who constantly and consistently help me present my vision more clearly.

Arvin Loudermilk and Mike Iverson have been my creative foundation and friends for over twenty years. They continue to help me make my work stronger (and less convoluted!) online and on the page. I don't know where I'd be without you both.

Thanks to my agent, Linda Roghaar, for her belief in my work and my stories even when the world doesn't, and Keith Haynes for listening to this story for years over coffee, helping with sentences, and for loving Elle and Remmy and Helen and Frank and me.

And Jeffrey Hartgraves, thank you for sharing your Magical San Francisco with me. I will always remember you. Your spark is in every page I write.

Reader's Guide

1) The poet T.S. Eliot wrote, "to make an end is to make a beginning. The end is where we start from." *Gathering Lights* features many characters experiencing some sort of conclusion to some aspect of their life and, simultaneously, a new beginning. What are the most prominent examples of this ending/beginning paradox? In what way is Elle's recovery of her fiddle an end as well as beginning? Does it seem that Frank and Helen's marriage ends, in a way, while it begins anew?

2) *Gathering Lights* presents many different perspectives on the city of San Francisco. Broadly speaking, the novel's perspectives are either those of visitors (Frank and Helen) or those of natives (Remmy, Brian, and many other characters). How does Frank and Helen's experience of San Francisco differ from that of Remmy and Brian? How do the natives view the visitors, and how do the visitors view the natives? At what points does the novel adopt the perspective of the visitor, and at what points does it adopt the perspective of the native?

3) In addition to their similar sounding names, Helen and Elle also seem to be linked in time, Elle having died shortly before Helen is born. Do the two characters share any similar traits? What is suggested by the fact that Helen is the only character besides Remmy and Brian to perceive Elle? What is the nature of the connection between Elle and Helen? How does their connection link the past and the present, the year of 1967 with the year of 2007?

4) The 1960s were a tumultuous and transformative period in American history, and the Haight-Ashbury district of San Francisco has long been seen as the heart of the hippie movement. How did this time period mold characters such as Remmy, Brian and Elle? In what ways did they become trapped by the era? What are some of the positive and hopeful aspects of the hippie movement reflected in the novel? How does the novel also reflect the darker aspects of the era? Did certain aspects of the hippie movement also make its failure inevitable?

AUTHOR INTERVIEW WITH
LARAINE HERRING AND GAYLE BRANDEIS

GB: What was the seed of inspiration for *Gathering Lights*?

LH: I thought the protagonist would be a very old woman, living in the Tenderloin, having basically become Janis Joplin (in terms of alcoholism). But then I couldn't get very far. This book took eight years to come together, and it wasn't until I got Remmy's voice that everything fell into place. Once I found him, which came in a dream, the whole book snapped together.

GB: Your fiction often features ghosts. Can you talk about why ghosts are such an important part of your writing life?

LH: I don't think the past, as Faulker reminds us, is ever really past. I don't move in the world as if there were hard endings to things, and I have always been able to see layers in objects—whether it's antique furniture, or walls in an apartment, or a cemetery—I seem to be able to imagine what all the different stories connected to those objects are. I think the idea that things are gone forever is just incompatible with me, so I write stories where that's not the case.

GB: Letting go is also an important theme in much of your work, including this novel. Why do you think this is a theme you keep returning to in your writing?

LH: See above question! I don't let things go, and I think a large part of my personal work involves learning how to release what isn't serving me anymore.

GB: *Gathering Lights* feels like a breakthrough novel for you—how did writing this book feel different from other work you've written?

LH: I think this book marked the introduction of plot to my work! It is also a book that I feel is truly fiction. Not that the themes are not personal, as they always are in a novelist's work, but I don't feel like I'm exorcising my father (he died in 1987) anymore. I feel liberated with this book, and I was honestly afraid I didn't have another book in me, so this came as a great relief.

GB: San Francisco is really a character in itself in *Gathering Lights*. What is your own connection to San Francisco?

LH: My amazing friend, the late Jeffrey Hartgraves, first introduced me to San Francisco about fifteen years ago. It was love at first sight. I go back every chance I get and wander her streets and get lost. I think about the City as a heart-home for me.

GB: Remmy has a hard time remaining objective as he writes his newspaper; do you try to remain objective as you write your fiction (and if so, is this ever a struggle for you)?

LH: What a great question! I actually never try to remain objective in fiction. I don't think that's the role of fiction. Fiction isn't journalism (although in Remmy's case that might be a little different!) I try to tell the story as truthfully as I can through the perspective of the characters I've chosen as narrators. I think the story must be authentic to that lens, not any sort of attempt at objectivity.

GB: One thing that really struck me about this book was how beautifully you inhabit your male characters—how were you able to enter the male experience in such an authentic way?

LH: Thank you! I think one thing that was different for me this time is that I've really reached out to men as partners, friends and colleagues in ways I wouldn't have considered doing before. I think that once I really stopped thinking and feeling that men are the 'other', I was able to inhabit male characters with the compassion and empathy I knew I needed to be able to do.

GB: What do you hope readers will ultimately take away from this novel?

LH: A belief in the power of art and love to change everything.

•

Gayle Brandeis' latest work is Delta Girls (Random House) and My Life with the Lincolns (Henry Holt & Company). She is the recipient of the Bellwether Prize for her novel The Book of Dead Birds (HarperCollins). Find out more about Gayle and her work at www.gaylebrandeis.com.

About the Author

Laraine Herring holds an MFA and an MA and directs the creative writing program at Yavapai College. Her work includes the novel *Ghost Swamp Blues* and *Writing Begins with the Breath*. She also teaches at the Kripalu Insitute for Yoga and Health and online at DailyOm.com. She lives in Prescott, AZ with four beautiful orange cats and whatever ghosts happen to be currently speaking. Visit her at laraineherring.com for updates, newsletters and more.

www.ingramcontent.com/pod-product-compliance
Lightning Source LLC
Chambersburg PA
CBHW061130200626
46817CB00016B/642